DEFENDER CAVE BEAR

PROTECTION, INC: DEFENDERS # 1

ZOE CHANT

CHAPTER 1

*S*omeone's following me.

Tirzah glanced behind her. The sidewalk was full of people, most briskly walking, plus a few elderly folk moving slowly and with the help of canes. No one seemed to pay any attention to her, let alone give her a sinister stare. But when she turned to face forward, she once again felt that prickling sensation at the back of her neck, as if the intensity of that unseen watcher's gaze was actually striking her skin. She shivered.

It wasn't as if anyone could do anything to her on a busy city sidewalk in broad daylight. All the same, it wasn't impossible that she could have a stalker. Someone could have found out about her little hobby. Or some creep could have just spotted her and decided that she looked vulnerable.

She *was* vulnerable, now. Maybe she should go home...

"No, screw that," Tirzah muttered to herself, and kept on moving. "If the grannies are out for their walks, I'm finishing mine."

No one so much as gave her a curious glance. You had to do a lot more than talk to yourself quietly to get people's attention in Refuge City. Screaming at yourself might get a raised eyebrow or two—

"Excuse me!"

It was a loud male voice. Tirzah almost jumped out of her skin.

The man addressing her looked abashed. "Sorry to startle you. Do you love cats?"

"How did you—" Then she smiled as she noticed his Humane Society T-shirt and clipboard. "I'm already a regular donor. But yes, I do love cats. So if you're doing something special for them, I could chip in a bit more."

"We are!" Enthusiastically, he went on, "We're building a new, state-of-the-art shelter exclusively for them. They're very sensitive animals, and it stresses them out if they're housed in the same building as dogs."

"Good for you! I mean, good for the Humane Society. Will it be a no-kill shelter?"

He looked horrified at the very idea of it being anything else. "Of course!"

"Sold." Tirzah took out her purse and wrote the Humane Society a check.

"Thank you so much..." He looked at the name on the check before carefully tucking it away. "...Tirzah. And pleased to meet you! I'm Jerry. Do you have cats yourself?"

"No."

"Would you like to? Or doesn't your landlord allow them?"

Tirzah dodged the landlord question. "Just haven't gotten around to it. It's been a busy year."

That was certainly true. She'd intended to get a cat a year ago. And then, well, there'd been a whole lot of things she'd been too busy to do. But there wasn't anything stopping her now.

Though she should renovate her apartment *before* she got

a cat. As Jerry had said, they were sensitive animals. If Tirzah herself hated having construction going on and her place all torn up so much that she'd put it off for an entire year, a cat would probably be terrified.

But Jerry obviously knew the look of someone who didn't have a cat and wished she did. An eager gleam lit his eyes as he asked, "Would you like to take a look at our kittens? Someone left a basket of them on a church doorstep yesterday, and we're keeping them in here. Our very first guests!" He indicated the door behind him.

"Oh, is this the place you're converting into a shelter?"

He nodded. "It's still very much under construction, but we made some space for the kittens. Come on in and meet them. They like sleeping in the basket, so we kept it in their cage for them. It's the cutest thing you've ever seen!"

She knew that if she met the kittens, she very likely wouldn't escape without adopting one. But she couldn't resist the invitation to pet a litter of kittens—in a basket, no less! Anyway, it was about time for her to start moving on with her life.

Jerry held the door open for her, and she wheeled her chair up the ramp.

Tirzah knew the building well, though she'd never been inside. Locals here at Refuge City called it Sucks To Be You Square. It had last been occupied by a travel agency, Fly You To The Moon. The agency's logo was the man in the moon, with craters that made him look like an ad for Clearasil and a distinctly sinister smile. Tirzah hadn't been surprised when it went out of business.

Before that, it had been a pizza parlor, Hollywood Pizza, with a logo of palm trees with pizzas instead of fronds, dripping melted cheese on to the Hollywood sign. Refuge City was famous for pizza, but East Coast style; the worst insult anyone could throw at a pizza here was that it tasted like it was from Los Angeles.

Before that, it had been a plus-size clothing store called Bright. Its dresses made up in cheapness what they lacked in colorfastness. Tirzah had gotten an earful about that from both a plus-sized neighbor and the plus-sized neighbor's teenage son, who had owned a number of black T-shirts with white images and writing. His skulls and angry slogans were now a bubblegum pink that was very bright indeed.

And before *that*, the building had been No Pain Dentistry, which immediately had several letters of its neon sign burn out so it seemed to ominously advertise "Pain Dentistry."

If a cat shelter with baskets full of darling kittens couldn't turn around the luck of Sucks To Be You Square, it had no hope.

Tirzah winced as her chair went over a bump at the top of the ramp. She hated that jolt.

Jerry closed the door behind her as she glanced around. As he'd said, the place was still under construction, with the old office cubicles still in place. The Humane Society hadn't even had a chance to replace the creepy Fly You To The Moon posters with some cute cat photos. The pimply man in the moon leered down at her from every wall.

"Okay, where's these kittens you promised me?" Tirzah asked, grinning. "I gave you a nice fat check, so they better be adorable!"

Only silence met her words. No answering chuckle. No meows. And then the unmistakable sound of a door being bolted.

That eerie prickling sensation she'd felt earlier and then had been distracted from returned in full force. Tirzah twisted around.

The man who'd lured her inside was standing in front of the closed—and padlocked—door, tauntingly dangling a key

4

just out of reach. His contemptuous sneer was a nearly perfect match for that of the Fly You To The Moon man's, only with less crater-acne.

I can't believe I fell for that, Tirzah thought. *He might as well have said, "Want some kittens, little girl?"*

"You open that door right now," she demanded. "Or I'll scream for help."

Jerry—she supposed that wasn't his real name, but that was the only one she had—gestured with his other hand at the base of the door. "It's soundproofed."

She looked, hoping it was a bluff. It wasn't. That was what that bump at the top of the ramp had been: high-grade industrial soundproofing. He was right: no one would hear her scream.

Tirzah considered the key. Jerry obviously didn't know it, but she *was* capable of standing. If she stood up fast, held on to her chair, and leaned forward, she could snatch the key right out of his hand. Unfortunately, she could only stand on one leg, and she hadn't brought her crutches with her. Why would she, when she hated them and had a perfectly good wheelchair? So even if she managed to get the key, Jerry would grab it back while she was still opening the lock, let alone opening the door and maneuvering her wheelchair out.

"You want money? Fine. Just let me go. You can have my wallet. Here…" Tirzah reached into her purse. But she felt for her phone, not her wallet. She'd rigged her phone with an emergency button, among some other little alterations she'd made in her spare time, and could dial 911 with a single tap. The operator would hear any ensuing commotion, and would trace the call and—

"Ah-ah-ah," said Jerry, wagging his finger at her like she was a toddler. "Don't try calling the police. If you do, I'll tip them off about the *real* criminal they should arrest... Override."

Tirzah froze at the sound of the name that she'd never heard spoken aloud before, though she'd read it on a screen a million times.

Override was the notorious hacker who broke into corporate databases, ferreted out their dirty secrets, and sent them to journalists. Override had been the catalyst for class action lawsuits against factories that dumped toxic waste near communities, and was responsible for handing actual jail terms to executives who had suppressed studies showing that their new wonder drug had the nasty little side effect of making patients drop dead.

Override was also Tirzah's secret identity.

She withdrew her hand from her phone. As far as the law was concerned, it was irrelevant that she'd never stolen a cent from the multi-billion-dollar corporations she'd spied on, or that she'd only revealed their secrets if they were harming others. Hacking was illegal, plain and simple. So was corporate espionage. If the police ever found out what she did in her spare time, she'd go to jail.

"What do you want with me?" Tirzah tried not to let her voice waver. She didn't succeed.

"Nothing important," Jerry replied with an unconcerned shrug as fake as his Humane Society clipboard. "Just your password."

There was a pause as he waited for her to obey and she waited for him to be more specific.

"Give it to me," he said impatiently. "Now."

"Er..." Tirzah could hardly believe that a man smart enough to lure her with kittens could be that ignorant about computers. "Which one?"

She caught the brief flash of confusion that crossed his face before he covered it up. "Both of them."

Tirzah felt like she was back in college and working part-time on a technical support hotline. Using the calm tone she'd used then, the one that soothed frantic students who'd spilled a venti latte over their keyboard right after they'd finished a last-minute essay that was due in an hour, she said, "Why don't you tell me exactly what you want?"

"Just give it to me!" His voice rose angrily.

"I have hundreds of passwords. All hackers do."

Jerry stared intently into her eyes, then nodded as if he'd seen that she was telling the truth. "What's the password for your Amazon account?"

That was random. And something about the way he was eyeing her made her skin creep even more than it was already creeping. She decided to give it to him. The worst he could do was order a widescreen TV or a whole lot of books on her credit card. "Um... Capital L numeral 4 exclamation point pound key pound key capital Z small h numeral—"

"That's enough," he snarled. "You can get into everything with your phone, right?"

She considered bluffing and saying she needed to use her computer at home, but if he didn't already know where she lived, she didn't want to be forced to lead him there. Tirzah nodded.

"Last week you downloaded an encrypted file labeled Apex 3.0," he went on.

That was what he wanted? Out of all the valuable data she had, he wanted a file she'd come across by accident while looking for something else, downloaded out of nothing more than idle curiosity as to why it was encrypted, and had never gotten around to decrypting?

"Did you make a copy of it?" Jerry asked.

"Yes. I sent it to a friend of mine, a hacker who goes by—"

"No, you didn't," Jerry said. She felt pinned against the

7

back of her chair by his intense stare. "You didn't make any copies, either. Did you decode it?"

"No."

He again stared deeply into her eyes, then gave a satisfied nod. Was she really that transparent? He seemed to always know whether or not she was telling the truth.

"Good. I want you to delete it. Can you do that from here?"

Tirzah nodded.

"Then do it. Now."

"I will," she said. "But before I do, I want you to know that I have a dead man's switch. If I don't log in every day, all my files get sent to all my contacts—the New York Times, the Refuge City News, everywhere. Your file included."

He gave her that searching look again, then relaxed. "Don't worry. I won't hurt you. Once that file is deleted, I'll let you go."

Icy fear struck into Tirzah's heart. It would've been easy to set up that sort of dead man's switch. But she hadn't done it. And just like he'd known she was lying, she intuitively knew that he was. Once she erased that file, he'd have what he wanted. And then he'd kill her to keep the secret.

She took her phone out of her purse. Her hands trembled as she punched in the password to unlock her phone.

Jerry smirked. He was obviously pleased that she was afraid of him. More than that, he seemed completely unafraid of *her*. He was standing between her and the door, but he hadn't bothered to pull a weapon on her or even step out of her reach. He obviously thought a woman in a wheelchair was completely helpless.

That made her fear smolder into anger. Sure, she couldn't win a wrestling match with him. But she couldn't have before the accident, either. And she wasn't only Tirzah Lowenstein, disabled cyber security expert. She was also

Override, hacker extraordinaire. Override fought wealthy, powerful corporations—and won! Sure, she did it by sneaking in through their virtual back doors rather than by punching them in the face, but a win was a win.

She needed to stop thinking of herself as a woman who couldn't even run away pitted against a man who could pin her down with one hand, and start thinking of herself as Override versus some idiot who probably kept his password on a post-it note stuck under his keyboard, reading "Password: mypassword."

Tirzah's hands stopped shaking. Since Jerry was obviously good at reading her expressions, she lowered her head. Her hair fell across her face as her fingers danced over her phone.

An ear-piercing siren went off, and a gruff voice blared out from a bullhorn, "FBI! STEP AWAY FROM THE DOOR!"

Jerry leaped like he'd been goosed. Tirzah dropped her phone back into her purse and moved her wheelchair forward like she was in the last stretch of a Paralympics sprint. Her front wheel, plus the entire combined weight of her chair and herself, ran over her enemy's toes.

Now that was a bump she didn't mind rolling over. His shriek of pain and fury was satisfying, too. Almost as satisfying as the jingle of the key falling to the floor.

Tirzah leaned over and snatched it up.

"Hey!" Jerry had been doubled over, but he started to straighten up.

She spun her wheels in reverse, rolling over his toes again. The sound he made then indicated that he wasn't going to chase her or anyone any time soon. She unlocked the padlock and took it with her as she opened the door. Then she rolled over the soundproofing bump (not as big a bump as his toes had been) and twisted around to slam the door behind her. His second anguished scream was cut off.

A few people were looking at her. Apparently her phone and Jerry had made enough noise to attract attention. Tirzah looked down in simulated alarm, pulled her phone out of her purse, and made sure to fumble around a bit before hitting the mute button. The cop movie she'd been playing in the directional sound mode she'd installed in her phone, so it sounded like it was coming from outside, was silenced as instantly as Jerry's scream. The looky-loos lost interest and went on their way.

Tirzah carefully stood up on her left leg and padlocked the door. Then she rolled sedately down the ramp, keeping an innocent smile plastered to her face. *Just a harmless woman in a wheelchair enjoying the fresh air on this lovely day, nothing here to see, folks.*

Just in case Sucks to Be You Square had a rear exit, Tirzah took a roundabout way back, keeping to side streets with plenty of foot traffic, until she was satisfied that she hadn't been followed. Only then did she turn toward home.

By the time she got back to her apartment building, the jigsaw puzzle of the sky as seen between skyscrapers had gone from the deep blue of late afternoon to the gold and pink clouds of sunset. The old men playing chess on a folding table they'd put out on the sidewalk smiled at her, the chatting women holding grocery bags broke off their conversation to greet her, and the sullen teenager staring at his phone, hunched over to hide the bubblegum-pink anarchy symbol on his T-shirt, straightened up and word-lessly held the door open for her.

"Thanks, Jamal," Tirzah said. "Hi, Miriam. Hi, Khaliya. Yeah, I had a great stroll. I'd love some cookies, thanks! Just knock on my door when you bake them."

As she went up the ramp, Tirzah relaxed. Even if her

mysterious enemy had figured out where she lived, he wasn't likely to try ambushing her at home. Her apartment building was crowded and bustling, everyone knew everyone, and there were always plenty of people there. If she screamed, ten people would call 911 within seconds, and she'd have burly men breaking down her door only seconds after that, with grandmas and grandpas lurking behind them, ready to bash any evildoers over the head with their canes. She was as safe in her apartment as it was possible to be.

She took the elevator up to the fifth floor and headed down the hallway, nodding at the neighbors who had their doors open, until she got to her front door. Tirzah unlocked the doorknob, then braced her hand on the arm of her chair so she could stand and fit her key into the high top lock.

"I got it!" squealed Amy, the six-year-old next door.

She darted out of her apartment, carroty hair flying out behind her, then skidded to a stop in front of Tirzah at her father's yell of "Ask first!"

"Want me to open the door?" Amy asked belatedly.

"Sure. Thanks, Amy." For at least the 365th time, Tirzah promised herself that she'd call that renovator tomorrow and have her apartment made more accessible. It wasn't like there would be any problem with the landlord, and while she *could* stand up to reach the top lock and high shelves and everything else that was otherwise out of reach, it made more sense to move them lower down so she could use both hands.

On the other hand, it wasn't as if she ever had any trouble finding a neighbor to give her a hand, or that she minded giving Amy an excuse to come over and look at her collections. Sure enough, Amy stood on her tiptoes to unlock the deadbolt, handed Tirzah the key, then hung around with a hopeful look on her face.

"Want to look at my dollhouses?" Tirzah asked, grinning.

Amy nodded eagerly and followed her inside, yelling over her shoulder, "Looking at Tirzah's dolls!"

"Yeah, sure!" her father yelled back.

"Okay if I give her a cookie?" Tirzah called.

"Please, Daddy, please please please?" Amy begged.

"Just one!" her father shouted.

Tirzah went to the kitchen, poured milk into a teacup, and opened the cabinet. "Khaliya's lavender shortbread, Ruben's oatmeal squares, or Circus Animals?"

"Circus Animals!" Amy exclaimed gleefully.

It was part of their ritual. Tirzah was well-supplied with delicious homemade baked goods by the other tenants, but she always kept some kind of brand-name supermarket cookie on stock for Amy. To her parents' everlasting despair, Amy disdained all home cooking in favor of junk food, and the more artificially colored, preservative-filled, and heavily advertised, the better.

Amy dashed back to the door and shouted, "Can I have two? They're small!"

"Yeah, sure!" her father called back. "But no refusing to eat your dinner! Yes, Amy, even it doesn't come out of a box."

"I won't!" Amy shouted, clearly lying.

"Your dad's a pushover," Tirzah remarked.

Amy gave her a blank look. "He's too big to push over."

Smiling, Tirzah got out the fancy saucer with roses painted around the rim. Amy had already vanished into Tirzah's bedroom, where the dollhouses were. Tirzah placed one pink and one white Circus Animal cookie on the saucer, then followed Amy in.

"I want to look at the lacy house," Amy said, and pulled up a chair in front of the Victorian dollhouse, her favorite. She watched it like a TV set as she nibbled her cookies and drank her milk. "The red-headed doll looks like me."

Tirzah considered the Little Orphan Annie doll, which

she'd posed in front of a closet of tiny dresses, her arms raised to select one. "Yeah, she does. If you had curly hair."

"You should get her a friend with straight red hair, like mine. Then they could be sisters."

"Okay. I'll keep an eye out for one."

Amy finished her cookies and milk, gave Tirzah her plates, washed and dried her hands, then gleefully approached the Victorian dollhouse. "Can I move the doll who looks me?"

That, too, was part of their deal: Amy could touch all but the most fragile dolls and animals, but she had to have clean hands and ask permission first.

"Go for it."

Ceremonially, Amy closed the closet door, lifted Little Orphan Annie, and placed her in a bedroom occupied by a Mexican doll in an embroidered dancing dress. She posed the two dolls sitting on a bed, their heads close together as if deep in conversation.

"Now she has a friend," Amy said with satisfaction, and headed back out. Over her shoulder, she called, "Next time I want to look at the ninja house!"

"Any time!" Tirzah called back. "Just knock!"

Any time Amy wanted to look at Tirzah's dollhouses, she could knock. If Tirzah was working or just didn't want to be bothered, she wouldn't answer the door. If she didn't mind a visit, she'd let Amy in.

The door closed behind Amy with a solid thud. Tirzah could still hear the sounds of people talking, cars driving in stop-and-start traffic, the calls of crows, and the rumble of the subway. But they were faint and distant. The apartment suddenly felt very quiet and alone. And, though she was surrounded by friends and neighbors, not quite safe.

Tirzah shivered, remembering the solid thunk of the bolt

13

sliding into place as Jerry had locked her inside. She'd escaped once, but would he try again?

There was one thing she knew for sure: she had to find out what was on that file he'd wanted her to delete.

Tirzah opened her laptop and got to work. First she set up the dead man's switch she'd told Jerry she already had. Once she was finished, that file would be automatically mailed to all her media contacts, along with a note explaining why they were getting it, unless she manually turned off the switch every 24 hours. Then she pulled up the file itself.

She prided herself on being able to decode any file or break into any system, but the mystery file was a tough nut to crack. Three hours later, she'd barely made any headway, and took a break to eat something. Hunger made her lose focus.

As she sat munching on a hastily slapped-together peanut butter sandwich, she thought about how ironic the whole thing was. She'd downloaded the file out of nothing more than idle curiosity. It could have sat on her laptop for months or even years before she'd ever gotten around to looking at it. She might even have eventually deleted it unread while doing some virtual tidying-up. If she had tried to decode it, with no reason to believe it was anything special, she'd probably have decided it was too much work for too little clear reward, and *then* deleted it.

"But now?" Tirzah muttered to herself. "Nobody messes with Override!"

She returned to her laptop. It was hours later, well into the early morning when even most of Refuge City was asleep, that she finally cracked the code.

She read the file.

What the hell...?

It had been a stressful day and she'd stayed up all night;

she needed to analyze this with a clear head. Tirzah went to the bathroom and splashed some cold water on her face, then returned to her laptop and read the file again.

No way.

She made herself some coffee, drank a cup, and took a second cup back to her desk to read the file for the third time.

What's the only thing more ironic than Jerry making sure I read this file by trying to make me delete it? Tirzah thought. *Jerry making sure I* believed *this file by trying to make me delete it.*

The file labeled Apex 3.0 was a set of notes on an experiment with human subjects. Tirzah had come across that sort of thing before, and had been instrumental in getting a drug company exposed for falsifying the results of their studies on a medication. (Information removed: the part about it occasionally making people drop dead.) But this was a whole 'nother ballgame.

If she hadn't been locked in and threatened, she'd have assumed the file was part of a fantasy novel some government employee had been writing in their spare time and storing on the department server, and the only reason it was coded was that they were paranoid about being plagiarized. In fact, she still wasn't one hundred percent sure that *wasn't* what it was.

"Secret black ops experiments on kidnapped soldiers," she said aloud, incredulous. "To give them super powers and make them into shapeshifters. And not even just regular shapeshifters, but shapeshifters that turn into magical or extinct animals. I'd watch the hell out of that movie!"

She read the file for the fourth time, skimming over the more technical parts and focusing on the nitty-gritty, which included an awful lot of To Be Determineds:

Subject: Thirty
Name: Pierce, Ransom.
Occupation: Recon Marine.
Previous/Other Occupations: [Redacted]
Shift Form: Hellhound.
Powers: TBD. Possible clairvoyance?
Limitations: Ability to recognize and bond with mate has been severed. As a mythic shifter, he cannot shift while touching shiftsilver.

Subject: Thirty-One
Name: TBD.
Alias: Merrick, Merlin.
Occupation: Recon Marine.
Previous/Other Occupations: Circus performer, talk show host, rodeo clown, private language teacher, short order cook, fortune cookie writer, Olympic gymnast, stunt man, chicken sexer. [Attn: Dr. Lamorat: There were more but I stopped noting them down before he stopped talking. Do you want every occupation he claims to have had listed on this form? Unclear as to whether any of them are even real so could be a lot of work for Investigations to verify them, with no obvious benefit.]
Shift Form: Raptor.
Powers: TBD.
Limitations: Ability to recognize and bond with mate has been severed.

Subject: Thirty-Two
Name: Valdez, Pete.
Shift Form: Cave bear.
Occupation: Recon Marine.
Previous/Other Occupations: Police Officer. [Attn: Dr. Lamorat: Portions of his police file appear to have been

16

deleted and/or altered. Do you want me to have Investigations look into this?]

Powers: TBD.

Limitations: Ability to recognize and bond with mate has been severed.

Tirzah leaned back with a sigh. The file left her with so many unanswered questions.

What was a mate, and why did it matter if the men couldn't recognize or bond with one?

What were the men's powers?

Who was Dr. Lamorat?

Most importantly, was any of it even real?

Cave bear, Tirzah thought. *Raptor.* Hellhound. *Seriously?*

But Jerry had sure been serious about threatening her. If she'd obeyed him and deleted the file, she was sure he'd have killed her. And then the cover-up would be complete. The whole thing made no sense if the file was fiction. At the very least, *Jerry* must believe it was for real.

And he'd somehow figured out that she was Override. Tirzah's fingers drummed nervously on her desk. Journalists, the FBI, and powerful corporations had tried to track down Override's identity, and all of them had failed. She hadn't gotten to be Override by failing to cover her virtual tracks. But Jerry—or the people behind Jerry—had managed to identify her.

The fear she'd kept at bay until that moment washed over her in an icy wave. Jerry knew who she was. He knew she gave money to cat rescues. He knew the streets where she took her daily walk. (*My daily roll,* she sardonically corrected herself.) He had to know her address, too. He—or someone worse than him—could be coming up the stairs, right now, while most of her neighbors were asleep...

"Stop," she said. The sound of her own voice calmed her.

17

She spent so much time alone, she'd gotten in the habit of talking to herself. "If he wanted to do that, he'd have tried that first. He obviously doesn't want to risk drawing attention to himself."

But now he knew she'd been alerted. He might decide that keeping his bizarre secret was worth taking more risks. Besides, she couldn't just stay in her apartment for the rest of her life.

She needed protection. And she couldn't go to the police.

For the first time since Amy had left, Tirzah smiled. Maybe nothing else going on was simple, but that particular problem had a very simple and easy solution. She'd just hire a personal bodyguard. She sure wasn't going to mention Override, but she could just tell the bodyguard and her curious neighbors that she had a stalker.

The nice thing about being a hacker was that if you had the skills to hack, you also had the skills to make money legally. She could afford the best. And she could do better research than googling "What's the best security agency in Refuge City," which would just get her every agency that put that phrase on their website. Her fingers flew across the keyboard.

It wasn't long before she'd figured out that the answer was Defenders, which was the new East Coast branch of the security agency Protection, Inc. Their website was nice and professional. The names of the individual bodyguards weren't listed, unsurprisingly, but it was child's play for Override to find that out...

A few minutes later, Tirzah sat dumbstruck, staring at her laptop screen.

"You have *got* to be kidding," she said aloud. "Defenders is the hellhound and the cave bear and the velociraptor?"

And some other guy, too, the boss: Roland Walker. She looked him up, but found nothing but an exemplary Army record. Then again, the Apex 3.0 file had records for subjects thirty through thirty-two. For all she knew, Walker was subject twenty-nine or thirty-three.

She tried digging deeper, both into Defenders itself and into the individual men, but hit a wall. Their servers had better protections than the Pentagon, and the men's information seemed to have been wiped beyond some public record stuff that didn't tell her much.

"Okay," she muttered. "So this'll be a challenge."

She organized the few photos she'd found of the bodyguards/experimental test subjects into a neat collage. Which one to research first? The cave bear who used to be a cop before...something? The hellhound with the top secret past? The raptor who either had a lot of weird jobs or a quirky sense of humor? The boss who might or might not be some sort of strange shapeshifter too?

Tirzah decided to start with the cave bear cop. A clumsily falsified police record would probably be the easiest thing to sort out. She quickly broke into the police database and pulled it up. Whoever had written up the Apex file had been correct about Pete Valdez's police records: someone who clearly wasn't used to falsifying records had indeed altered portions, inserting assorted minor infractions and acts of poor judgment in an apparent effort to make him look bad.

Further digging uncovered the intriguing tidbit that much of his department had been indicted for corruption and drug trafficking shortly after he'd resigned from the force. Coincidence? Had he left in disgust at what the other cops were up to? Or had he been involved, but had been smart enough to flee before everyone else got scooped up?

Her gaze returned to one of the photos she'd found of him. It was from a few years ago, and was part of photo-essay on Recon Marines by a war reporter. The caption read, *Wounded Marine waits for medical evacuation.*

A Marine lay on a stretcher, with a medic crouched beside him. Valdez stood over them both, guarding them. His handsome face was streaked with blood and grime, and his camouflage shirt was ripped half off his body, exposing muscles way more impressive than anything she'd seen at the gym. Not that she spent much time in gyms.

But what kept drawing her attention was his eyes, which were big and brown, with an unexpected depth of feeling, and his stance, which looked like you could push the world out from under his feet sooner than you could move him away from the men he was shielding.

He did not look like a crooked cop. He did look like he'd be one hell of a bodyguard.

He looked like he'd be one hell of a boyfriend, come to think of it. Those soulful eyes... Those enormous biceps... That fiercely protective expression...

Tirzah cut off that line of thinking right away. What she needed was a competent person to do a job for her, not a soulmate or a roll in the hay. She had way too much on her plate to deal with a relationship. Just the thought of a first-date conversation made her shudder:

"Hi, I'm Tirzah Lowenstein. I've spent most of the last year recovering from some injuries and adjusting to using a wheelchair. NO I don't want to talk about how the injuries happened. Anyway, I only recently got back to what I normally do, which is illegally hacking for the greater good. Oh, and yesterday someone tried to kill me because I found out about secret government experiments to turn Marines into dinosaurs. And you? What do you do?"

Ugh!

Well, no point brooding over things she couldn't have. She'd stayed up so long that the scrap of sky outside her window was brightening with dawn. No, she didn't need a man. What she needed was more coffee. Tirzah started to push herself away from the desk.

Something slammed into the window, making it rattle in its frame. The thing that had struck the window stayed there, a black blob clinging to the screen.

Tirzah recoiled, instinctively scrabbling for a weapon. She snatched up her phone in one hand and a pen in the other.

The black blob opened a rose-pink mouth and let out a tiny meow.

Her pen fell unnoticed to the floor. She barely managed to lay her phone back on the desk rather than dropping it as well. The creature hanging on to her screen was a very tiny, very furry black kitten.

Five stories up. How had it managed to get that high? More importantly, how could she get it in without scaring it and making it fall to its death?

Her heart pounding, Tirzah reached up very slowly, giving the kitten plenty of time to see her coming, and eased the window open a crack. To her immense relief, the kitten did nothing but stare at her with huge golden eyes, brilliant against its black fur. Even more slowly, Tirzah pulled the window inward.

When the kitten, still clinging to the screen with tiny translucent claws, was inside the apartment, Tirzah heaved such a sigh of relief that she ruffled its fur. The kitten meowed indignantly, then jumped from the screen to her thigh. Tirzah hurriedly slammed the window shut and latched it. The kitten yawned and stretched, arching its back and digging in its pinprick claws.

A pair of wings, as furry and black as the rest of the kitten, unfurled and spread out before Tirzah's disbelieving eyes. The kitten's hindquarters bunched, its little tail twitched, and it launched itself off her thigh.

"No *way*," Tirzah said aloud. "That is *impossible*."

As impossible as hot Marines who turned into cave bears,

she supposed.

The impossible and absolutely adorable flying kitten flew into her kitchen. A few black hairs drifted down in its wake, catching the slanting rays of early dawn light through the blinds that Tirzah thanked her lucky stars she'd pulled.

She followed it into the kitchen, where it was circling below the ceiling like the world's cutest vulture. It looked down at her and meowed like it hadn't eaten in days. Maybe it hadn't. She didn't have any cat food, of course, but she did have some lox in the refrigerator. She wasn't sure how cats felt about smoked salmon, but it was fish so she figured it was worth a try.

Tirzah got it out, then went to get a knife. The kitten let out a triumphant meow and plummeted down like a hawk. It landed with a thump on the cutting board, with all four paws planted in the lox.

"Hey!" Tirzah protested. "I was just going to cut you off a kitten-sized piece. The rest of that was for *my* lunch."

The kitten made a sound that somehow conveyed the message of "finders keepers," despite the fact that it consisted of a meow and was muffled by a giant mouthful of lox.

"I have to cut it up," Tirzah explained. "You'll choke."

The kitten ignored her, growling as it worried at the lox. Tirzah put down the knife and pried the kitten off the pink slab. It flapped its wings, shedding more black hairs, then gulped down a mouthful and choked.

Tirzah swatted it on the back, then held the struggling kitten in one hand and a knife in the other as she cut the lox into kitten-sized bits and scraped it into a saucer. She plunked down the saucer and released the kitten, then watched in amazement as it flew rather than jumped to the floor to devour its meal.

A part of her still wondered if she was having an incredibly vivid dream. But the shed fur all over her clothes, the scratches on her hand, the paw-prints in what remained of the smoked salmon, and the sound of the kitten greedily gobbling up her lox had the unmistakable feel of solid reality.

Tirzah supposed she needed to get some real kitten food. And a litter box. She didn't feel like going out again, especially when that meant leaving the winged troublemaker alone in her apartment, but luckily she could order everything she needed online and get it rush-delivered to her doorstep within the next few hours.

Unless the kitten was like those talking animals from the folktales Grandma used to tell. Those all went on their way once the princess helped them out, returned when she needed help herself, and left for good once she got to her happily ever after. When Tirzah had been a little girl, she'd have preferred the talking horse or hound or hunting cat to the prince. When she'd gotten older, she'd wondered why the princess couldn't have both.

Tirzah really hoped she wasn't living in that sort of fairytale. The kitten had only arrived ten minutes ago, but she loved the little hellraiser already. The idea of a kitten-less apartment suddenly seemed very lonely.

The kitten finished its meal, licked itself thoroughly, then waddled to Tirzah and climbed up her legs, digging in its claws with every step.

"Ow!"

But before she could scoop it up, the kitten was in her lap. There it turned round three times, curled up into a ball that could fit into the palm of her hand, and closed its golden eyes. A disproportionately loud purr rumbled up.

Tirzah guessed the fuzzball was staying.

"And now for you, Pete Valdez," she muttered to herself. "Mr. Hot Marine Bodyguard Cave Bear. Let's see how good you really are before I decide to hire you…"

CHAPTER 2

*P*ete Valdez shook a frying pan over the blue flame of a gas burner. The hash browns were getting nice and crispy, just the way his daughter had always loved them. Sure, his return to civilian life and being a live-in dad had been a little rocky. Okay, it had been incredibly rocky. But he was determined to make it work. Starting with fixing Carolina her all-time favorite breakfast before she headed off to school.

Right on cue, his daughter wandered into the kitchen, yawning and rubbing her eyes. Her long black hair hung straight down her back. She was in a nightgown he remembered, white with a faded print of rearing black horses. When he'd last seen her in it, the hem had hung to her ankles. It was now nearly up to her knees. He couldn't believe how much his little girl had grown up. He kept having to remind himself that she was an actual teenager now.

"Morning, Lina," he called. "Made you breakfast."

"Caro, remember? I haven't gone by Lina for *ages*." Then she looked abashed. "Thanks for making breakfast, Dad."

"You're welcome, Caro. I swear, I'll get used to it any day now."

"Just in time for her to change it again," teased Pete's mother as she came into the kitchen and made a beeline for the coffeepot. "What's wrong with Lina? Lina is cute!"

"Right, Abuelita," Caro replied. "Lina is *cute*. I don't want to be cute little Lina. I want to be sophisticated, teenage Caro."

Pete poured his mother a cup of coffee, then turned to his daughter. "You shouldn't be in such a hurry to grow up. Enjoy being a kid while you can, kid."

To his dismay, Caro looked genuinely hurt. "Don't you like Caro? Is that why you keep calling me Lina?"

"No!" Pete started to reach out to pull her in for a hug, then stopped himself just in time. *Goddammit.* He tried to cover up the movement by picking up the spatula, but Caro had registered it. That kid always had been too sharp for her own good. Her brown eyes were starting to brighten with tears.

"Hey. Hey, come here, Caro." Pete put down the spatula, mentally braced himself, then beckoned her into his open arms.

Caro stepped into his hug, laying her head against his chest. He forced himself not to flinch. No matter how often he experienced it, the pain was always worse than he remembered. Wherever she touched him, his skin burned like she was a living flame. Every fiber of his being screamed out that he needed to let go of her, before he did himself irreparable damage.

Pete held on to his daughter, forcing himself to hug her for long enough for her to be reassured. But he was gritting his teeth so hard that he couldn't speak while he held her. Reluctantly, he broke off the hug and took a step back.

Always before, Caro had been the one to let go. And she

obviously remembered that too. The tears in her eyes threatened to spill over.

"Caro is a beautiful name," Pete said. "You're right, it's more sophisticated. And it suits you. I just need to get used to it, okay?"

She nodded, a little doubtfully.

"Don't tell me you've grown up so much that you don't like hash browns any more," he added, shaking the pan under her nose.

That distraction succeeded. She grinned. "Nope. Gimme."

Pete divided them onto three plates, then cracked eggs into the pan. Scrambled for Mom, fried for himself, and an omelette stuffed with pepperjack cheese for Caro. At least that much hadn't changed.

When he'd been a Recon Marine, Pete had never minded the stress or the exhaustion or the danger. The lack of life's little pleasures like beer and baseball and burgers had annoyed him, but no more than that. But he'd hated spending so much time away from Carolina, especially since his missions were often so secret or remote or both that they couldn't even exchange phone calls or emails. She was the best thing in his life—always had been, ever since she was born—and the job he'd taken to provide for her had meant they rarely saw each other.

When he'd been forced to leave the Marines, after getting kidnapped, experimented on, and given "powers" that felt more like a curse, he'd figured the one good thing would be that he could live with Caro and be an in-person Dad, not a mostly absentee one. And it *was* good. Just…

Well, he'd make it work. That was what a Marine did. You got handed some shitty situation, you didn't complain, you fixed it if it was fixable and made the best of it if it wasn't. If he couldn't fix his… whatever the hell was wrong with him… he'd learn to live with it. Because there was one thing Pete would endure any amount of pain for, and that was to make sure his Caro always knew she was loved.

"Hey!" Caro broke into his thoughts. "Dad, can you drive me to the subway station this weekend?"

"What's at the station?" Pete asked, grating cheese into her omelette.

She rolled her eyes at him. "The subway. Duh."

"The subway to where?"

She coughed, then mumbled, "Refuge City," as if he'd more likely to let his little girl go into the big city all by herself if he didn't quite hear its name.

The cave bear inside Pete's mind, a vast and brooding presence, stirred and growled, *Protect our cub.*

On it, Pete replied silently. To Caro, he said, "Not a chance."

"Daa-aad! People my age who live in the city take the subways by themselves all the time!"

Pete was unsurprised but relieved to see his mother's silent head-shake. Caro saw it too and scowled, deprived of the opportunity to appeal to her Abuelita.

"I don't care what other people's parents let them do," Pete said. "It's not safe. You can go to the city this weekend if you want, but not without your Abuelita or me."

Caro scowled harder. "I hate it here. There's nobody my age. There's nothing fun to do. If we were in the country, I could take riding lessons, and if we were in the city, I could find fun stuff to do just stepping outside. This is the worst of both worlds." Dramatically, she declared, "Suburbs are the soulless embodiment of the death of the American Dream!"

Pete and his mother stared at her, then Caro burst into giggles. Pete chuckled, but there was also an ache in his chest. When he'd been her age, he'd desperately wanted to be treated like a man, but had all the emotional maturity of a toddler. Caro too was poised between worlds, swinging between acting like a little kid and talking like a college professor.

"Don't live in the suburbs once you leave home, then," Mom said.

"I won't! Look out, Refuge City University, here comes Caro!"

Caro had a point about the suburbs, and it was true that this neighborhood was almost entirely populated by retirees. But it was safe. And right now, with... things... the way they were, safety was more important than anything.

Pete slid the omelette on to her plate. "Eat up. You'll need that protein for energy, so you can get good enough grades to get in."

Caro dug into her omelette with an enthusiasm that couldn't be faked. Gulping down a bite, she declared, "Discussion topic! Is a hot dog a sandwich? Support your reasoning."

Pete grinned. She'd been amusing herself with discussion topics since before he'd left, and could spin them out for hours if they were on a long car ride. Obligingly, he said, "It's not a sandwich. A sandwich has bread, not a bun."

"Not a sandwich," said Abuelita. "Just because something has a filling doesn't make it a sandwich. A taco isn't a sandwich, and neither is a ravioli."

They both waited expectantly for Caro, who always took the contrary position if Pete and his mother agreed.

Caro held up a finger. "I say it's a sandwich! Dad, would you define a hoagie as a sandwich?"

He saw the trap coming, but had to say, "Sure."

"And what is used to enclose the filling in a hoagie?" Caro asked.

"A bread roll," said Pete.

"A BUN!" said Caro triumphantly.

"A bread roll!" retorted Pete.

"Define the difference between a bread roll and a bun," said Caro.

They had an enjoyable argument about the definition of sandwiches over breakfast, during which Mom got out her phone and pulled up the USDA's definition of "sandwich," which specifically ruled out both hot dogs and tacos as sandwiches, and Caro countered by taking out her phone and producing the New York State definition, which defined them "any bread product surrounding a filling and meant to be eaten with the fingers."

"An excellent and productive discussion," Caro announced, having finished her omelette. She ran off to shower.

"Don't slam—" Mom began to shout after her.

BANG! The bathroom door slammed with a sound like a gunshot. Pete, who had gotten used to that, didn't so much as blink.

A second later, the door popped back open and Caro stuck her head out. "Dad! Forget Refuge City. Let's do a cook-off this weekend! You, me, and Abuelita. We each cook something delicious—possibly sandwiches, which as we now know include any bread product with a filling and meant to be eaten with the fingers—and then we all vote on our favorites."

"Sounds great, Caro," Pete said, inwardly crossing his fingers that he wouldn't get any 24-7 bodyguarding jobs between now and then. "Are you in, Mom? How about your famous taco sandwiches?"

His mother hesitated, then said, "Of course I'm in. Let's do it Sunday."

"Oooooh," Caro sang out. "Abuelita's got a hot date Saturday with her booooooooooyfriend!"

Pete chuckled, thinking Caro was teasing her grandmother over her book group or yoga class or something like that. But to his surprise, Mom looked genuinely put on the spot. "Caro, be respectful. It's not a 'hot date,' it's Shakespeare in the Park."

In the exact same teasing sing-song she'd used before, Caro said, "Abuelita's got a hot date Saturday with her booooooooooyfriend—and Shakespeare!" Her final word was punctuated with another slam of the bathroom door.

Pete and his mother looked at each other. That was the first he'd heard of his mother dating. It was hard to wrap his head around.

"A boyfriend, huh?" Pete asked.

A faint blush darkened her cheeks. A little defensively, she said, "He's not my boyfriend. He's someone I met at my yoga class. This will be our first date. I've never brought him home. Caro's just heard us talking on the phone."

"Whoa, whoa!" Pete held up a hand. "It's fine, Mom. You're allowed to date." He wasn't entirely joking when he added, "If you give me his full name and date of birth, I'll run a background check."

"You'll do no such thing," she said, then added thought-fully, "If I get serious about him or anyone else, though, I'll give you all the info."

Pete stared at her. That sure sounded like she was ready to take a flying leap into the dating pool.

His mother, dating for the first time in ten years. His little girl, growing up. Himself, changed. Everything that used to be solid was unsteady under his feet.

"Go to work, mijo," his mother said. "I'll drive Caro to school."

Pete knew perfectly well what that meant: his mother, who was just as sharp as her granddaughter, hadn't missed what had gone down between them at breakfast, and intended to have yet another talk on the subject of "War changes people, you can't expect your father to be exactly the same as he was the last time you saw him, but he still loves you more than anything."

"Yeah. Okay." Automatically, he bent his head to let her kiss his forehead, their old ritual to wish him safety. And then flinched away from the searing agony.

"I—" Pete's voice ran down. He couldn't tell her what was going on. He didn't even understand it himself. But he did know that revealing that there was a hell of a lot more wrong with him than combat trauma could do nothing but bring pain and danger down on the ones he loved most.

If anyone needed to bear that pain, it was him.

The wrinkles deepened around his mother's brown eyes. He'd hurt her anyway, and he knew it. There was nothing either of them could say.

Mom gestured with one hand. "Mijo. Go, before Caro comes out and starts an argument."

Pete went. But he didn't get two steps before Mom reminded him, "Your laptop?"

He scooped it up from the sofa where he'd left it the night before, still in its carrying case. There was another thing he found hard to get used to: he was working a job where they actually issued laptops to employees. Not that Pete had ever used his for much.

He got into his car and tossed the laptop into the back seat, then set out through the placid suburbs and toward the city.

It was over an hour later when he finally made it to the underground parking lot of the Defenders office, and his temper was frayed by the endless traffic jams and all the assholes who'd cut in front of him, making him even later. It was obviously going to be one of those days.

Pete scowled even harder when he saw all the other cars in in the lot. He'd hoped to not have to deal with anyone but his boss, Roland. And Roland's sensible, sturdy car was there, parked neatly in the slot reserved for him.

But so was Ransom's latest rental car, every one of which seemed to have been selected for anonymity and which he switched out every month, like he was some kind of fugitive dodging the cops. This month it was a dull red Honda. Merlin's ridiculously tiny British sports car looked like a toy beside it. And as if that wasn't bad enough, Carter Howe, who wasn't even a member of the team, was back again. He'd parked his show-off Ferrari across two spaces. The lot was full of empty spaces, so it didn't squeeze anyone in. But still. It was the principle of the thing.

Pete parked his Ford as far from Carter and Merlin as he could manage, then reluctantly headed for the elevator. He paused with his finger hovering over the button. Carter *wasn't* on the team—he just showed up occasionally to do tech stuff, then disappeared again. For all Pete knew, he'd come in early and was already on his way out. And a pampered rich guy like him would definitely take the elevator rather than the stairs.

Pete headed up the stairs, taking them two or three at a time. Even if he missed Carter, there was still Merlin and Ransom to contend with. And if you weren't looking forward to something, the best thing to do was get it over with as fast as possible.

He stepped onto the first landing, and came face-to-face with a velociraptor. It stood as tall as he did, lean and predatory, its fangs glistening white against its black hide.

Pete jerked backward. Only his quick reflexes in grabbing the rail saved him from taking a very bad tumble down the stairs.

"Goddammit, Merlin!" he yelled.

The velociraptor grew to the size of a pony, forcing Pete to step back again, then shrank to the size of a St. Bernard. It let out a frustrated hiss that reminded Pete of Mom's tea kettle, then suddenly became a blond man in blue jeans. His T-shirt had a drawing of cavemen hunting a woolly mammoth, with the slogan, *The REAL paleo diet.*

"Sorry," Merlin said, not sounding particularly sorry. "No one ever uses the stairs, so I figured it was a good place to practice. I forgot that Carter was here."

"What the hell does Carter have to do with it?"

"You were taking the stairs to avoid him, weren't you?"

The cave bear in Pete's mind snarled. Pete held it in tight check as he glared at Merlin, but he knew the beast was looking out of his eyes. Most men would've stepped back. Even most *Marines* would've stepped back.

Merlin just smiled that bright, annoying smile of his. "Carter's checking all our laptops for viruses and stuff. Did you forget yours at home? He'll be pissed."

That was when Pete realized that he'd left the laptop in the back seat of his car. Swearing under his breath, he started back down the stairs.

Yeah. It was obviously going to be one of those days.

Pete took the elevator up. Sure enough, Carter was in the lobby, sitting on the sofa in front of a coffee table with a set of laptops on it. He was dressed to the nines, as usual. Pete was willing to bet that his shoes alone cost more than Pete's car.

Carter glanced up at Pete. "Thanks for gracing us with your presence, Valdez. I hope you haven't been surfing any porn sites. They're full of viruses."

"You would know." Pete shoved his laptop case at Carter, making sure their fingers didn't touch.

"Purely academic knowledge," Carter retorted. "I'd never pay for that stuff."

"You get porn for free?" Merlin inquired innocently. "Where?"

Ransom glanced up from his seat in the corner. The grim lines of his angular face brightened slightly as he remarked, "If you can make a billion off tech, you can figure out how to hack into porn sites."

Carter shot an annoyed look at him. "You're done, Pierce. No viruses, no hijacking. No search history. You ever actually use this thing?"

"I don't need it," Ransom said.

A brief silence fell as everyone looked at him. It was true as far as Pete knew—Ransom's power seemed to give him the ability to know things, from being aware of events happening far away to learning secrets about people—but it was rare for him to talk about it and Pete had the impression that he didn't like using his power.

"I have search history," Merlin volunteered.

"I'm aware, Merrick," Carter said, rolling his eyes. "I can teach you how to wipe it—"

"Oh, I know how," Merlin assured him. "I just thought it would be more fun for you if I left it up. In case you wanted to check out any of the cool links I found."

"Not particularly," Carter replied. "And you're—"

"Let me show you this amazing link I found on how to make a goldfish out of hot sugar!" Merlin broke in, leaning over Carter and typing on his laptop. "It comes out looking just like blown glass!"

"You're done." Carter shoved Merlin's laptop into his hands as if he was fending off an over-eager golden retriever.

"But—" Merlin protested.

"DONE," Carter said.

He spoke just as the door to Roland's office opened. The Defenders boss ran his hand over his silvering hair and said, "Want a break, Carter? Or a drink?"

"I've just got Pete's left," Carter said.

"But—" Merlin began.

34

"Whatever it is, the answer is no," Carter snapped. "I don't even know why I bother coming here."

Roland said, "Because we like having you around."

Carter frowned, staring at the Defenders boss as if searching for sarcasm, but found none, just Roland's steady, straightforward gaze. He seemed at a loss for how to reply.

Pete, watching their silent regard, was reminded of how, in the middle of a desperate battle, he'd once seen Roland step calmly forward and raise his arms, and fire had blossomed along them. Pete only once seen the phoenix that Roland could become, but he'd never forgotten it; beneath that exterior of calm authority smoldered a fire that could light the world.

"Thanks," Carter said, as if the word had been dragged from his lips against his will. "I'm about to go, though."

Merlin flipped open his laptop and held it up. "No, wait, this is really amazing."

"Get that thing out of my face," Carter said.

Undaunted, Merlin went on, "You know I was raised in a circus—"

"Oh, God, not that again," Carter said.

"—and my best friend, Natalie, was apprenticed to the lion tamer—"

Quietly, Roland retreated back into his office and shut the door.

"—who was the third cousin twice removed of the former empress of Moldavia, which doesn't come into this story but I do think it's interesting—"

"Maybe *you* do, but nobody else does," Pete broke in.

"—but the important part is the feud between the lion tamer and the seal trainer, which started three years before Natalie and I were born—"

Ransom picked up his laptop case and headed for the elevator. Merlin glanced from Roland's closed office door to

Pete's glare to the top of Carter's head as it bent over Pete's laptop, and apparently decided that the best audience for his ridiculous bullshit story was Ransom's back. Merlin pursued him out the door, still talking.

"—over a little matter of a missing camel—"

The door slammed behind them both, cutting off Merlin's voice and leaving Pete and Carter alone together. Pete could hardly believe that he was glad of that, but at least for the moment, he was. With any luck Carter would spend five silent minutes checking his laptop, and then Pete could—

"Whoa!" Carter said. "Valdez, your laptop's been hijacked."

Pete had no idea what that meant. "I have a virus?"

"No, I mean that some hacker took over your camera and is using it to spy on you. Every time you open it, they can see whatever the computer sees."

Pete stared at the screen, which now seemed to glow with a sinister light. "Someone is looking at us now?"

"No." Carter tapped his finger on the screen. Once he'd pointed it out, Pete could see the little black square Carter had stuck over the camera. "I put that on before I opened it, so the hacker hasn't seen anything yet. I disabled audio too. But if you've used your computer in the last..." His fingers flew over the keys. "Two days, then..."

Pete shook his head. A slow-burning rage was heating him from within, stoked by the ferocious growling of his cave bear. Thank God, that hijacker hadn't seen his home. He hadn't seen Mom. He hadn't seen Caro. But he'd tried to. "Where is he?"

Carter typed, typed, typed, while Pete's fury grew until the room seemed hazed with red. When Carter finally spoke, Pete could barely hear him over the snarling in his head. "I've got an address for you. There's no guarantee they're still there, though..."

"Give it to me."

Pete took the address, and his laptop too. He stormed out of the office, the case swinging from his hand. He'd break it over the hacker's head.

But the heavy rush hour traffic gave him enough time to cool down, just slightly. Just enough that when he saw that the address was in a large apartment building, he made sure to park well away and approach stealthily. People stood chatting at the front, and might well notice that he didn't belong. But he was prepared for that. He pulled on a red jacket and walked up with a pair of empty pizza boxes, and nobody gave him a second glance.

Once Pete was on the fifth floor, where his target lurked, his rage returned, filling his veins like boiling water. He stashed his pizza boxes and jacket in a utility closet, then approached the hacker's door. He picked the lock as quietly as he could, remembering Merlin, who had taught him to do it, saying, "Pretend it's a raw egg at the bottom of a Jenga tower made of fifty more raw eggs." At the time Pete had thought that was a typically ridiculous thing to say, but now it helped to guide his hands.

First the bottom lock, then the top opened with the softest of clicks. Pete threw open the door and kicked it shut behind him. That spy would wish he'd never—

A pair of startled brown eyes met his. The hacker was a very pretty woman of about his age, with a tumble of curly brown hair, soft full lips, and a determined-looking jaw. Her slim hands were frozen on the keyboard of a laptop, and her bare feet rested on the foot supports of her wheelchair.

They stared at each other, both too surprised to speak.

And that was when he got a faceful of flying kitten.

CHAPTER 3

*T*irzah was too startled by the unexpected entrance of Pete Valdez, Hot Cave Bear Bodyguard Who Never Opens His Laptop, to say a word. She did, however, hear herself emit a faint squeaking noise.

And that was apparently all it took to set off Batcat's protective instincts. She dove from her perch atop the ceiling light like a very tiny, very fluffy missile, right into Hot Home Invader Bodyguard's face.

He staggered backward and fetched up against her front door. Batcat resisted his attempt to pry her off, wrapping all four legs around his head and hissing like a tea kettle.

"Be careful with her! She's just a kitten!" Tirzah sent her chair rocketing forward to remove Batcat herself.

Just as she reached his side, what sounded like every tenant on the fifth floor began shouting and pounding on her door.

"Tirzah! Are you all right?"

"Tirzah! Do you need help?"

"Tirzah! Should we call the cops?"

The door opened a crack before Pete Valdez's weight

thudded it shut. She grabbed the doorknob and hauled herself to her feet. Once she was up, Tirzah caught Batcat by the scruff of the neck and pulled.

Reluctantly, the kitten came loose. And then Tirzah realized that she was standing with only a door between her and a whole bunch of very concerned neighbors, holding a flapping, spitting, winged kitten.

She was so desperate for help, she looked up at Pete, who was the cause of the entire problem. Their eyes met. He had the most beautiful eyes, big and brown and soft. Gentle eyes in a hard man's face.

He bent down, and the dog tags he wore on a chain around his neck clinked together as he murmured in her ear, "Turn on something loud. I'll hide the kitten."

There was a split second in which she wondered whether to trust him. He *had* broken into her apartment…

…but it was obvious why. More than that, it was justifiable. And though she'd thought she'd covered her traces, he'd somehow managed to not only figure out that his laptop had been hijacked, he'd tracked it back to her. If he was that good of a hacker, or had that good of a hacker on staff, she *definitely* wanted to hire him.

That was, if he'd be willing to take her business after she'd spied on him and her flying kitten had scratched up his face.

But that could all be dealt with later. Right now, she needed to hide Batcat. And though she knew looks could be deceiving, she found it impossible to believe that anyone with eyes like that could do anything with a kitten but cuddle it.

"Hide yourself too," she murmured back. "I don't want to have to explain how you got in here."

A glimmer of humor sparked in his eyes as he whispered, "Me neither."

Tirzah transferred Batcat to him (a procedure which

39

involved him getting a number of scratches on his hands to match those on his face), and locked her door, shouting, "I'm fine!" to cover the sound of the click.

She quickly wheeled to her laptop, typed even more quickly, then returned to the door.

"Don't rush in!" Tirzah called. "I'm right at the door."

She put a hand on the wall for balance and glanced back to make sure that Pete Valdez and Batcat were both out of sight. Then she opened the door to one Jewish grandma waving a cellphone and another brandishing a cast iron frying pan, a beefy biker with a baseball bat, one of Amy's dads coming to Tirzah's aid and the other shooing Amy back into their apartment, a Filipina Navy vet with a prosthetic hand and a "No one messes with my neighbor" expression, and a teenage boy in a black hoodie with bubblegum-pink lettering reading *No more throne, no more crown, fuck shit up and burn it down.*

Tirzah smiled. There they were, her neighbor family, all rushing to her rescue.

Right on cue, the sounds of hushed arguing from the movie playing on the laptop suddenly rose into a blast of noise, then subsided.

"Sorry," Tirzah said. "I'm fixing a laptop with a volume-control issue, and my headphones fell off."

"Man," Jamal said, peering at it from within the depths of his black and pink hoodie. "It really sounded like there was some kind of fight going on in here."

"Only onscreen," Tirzah said. "But I really appreciate you all looking out for me!"

Amy's head popped out of her apartment. Tirzah waved at her. "I'm fine! I was just playing a movie too loud."

"Daddy says that's rude," Amy said disapprovingly, and vanished.

The crowd began to sheepishly disperse. But Esther,

frying pan now dangling at her side, fixed Tirzah with a gimlet eye. "That's some movie. My walls shook."

"Low-frequency sound can do that," Tirzah replied.

"Hmph." Esther was clearly unsatisfied, but didn't know enough about the relevant technology to argue.

"Thanks again!" Tirzah said brightly, and closed the door.

She sank back into her chair, then spun it around. Where had Pete gone...? Her closet door opened, revealing him with a napping Batcat cradled to his chest. The sight of the tall, strong, muscular man gently holding an adorable fluffy kitten made Tirzah melt inside.

He's your bodyguard, not your boyfriend, she reminded herself. *And maybe not even that, depending on how ticked off he is over the laptop hijacking.*

Then, to provide a plausible explanation for any warm fuzzy feelings that might have showed on her face, she said, "I'm glad that... you're in my closet! That is, I was worried that you'd gone into my bedroom."

Pete looked genuinely offended at the suggestion. "I would never go into a woman's bedroom without her permission."

"You came into my apartment without my permission," Tirzah pointed out.

"Because you spied on me! Anyway, I didn't know who you were." He looked at her, then down at the snoozing Batcat draped over his right hand. "Who *are* you? Why did you hijack my laptop? Where did you get this kitten?"

"Wow, that's a lot." As a scowl started to darken his face, she hurriedly said, "I'll tell you! I just meant, it'll take a while. Also I have some questions for you, too. But the short answers are, I'm Tirzah Lowenstein, I hijacked your laptop because I wanted to hire you as my bodyguard so I needed to check you out first to make sure you're on the up-and-up, and the kitten just appeared at my window."

41

"It just appeared at your window," he repeated, laying on the disbelief with a trowel.

Irritated, Tirzah said, "Is there some other explanation of where I got my *flying kitten* that you think would be more plausible? A pet shop? The Humane Society?"

Pete rubbed his jaw. He had a little streak of stubble he'd missed shaving that morning, a sharp black line against his smooth brown skin. Tirzah couldn't help wanting to touch it. Watching her closely, he said, "A lab, maybe?"

"Oh! Yeah, sure, that makes sense. I guess she must be genetically engineered." She didn't want to admit that she'd thought the kitten might be magical. Then again, she was talking to a man who supposedly could turn into a cave bear.

Who'd supposedly been altered *in a lab* to make him turn into a cave bear. Tirzah's mind, always her best asset, assembled the bits of scattered data into a clear, if incomplete, picture. "Did you see something like her in the Apex lab?"

Pete's head snapped up. "What do you know about Apex?"

He spoke in a quiet voice that she bet had terrified the criminals he'd caught when he'd been a cop. It might have scared her too, if he wasn't still holding her kitten cupped in one of his big-knuckled hands. But she found it impossible to be afraid of a man who was so gentle with a baby animal.

"I downloaded one of their files," she said. "It's kind of a long story."

"I got time."

Tirzah swallowed. He'd spoken simply, a statement of fact, but something about the deep timbre of his voice made her think of other contexts he might say those words in. Such as lying naked in bed, his brown skin and black hair striking against her white sheets. *We can make love all night. I got time.* Or maybe just sitting in her living room, his strong arm warm around her shoulders. *"Let's just stay here a while. I got time."*

Like that would ever happen.

Pete lifted his free hand and touched one of the scratches Batcat had left in his face. Most of them were nothing more than pink lines, but a few had drawn blood. His fingers came away spotted with red.

"Let me put some hydrogen peroxide on those," Tirzah offered.

He waved her offer away. "Nah, nah. It's nothing."

"Oh, come on. It makes me feel weird watching you bleed and not doing anything."

"I'm not bleeding."

"What's that, then? Ketchup?" Tirzah reached for his hand. He started to pull it away, but stopped the movement in mid-gesture. She caught his hand and turned it over, showing him the blood on his fingertips. "See?"

Pete didn't answer. His pupils were so big that his eyes looked black. His hand trembled slightly, then closed convulsively over hers. His grip was strong, almost crushing, just short of pain.

Tirzah swallowed. She hadn't meant anything by the gesture—well, okay, if she was being honest with herself, she supposed she'd jumped at the opportunity to touch him, even for a brief instant. But she'd meant to keep it light, then let him go. Now he was hanging on to her hand like he was drowning and she'd reached out from a lifeboat.

The air in her apartment felt hot and thick, like the world had skipped from late autumn to the height of summer. She was suddenly very conscious of the heat of his own body, and of his clean masculine scent. He was running his thumb over the back of her hand, a tiny movement but one which focused all her attention on that half-inch of her skin. It sent tingling electricity straight down to her core. She shifted in her chair, squeezing her thighs together.

43

Pete abruptly released her hand, looking stunned. His voice was husky as he said, "Yeah. Yeah, okay. You do that."

For a moment she had no idea what he was talking about. Do what? Then she remembered her offer of hydrogen peroxide. "Right. Um, this way."

She spun her chair around and headed for the bathroom, leaving him to follow. The slight breeze created by her movement cleared her head. By the time she got to the bathroom, she was able to wave Pete inside and speak in a businesslike tone. "Sit down there."

She indicated the plastic stool she sat on to take a shower. He sat, a bit gingerly as if he was afraid it would collapse beneath his weight. Batcat woke up, stretched, fell off Pete's hand with a startled meow, snapped out her wings, and arrested her fall at the last moment, skimming so low over the floor that her tail brushed it. Tirzah and Pete watched her go until she turned the corner and vanished from their view.

"That is some cat," Pete remarked. "My—One of my co-workers would love it." Tirzah could have sworn he'd started to refer to someone else. But before she could inquire, he went on, "Does it have a name?"

"She. It's Batcat."

Pete chuckled. "Good name. Yeah." Another fractional pause. "Merlin would love her."

"Your co-worker?" Tirzah just barely stopped herself from saying, *"The one who turns into a raptor and claims to have been a rodeo clown?"* "Uh, another bodyguard?"

"Yeah."

Tirzah leaned on the sink as she stood up to collect her supplies from the cabinet over the sink. She hadn't used hydrogen peroxide since her accident, apparently, as it was way on the top shelf gathering dust. The doctors had given her prescription stuff to use on her own injuries. Her fingers brushed against it, but she couldn't grab it.

"Want me to get that for you?" Pete's deep voice filled the small room.

"Yeah, thanks."

He didn't even have to stand to reach it down for her, and a bag of cotton balls as well. Noticing her staring, he remarked, "Monkey arms."

That wasn't at all what she'd been thinking, but she could hardly say, *"No, actually I was thirsting for your sexy biceps."*

Hoping she wasn't blushing, she poured some peroxide on to a cotton ball. "Shut your eyes. The peroxide will sting if it gets in them."

He tensed, just slightly but she noticed it. They were so close that she could feel the heat of his body. He seemed too big for the room, like it had become one of her own doll-houses and he was the real person reaching inside. And yet, as she watched him watching her, she could have sworn that he was afraid. He was actually trembling.

PTSD, maybe? He'd been in combat. Maybe he'd been ambushed on a dark night, or taken hostage and blindfolded. Whatever it was, she guessed he didn't like being touched when he couldn't see who was touching him. And of course he was such a man's man, he'd never admit it.

It wasn't like Tirzah didn't understand trauma-related phobias, or being too embarrassed to admit to them. A warm rush of sympathy filled her. But she knew how she could make it easier for him.

"Actually, keep your eyes open," she said. "I'll shield them for you. Here."

Tirzah laid her hand on his forehead.

CHAPTER 4

*P*ete was glad he was sitting down when Tirzah laid her hand on his forehead. If he hadn't been, his legs might have gone out from under him.

That first time she'd touched him, it had nearly knocked him off his feet. Her hand had been warm against his, her palm velvet-soft with a few thickened areas, probably from propelling her wheelchair.

And it hadn't hurt.

He drew in a shaky breath, marveling again at the joyous shock of that moment.

It hadn't hurt.

Ever since he'd been kidnapped and experimented on, any human touch had been agonizing. But when Tirzah had touched him, taking his bare hand in hers, it had felt... good.

Pete had almost forgotten what it felt like to enjoy the touch of skin to skin. It was like a jailhouse door opening, letting in a flood of sunshine and fresh spring air. Like when you're so exhausted that you can't even raise your arms, and your buddy lifts the eighty pound rucksack off your back.

Tirzah's touch was like life itself.

And now she had her hand on his forehead, protecting his eyes as she dabbed at some tiny scratches that in no way needed any medical attention, but he sure wasn't going to complain.

That feels good.

Pete repressed a start. It was the voice of his cave bear. He still wasn't used to it. The bear rarely spoke, making it startling every time. Usually it was a silent, brooding presence within Pete's mind, vast and primal and filled with rage. But the bear wasn't angry now.

I like her. His cave bear spoke in a rumble that suspiciously resembled a vastly deeper version of Batcat's purr.

I like her too, Pete admitted.

A part of him didn't want to. Tirzah had no right to spy on him, though he was getting the idea that she'd had some fairly good reasons for doing so. But he'd been expecting some sinister criminal, not a pretty, independent, whip-smart, kind-hearted woman with beautiful brown eyes, hair he wanted to run his fingers through, and hands he wanted to hold forever. Her skin, my God, the touch of her soft, smooth, warm, living skin...

I shouldn't be thinking like this, Pete thought. *I can't. She wants a bodyguard, not a boyfriend. And even if she did, I'm not boyfriend material. Not anymore.*

But that thought did nothing to stop his hypersensitivity to her touch. Tirzah dabbed his forehead dry, then cupped his cheek with one hand, holding his face still while she doctored whatever microscopic scratches he had on his other cheek. Pete sent silent thanks to Batcat for the blood she'd drawn, and an invitation to scratch him up some more, any time.

Why can she touch me? Pete asked his cave bear. *What does it mean?*

His cave bear sent him the image of a shrug of his massive

47

shaggy shoulders, followed by the sensation of blissfully dozing in warm sunlight.

Pete couldn't look Tirzah in the eyes, because what he wanted to do right now was a lot more down-and-dirty than sunlit snoozing. Especially the way she was leaning over him with her breasts nearly touching him. He tried hard not to look down her cleavage, and almost succeeded.

She was so close that he could feel the warmth of her body and breathe in her distinctive scent. His senses had gotten sharper since his change, and he could identify the floral scent of her soap and shampoo, a sweet cozy smell of fresh-baked cookies, a sharper undertone of metal and chemicals on her fingers, and over it all, a spicy scent, like nutmeg but warm and human, that he knew was Tirzah herself.

He drew in a deep breath, trying to regain control of himself. So the hacker was a likable, pretty woman whom he could touch without pain. Of course he was attracted to her. But that didn't mean he had to do anything about it. Pete had his hands full trying to make a good life for his family. He had nothing to spare for himself, let alone for a relationship.

She released his face and picked up his hand, carefully dabbing each scratch with peroxide. Then his other hand. For all that he knew he could never have more than this, he couldn't help reveling in her touch. It was all he could do to not toss aside the cotton ball and close his hands over hers. And then...

"Done!" Tirzah released his hands.

A sense of loss hit him like a punch to the gut. What if that moment had been a fluke? What if he'd never enjoy the touch of skin to skin again? Maybe he should lean in, right now, and find out...

Yes, rumbled his cave bear.

No, Pete replied firmly. His mother had always said,

"Never date a woman with more problems than you have." Now Pete was the man with more problems, and he had no intention of inflicting them on a sweet, if not totally law-abiding, woman like Tirzah.

He stood up, ducking to avoid banging his head on the showerhead. "Whoa. Nearly gave you another cut to put peroxide on."

Wish I had, he thought.

"Next time you get banged up, come on by. Or, actually, maybe you'll be here already." A flush of pink spread across her cheeks. A bit flustered, she added, "I mean, if you take that bodyguarding job I wanted to hire you for. Which I still do. Especially since you already know about Batcat and haven't called... whoever you call to report a flying kitten."

Pete couldn't resist. In his best *Ghostbusters* voice, he said, "Who you gonna call?"

"Catbusters!" Tirzah replied.

They both laughed. He wasn't sure exactly how or when it had happened, but they'd somehow gone from being suspicious to awkward to comfortable with each other. There was just something about her that made him feel at ease.

"I'm *not* gonna call," Pete said. "And it sounds like you have an idea why not. Tell you what. You tell me your story, then I'll tell you mine."

"What, so you can know what to leave out based on what I already know?" Tirzah didn't sound angry, just frank.

"You don't miss a trick. Look, it's nothing personal. Some stuff involves other people, and some is secret—official, US military top secret—and some..." Pete trailed off. Then, looking into Tirzah's sharp brown eyes, he said quietly, "Some I just don't talk about. That's all."

To his immense relief, she didn't pursue it. "Fair enough. So, about that bodyguarding thing—and all the other things... Would you like some coffee while I explain? I just made a pot. Cookies? I have homemade lavender shortbread, homemade pecan bars, Circus Animals—"

"I'm not much for cookies."

"A bagel with lox? No, wait, the lox all got eaten or stepped on. I might have some of Jim's Irish soda bread..."

Pete realized he wasn't going to get a thing out of her until she fed him. "Okay."

"Okay coffee? Okay bagel?"

"Okay coffee and soda bread, if there's any left. I never even heard of it and I'm curious what it is. Is it like 7-up cake?"

"No, that's soda as in baking soda. It's sort of like a scone, but not sweet. Still want it?"

"Sure. I'll give it a try."

They headed out into the living room. Batcat ran alongside Tirzah's wheelchair, squeaking indignantly, until Tirzah reached down with one hand, scooped her up, and settled the kitten on to her shoulder.

"Can't she take off from the floor?" Pete asked.

"I'm still trying to figure that out. Might just be harder for her."

"Or maybe she likes being picked up," Pete suggested.

"Oh, she *definitely* likes that."

Pete followed Tirzah into the kitchen. "Can I help you with anything?"

"Hmm." She gave him a speculative glance before she apparently decided he could be trusted with her dishes. "Yeah, sure. Saucers are there, mugs are there."

Pete took out the dishes, realizing as he did that Tirzah would not only have to stand to get them, but would probably have to reach so high that she'd have to feel around for them. He wondered if her disability was recent and she hadn't had time to renovate yet, or if she couldn't afford to. Then, remembering the multiple shiny new laptops in the living room, he decided that she had to be able to afford it. And not enough time didn't make sense either, because she clearly knew her way around the wheelchair and he could build her a basic wheelchair-level cabinet in a day. A week, if he made it fancy.

As he watched her pick up the coffee maker from the counter and pour out the coffee, he was torn between wanting to offer to build her that cabinet, and the knowledge that if she didn't have it already, there was probably a reason why. And she *could* manage on her own, that was obvious. He just found himself wanting to smooth her path a bit.

"Milk? Sugar?" Tirzah asked.

"Both, thanks."

"Say when."

She slowly poured milk and sugar into his coffee mug until he said when, then gave hers a careless splash of each. Tirzah helped herself to one each of four different types of cookies, then warmed an English muffin-like thing—that had to be the Irish soda bread—in a microwave.

Pete tried not to openly stare at her, but he was fascinated. For all that she'd spied on him and didn't seem at all remorseful about it, there was so much sweet thoughtfulness in her nature, too. He'd barged into her apartment, and her response was to pry her kitten off his face, treat his scratches, refuse to get down to business until he had coffee and food, and make sure the coffee was exactly how he liked it and the food was hot.

As she turned to go into the living room, pulling the wheeled table with her, her curls fell aside and he saw that her shoulders were marked with the pink scratches of Batcat's claws. Pete looked closer, and saw the kitten digging in her claws for balance as Tirzah moved.

Like me with Caro, Pete thought. *She'd rather let herself get hurt than push away someone she loves.*

51

Tirzah gestured to Pete to take the armchair, and stepped from her chair to the sofa. She sank into the cushions, stretching out her body and rotating her shoulders. Pete could hear the soft pop of her joints.

"Long day waiting for me to open my laptop?" he asked.

"Yep. You ever use that thing?"

"Not if I can help it. I like to work with my hands."

"Me too." Tirzah tapped on the rolling table between them as if she was typing on a keyboard.

Pete scoffed. "Not like that."

"I figured," she replied, smiling. "So, how'd you find me, then? How'd you track me?"

"Oh, there's this guy who helps us out with computer stuff. He opened up my laptop and..." Pete imitated her tapping motion.

"Huh. He must be good. Because, not to brag, but *I'm* good."

"Yeah, I guess he is." Pete hadn't thought much about it before, but he supposed Carter had done *something* to earn his millions or billions or however much it took to have your very own private jet. But Carter wasn't the person on his mind.

Remembering his bodyguard training from Roland, Pete said, "Okay, I want to hear your story. Start at whatever you think is the very beginning. Don't leave out any details because you think they're not important. Let me decide that, okay?"

"Okay." But she obviously wasn't okay with telling him something, because instead of doing so, she fidgeted, cleared her throat, and petted Batcat. To put her at ease, Pete didn't stare at her, but picked up his coffee mug and took a sip.

"No no no, don't drink any coffee!"

Pete put it down, startled. "Why? Did you slip in a sleeping pill?"

"No!" Tirzah rubbed her head. "I'm just about to tell you something really shocking, or at least really surprising, and I didn't want you to spit it out."

Pete couldn't help laughing. "You were trying to rescue me from *doing a spit-take?*"

With immense dignity, Tirzah said, "Yes." Then, dramatically, she said, "You see... I'm Override."

A silence fell in which she obviously expected him to react. When he didn't, she said, "Override, the hacker!"

"Uh... That's your... hacker name? Like a pilot's call sign?"

Tirzah gave a long-suffering sigh. "Well, that was anticlimactic. Yeah, Pete, it's my hacker name. You're not going to arrest me if I confess to some crimes—some extremely justified crimes! Right?"

"I'm not a cop." Even all these years later, that sentence was bitter in his mouth. But he forged on. "Stop worrying that I'm going to turn you in for something. I'm not. Not for spying on me, not for Batcat, not for whatever hacking stuff you do. It's not my job." He stopped himself from saying *"anymore."*

"Good. Now eat your soda bread."

"Is it safe for me to wash it down with coffee?" Pete teased.

"Yeah. Apparently being America's most famous non-evil hacker isn't spit take-worthy."

"You're famous?"

Wryly, she replied, "I guess I'm not *that* famous."

"Up until recently, I was a Recon Marine," he pointed out. "I spent a lot of time in places that didn't have newspapers or TV, let alone the internet."

"Oh, right. Hmm. Okay, this one you might've heard of, even if you didn't know a hacker was involved. It was pretty recent, and I imagine it got talked about a lot in the military.

There was a big scandal at the VA, when it came out that some of the administrators were lining their own pockets with money that was supposed to pay for veterans' healthcare..."

Pete had heard about that one, all right. His cave bear snarled, echoing his own anger. "I heard. A vet died waiting for an operation that she should've gotten right away, and the people who'd been stealing money actually got charged with homicide... Wait. You were the one who blew the whistle on them?"

She nodded. "I hacked into the VA computer system and then their own personal computers, collected the evidence, and sent it to the FBI and a bunch of journalists. And that's what Override does. It's illegal, but it's to stop people who are doing much worse things than a little spying on the bad guys."

Now that Pete had gotten to know her a bit, her confession didn't quite surprise him. Of course she'd take it upon herself to risk jail time to help strangers, solely because she saw it as the right thing to do.

"So that's me!" Tirzah threw out her hands. "The notorious Override!"

Pete heard the nervousness underlying her bravado. Hoping she could see his sincerity, he looked into the depths of her brown eyes and said, "Listen to me, Tirzah. Sometimes what's legal isn't what's right. Legal isn't important to me anymore. Right is. If you need to go against the law because it's the right thing to do, well..." Pete bit back the impulse to say, *"Me too."*

No. He could never tell her what he'd done. Pete might not be computer-smart enough to understand exactly how Tirzah did her thing, but he knew it basically came down to illegal typing. If she'd ever done anything violent in her life, he'd eat his pizza delivery box. He could hear her confession, but his would do nothing but scare and horrify her. And that would be the last he'd ever see of those gorgeous brown eyes.

"…I got no problem with it," he concluded. "Personally, I think you ought to get a medal. You did what needed to be done and no one else was doing. Now, tell me why you need a bodyguard."

CHAPTER 5

irzah began with her encounter with "Jerry." Pete was a good listener, occasionally asking questions that served to jog her memory or get her to focus on details that she hadn't thought were important enough to include but which Pete clearly found relevant.

He didn't speak as she told him how Jerry had locked her in, but she could sense his building anger like a heat haze in the air around him. And when she said that she realized that Jerry was going to kill her, Pete interrupted.

"You don't have to worry about him. I'll protect you."

She stared at him, taken aback. "I haven't even finished my story. And, um, it involves you. Sort of. I mean even more than me spying on you. You might not want to make any promises till you hear it all."

The heat haze feeling intensified. Pete's voice was low and dangerous as he said, "You said that asshole meant to kill you. I believe it. As far as me protecting you is concerned, that's all that matters. If you still want to hire me, you got me. And if you don't want me, then I'll take you to the

Defenders office and you can pick someone else from my team. They're kind of, uh…"

She watched him struggle for words, too fascinated to stop him. Was he going to mention hellhounds or circus acrobats?

"…*different,*" he concluded. "But very competent. You'd be safe with any of them."

"I want you, Pete." The instant she said it, she realized that it sounded like the most blatant innuendo. Her cheeks flamed. "So, um, thanks for the offer! Anyway, back to me locked in with Jerry in Sucks To Be You Square…"

When she described running over Jerry's toes, Pete said, "Right on!" and held up his hand in a high-five gesture. She slapped it. The solid crack of their palms meeting sent a pleasant shock through Tirzah's body.

Pete rocked back slightly, his eyes widening as if he'd grabbed a live wire. The dog tags he wore on a chain around his neck clinked together. Then he snatched up his coffee mug so fast that some slopped over the rim and bent his head way down to drink, hiding his face.

She continued her story. But when she got to the contents of the Apex file, she stopped, feeling awkward about talking *about* Pete *to* Pete. "I have it here. You can read it for yourself."

She went to her desk, opened the file, came back with the laptop, and handed it to him. Pete began to read, the bluish light reflected in his eyes. And then Tirzah realized what she'd done.

Normally, she wouldn't let anyone else touch her laptop. But instead of printing the file and giving him the paper or emailing it to him for him to read on his phone, she'd passed him her entire laptop without so much as a twinge of concern.

Even now that she'd had that thought, she didn't worry

that he'd try to peek at anything but the file she'd opened for him. For all that he'd barged into her apartment, he'd obviously meant it when he'd said he'd never go into her bedroom without permission. Tracking her down had been a job, nothing personal; all he'd known about her was that *she'd* been spying on *him*. But her bedroom was intimate space, and there he wouldn't intrude without an invitation.

He's an old-fashioned gentleman, she thought. *I didn't know they made them any more.*

Pete was either a very slow or very thorough reader. Or else, like Tirzah, he needed to read the file multiple times before it sank in. Her coffee had cooled by the time he finally looked up.

"You believe this file?" Pete asked.

In reply, Tirzah pried Batcat off her shoulder, earning herself several more scratches, and held her up until she launched herself off Tirzah's hand and vanished into the spare room. Black hairs slowly floated down in her wake, caught in the slanting rays of sunlight through the closed blinds.

Pete spread his hands. "Fair enough."

"So," Tirzah said, when he didn't add more. "You can turn into a cave bear."

He nodded.

Fascinated, she blurted out, "Can you show me?"

"No!" Pete started halfway up out of his chair, nearly dropping the laptop.

They both grabbed for it at the same moment, and both caught it. Their hands touched. His were so tense that his tendons felt like steel cables. He froze momentarily, and she actually heard his startled inhale. Then he sank back down into the chair and passed it over to her.

"No," he repeated, and went on shaking his head word-lessly in what had become a very heavy silence. At last, he said, "You don't ever want to see that... that beast."

Tirzah was so curious about his reaction that she wanted to see it even more, or at least to know why he thought she shouldn't. But it was obviously all so tied up with something incredibly traumatic that she didn't want to push. To give him a break, she went on with her own story.

"So there I was, reading that file for the fifteenth time in the middle of the night, when something teeny and furry and black smacked right into my window..."

As she went on with the tale of how she'd acquired Batcat, the atmosphere lightened, and when she got to Batcat's appropriation of her entire slab of lox, he actually laughed. He went on chuckling as she explained how she'd hijacked his computer, then described her two days of unbelievable boredom waiting for him to turn it on.

"I was still waiting when you busted in," Tirzah concluded.

"Right. About that. Your apartment isn't very secure. I walked right in."

"I'm surprised there wasn't anyone outside the building. It's usually got people hanging out."

"There was. I put on a pizza delivery jacket and carried two empty boxes."

"Oh." An unpleasant heaviness settled into Tirzah's stomach. "I'd been hoping my nosy neighbors would put off anyone coming after me."

"Maybe they have. It's been a couple days. But I wouldn't count on that lasting forever."

"What do we do then? A hotel?" Tirzah caught herself looking nervously around the apartment. She felt so safe in it, and she knew she could get around in it. That wouldn't necessarily be true of anywhere else.

A yowl and a thud made both of them start. It was

followed by a series of flapping sounds, thuds, and frantic meows. Pete went to investigate, with Tirzah following.

She gave an exasperated sigh at the sight of her bedroom door, which was open just wide enough to let in a very small kitten. "I could've sworn I closed it. Nuisancy cat! She gets into everything."

Pete was blocking her way, standing in the doorway and giving her an excellent view of his long legs and extremely fine backside. She cleared her throat, and he stepped aside, plastering himself against the wall to let her pass.

Tirzah went into the bedroom, and immediately burst out laughing.

"What is it?" Pete asked. "Need any help?"

"I need you to take a look at my ridiculous kitten before I rescue her from her latest predicament. And yeah. I might also need some help."

Pete came in and also began to laugh.

Batcat had methodically yanked all the pillows on Tirzah's bed out of their cases, and dragged the cases on to the floor. Presumably in the middle of whatever the next step in her cunning plan was going to be, she'd gotten inside one of the pillowcases—a particularly nerdy *Star Wars* one—and had failed to figure out that the way in was also the way out. And so the disembodied and mostly flat head of Darth Vader was flying around the bedroom, meowing loudly.

Tirzah made a grab for it, but missed. "I'm going to order a butterfly net."

"Good idea. Maybe get a fruit picker too."

Pete reached up, snagged Darth Vader by the throat, and turned the case inside out, freeing Batcat. The ungrateful kitten spat at him, then arrowed to Tirzah, landed on her shoulder with all claws deployed to the maximum, and burrowed into her hair.

"Ow! It's like living with a raccoon. With wings."

"I was just thinking it's like living with a toddler," Pete said. "With wings."

Tirzah looked ruefully at the mess on the floor. "This is why she's not allowed in my bedroom. At least she didn't get into the dollhouses."

Oops. Naturally, that prompted Pete to look at them. Tirzah's face burned as the manliest man she had ever met walked over to examine her dollhouse collection. She could just imagine what he was thinking, that she was a case of arrested development or the world's biggest nerd (well, that was possibly true) or a plain old weirdo (also probably true) or—

"Love the ninja house," Pete said.

"You do?" Tirzah brightened.

She went over to join him as he examined it. She'd put her entire collection of ninja action figures into an antique pink dollhouse. Black-clad ninjas crouched atop four-post beds, shuriken dangling from their fists, where more black-clad ninjas peacefully slept. Ninjas sat around a dining room table on which a feast had been laid, daggers poised to slice hams and stab loaves of bread. Ninjas took baths fully clad, slid down banisters, stood balanced on the saddle of a rocking horse, perched atop mantelpieces, and crouched resentfully in a playpen.

"It's great," Pete said. "Makes me think I should take out my old action figures and give them a place to live in."

She grinned. "You totally should. Where are they now? In a bunch of dusty boxes in a closet?"

"Yeah. What's the point of that, huh?"

"If you have them, you should enjoy them."

"Right." He moved on to the next house over, which was a rare miniature of a big top circus. In the stage area, six dolls in frilly dresses balanced in a precarious pyramid with a rearing bear with a top hat standing over them. The

61

stadium seating was completely filled with an entranced audience of porcelain elephants, lions, tigers, seals, and bears.

Pete laughed. "Love it."

"See, that's what you should do with your action figures. Have some fun with them. What are they, toy soldiers?"

"Superheroes mostly. Batman, Superman, X-Men, that sort of thing. I was thinking maybe a military base. Make them go through an obstacle course, do rifle training, that sort of thing."

Inwardly, Tirzah rejoiced. So the manly man's man was a secret nerd, just like her. Or maybe not even that secret. He hadn't sounded the slightest bit embarrassed.

"You can find stuff like that online," she said.

He waved off the suggestion. "Nah, nah. If I do it, I'll build it myself. It'd be more fun."

"Build it yourself? Out of... clay? Legos?"

"Wood. And string, I guess, for the ropes course. Wire for the fences. Yeah, I should do that. Later. Right now, the work I need to do is on your place. I can get some things from the office to make it safer. And I'll stay with you, of course."

A flock of butterflies took flight in Tirzah's stomach. Pete was going to stay with her. Of course she'd known any body-guard would, but that was before she'd met her bodyguard. And then a completely different set of butterflies, or rather evil red-eyed moths, joined them at the thought of Pete leaving her alone, even for a brief office trip.

"While you're gone—" Tirzah began.

Pete shook his head. "I'm not going anywhere without you. You're coming with me. And so's Batcat, if you have a carrier."

Tirzah had, in fact, ordered a carrier with two layers of black wire mesh, advertised as being for extremely escape-prone cats, which obviously Batcat was given what she must have escaped to get to Tirzah. The mesh also had the advantage of being impossible to see into.

She hauled Batcat out of her hair, losing some of it in the process, and held her firmly as she told Pete, "It's in the closet. Not the one you hid in, the one in here."

Pete retrieved it. Just as Tirzah had guessed, Batcat did her best impression of the Tasmanian Devil at the sight of it, hissing, spitting, thrashing, and flapping. Pete held the carrier door open, Tirzah shoved Batcat in, and Pete slammed and latched the door.

"You carry her around before?" Pete asked.

Tirzah shook her head. "I assume she learned what they were... wherever she came from. I don't want to pry into, uh, anything you don't want me prying into. But any time you want to tell me... whatever you want to me... about that, I'd really like to know."

Pete made a noncommittal noise.

"You did promise," Tirzah reminded him.

"Yeah, I did." He sighed. "I'll tell you. Just not right now, okay? Let's get to my office, come back, get everything squared away, and *then* I'll tell you what I can."

"Is anyone else going to be at the office?"

"God, I hope not," Pete said in heartfelt tones.

"You can't see into the carrier," Tirzah pointed out.

"Wasn't what I meant. Though actually, if none of the guys are there, I might have to call one or two of them. I'm not much of a tech guy, but some of them are."

"Ooh," Tirzah said. "That should be fun. Well, fun for me."

"Oh, right." Pete chuckled. "You and Carter might actually get along. You can talk about computer... stuff."

"And my neighbors? They're going to see me leave with a cat carrier and the pizza delivery guy. How do I explain that?"

"The carrier's not a problem." He went into the hall closet

he'd hid in and took out Tirzah's biggest suitcase. "I'll put it inside this, just long enough to get it to my car. It's thick enough that no one will hear her meow. As for me..."

In the brief pause while Pete took a breath, Tirzah tried to think of any possible explanation for his 24-7 presence other than that he was her new boyfriend. She failed to come up with any that were actually plausible, after ruling out "roommate who accompanied her on strolls" and "personal assistant who lived with her," neither of which made sense.

Boyfriend it was, then. But how would she explain how she'd gone from dating to him moving in with her without ever saying a word about him and without him ever having come over before? A long-distance internet romance? Esther would probably hire a private eye to investigate Pete to see if he was a scammer or a serial killer or had a wife in every major American city, and then...

"...that's up to you," Pete concluded. "We could come up with some kind of cover story, if you want. Or we say I'm your bodyguard because you have a stalker, which is true. You can describe Jerry to them, so they can alert me if they see him. They're already protecting you; might as well get them working on our team."

Tirzah blinked. She was so used to keeping everything Override-related a secret, not to mention Batcat, that it hadn't even occurred to her to simply tell the truth about Pete. But he was right: in this case, honesty really was the best policy.

"Let's do that," she said. "If they're delaying me too much, you hurry me on. Say I have to go to the office."

They left the apartment together. To Tirzah's relief, the first person they ran into was Dalisay, the Navy vet, who clearly recognized a kindred spirit in Pete and took in their explanation with a businesslike nod.

"I'll tip off the rest of the building," Dalisay said. "Save you the trouble."

"Thanks for *your* trouble," said Tirzah.

They hurried out of the apartment and to Pete's car, where he popped open the suitcase to a series of indignant meows and stashed the carrier in the backseat. Tirzah slid into the front seat, lifting in her bad right leg, then instructed Pete in folding her wheelchair to fit it into the trunk.

It was the first time she'd been in a car in months. She occasionally took taxis, as the subway could be hard to navigate with a wheelchair, but almost everything she wanted or needed was either already in her neighborhood or could be brought to her. But as she rode with Pete, she couldn't help thinking of her car, gathering dust. She really needed to sell it if she wasn't ever going to use it. But if she sold it, then she'd be admitting that she *wasn't* ever going to use it.

I'm not missing anything by not driving, she told herself as Pete, swearing under his breath, maneuvered around a traffic jam consisting of a double-parked car, and an extremely slow bus. An electric scooter came careening out of nowhere, forcing him to slam on the brakes. As its rider flipped Pete off before speeding away (illegally, on the sidewalk), she thought, *Yeah.* Really *not missing anything.*

"Asshole!" Pete yelled, his face darkening with blood. Tirzah half-expected to see steam jet out of his ears. "Man, I hate it when people get away with that sort of crap. He could've really hurt someone."

"How long have you lived here?" she inquired, as they watched a sequence of pedestrians leap out of the scooter's erratic path.

Pete shook his head. "I don't, that's the thing. I work in the city, but I live in the suburbs."

"The suburbs are a whole 'nother world. Just watch…"

An old woman stuck her head out a window and shrieked, "Here, have another!"

She hurled a beer can at the scooter rider. It hit him smack in the small of the back, sending him flying and drenching his clothes. The pedestrians he'd nearly hit and everyone in the outdoor areas of cafes applauded, and Tirzah rolled down the window to join in. As the rider picked himself up and skulked off, angry and dripping, the old woman popped the tab on another beer can and raised it in a toast.

Pete chuckled, shaking his head in amazement. "It's like a three-ring circus."

"Isn't it great? I see stuff like that every day without even leaving my apartment."

He glanced at her curiously. "You really love it here, don't you?"

"I do. Sometimes it gets a bit much, and then..." She broke off. Pete didn't want to talk about the cave bear (*cave bear!*) and she didn't want to talk about what she used to do when it got a bit much. She concluded, "But mostly I love it. How about you?"

He stepped on the gas, neatly inserting himself into a tiny break in the traffic flow in true Refuge City style. "It's noisy and crowded and smelly. But I think it might be growing on me. A bit."

"Nothing like an old lady hurling beer cans to get you to see the city in a new light, huh?"

Pete smiled, the skin around his brown eyes crinkling. "I'll tell you what really made that moment for me. She kept the Bud Light Lime just to chuck at people. The can she was drinking from was a craft beer."

"That does make it even better," Tirzah said, who hadn't noticed. Pete must have eyes like a hawk. Or a cave bear.

As he approached the high-security-looking building

with an understated sign reading *Defenders, Inc.*, she wondered once again about him, his team, cave bears and flying kittens and secret experiments. She *did* respect Pete's request to discuss it later. But she was dying of curiosity, too. Override wasn't just a name, but a part of her, the part that pried and spied and learned secrets.

She'd given her word not to demand answers just yet. But she couldn't help hoping that some of Pete's teammates would be around. Merlin Merrick, for instance, the one who supposedly turned into some kind of raptor. He sounded like he might be a talker.

CHAPTER 6

*S*ince her accident, Tirzah had started noticing all sorts of things she never had when she'd been able to step over curbs and walk down stairs and use both her hands while she was standing up. The world was a completely different place when you used a wheelchair. With a very few exceptions, it just wasn't built for people like her. Even doctors' offices frequently had heavy manual doors without doorstops, so she could hold them open or move her chair through, but not both at the same time.

And don't even get me started about the height of supermarket shelves!

Whoever had designed the Defenders building had clearly considered the possibility that people might visit in wheelchairs. For every curb or set of stairs, there was a clearly visible ramp. The buttons for summoning elevators went low enough for her to hit without standing up or even stretching, and there was no unpleasant bump when she went in.

"This place is really accessible," she remarked to Pete, who was holding Batcat's carrier. He made a noncommittal grunt in response. An air of gloom had descended upon him once

68

they'd spotted the building, and it had only gotten darker and heavier when they'd pulled into the underground parking lot.

As the elevator ascended, she suddenly remembered something. "About Batcat—Is she a secret here? Or—"

The bell dinged, and the doors slid open.

A scene of unbelievable chaos met her eyes. And ears. Some small flying thing was zipping around the office, with one man in hot pursuit, another apparently trying to film it, and others trying to avoid both the flying creature and the pursuit. Tirzah tried hard to get a visual lock on it, but could see nothing more than a blur of color and motion, like a hummingbird's wings.

"Don't open the windows!" yelled a lithe blond man, who was vaulting over desks and chairs while making wild swipes at it with a butterfly net. She recognized him from her research as Merlin Merrick, the raptor shifter with a million probably-fake jobs.

A tall man with auburn hair and an angular face, whom she recognized as Ransom Pierce—the hellhound!—opened the nearest window, making Merlin let out a howl of outrage.

A burly black man with silvering hair and beard said with remarkable calm, "You're all probably scaring it. If everyone would just stay still and keep quiet, maybe it'd land somewhere."

"Hey! I have a client—" Pete's voice was drowned out in the general ruckus. He tried again, more loudly. "I have a CLIENT here! Everyone, shut up and sit down!"

This made no impression on anyone. Except for the flying thing, which whipped around and arrowed straight for Pete and Tirzah.

The next thing Tirzah knew, Pete had thrust Batcat's carrier into her arms and leaped in front of her.

She held her breath. The entire room seemed to hold its breath. In the sudden silence, she clearly heard the buzz of tiny, rapidly flapping wings as the creature circled Pete's head. Then it zipped out the window, and was gone.

"Ransom!" yelled Merlin. "I was about to get it!"

Not at all apologetically, Ransom said, "I couldn't hear myself think."

"Thanks a lot," said the man who'd been trying to film it. He had thick black hair and hazel eyes, and looked vaguely familiar. Maybe she'd seen him in her research too...? "I can tell you already that none of this footage is usable. Exactly how am I supposed to make your security system weird flying creature-proof when don't even know what it is?"

"Talk less, work more," Ransom suggested.

The burly black man cleared his throat. "We have a visitor. Let's try to make a sane impression."

From the looks everyone gave him, Tirzah guessed that he was the boss. He must have his hands full!

"Hi, I'm Pete's new client. Tirzah Lowenstein." She offered him her hand.

He shook it gravely. "Roland Walker. How did you manage to hire Pete without going through me first?"

"She, uh..." Pete trailed off, looking at her. He was obviously unsettled, though she wasn't sure if it was by all the commotion or by his boss finding out Pete had gone over his head.

As for her, she was still processing what had just happened. Pete had jumped to put his own body between her and some possibly dangerous, totally unknown *thing*, and he'd done it faster than she could blink.

That's his job, she reminded herself. *That's all.*

But she couldn't shake the feeling that it had meant something more.

Since Pete was clearly at a loss to explain her, she said,

"Should we show them?" She nodded at the cat carrier, from which forlorn meows were emanating. "Cut right to the chase?"

"Yeah." Pete squared his shoulders, like he was ready to spring into action all over again. "Yeah, let's do that. Let me close the window."

As Pete went to shut the window, Merlin's blue eyes gleamed. "You need to close the window before you open the cat carrier and showing us your cat will explain everything? Is it a flying kitten?"

Not one of the men reacted as if Merlin had made a joke or said something random and weird.

Ransom went white.

Roland folded his hands together and looked thoughtfully from Pete to Tirzah to the cat carrier.

"Oh, no," said the man with hazel eyes. "NO. I want absolutely nothing to do with this. Don't bother calling me for anything till you've got this completely squared away. I'll be in Bali. Or, actually, I'll be anywhere *but* Bali, because I don't even want to tell you where I'm going!"

With that, Tirzah recognized him. She'd heard that voice before, on podcasts and TV, and seen that face. She'd just never expected to actually meet the tech genius billionaire himself.

"Oh my God," she blurted out. "You're Carter Howe! You're my inspiration! When the news came out that your plane had gone down and they thought you were dead, I cried all day. And when I heard that you weren't, I—um." Her face burning, she said, "Sorry. Sorry. Fangirl moment. You must be so sick of that. Pretend you didn't hear it. Pleased to meet you."

But he didn't seem annoyed. In fact, Carter sounded quite sincere as he said, "Pleased to meet *you!* And not at all. Are you a fan of my phones?"

"I love your phones! But I'm a—er, I work in cyber security, you see, so—"

Carter burst out laughing. "Sorry. I just realized how you and Pete must have met. Very elegant hijacking; I was impressed. You really made me work to track you down, too."

"That means so much to me, coming from you," Tirzah said, beaming. Over Carter's shoulder, she saw Pete looking like a thundercloud. "Oh, sorry, Pete, I got distracted. Carter is such a hero of mine. I can't believe you know him... How *do* you know each other?"

It was like her words sucked all the cheer out of the room. A heavy silence fell, and even Merlin's bright smile faltered.

"Apex," Roland said quietly. "Let's see your cat."

Tirzah opened the cage. An angry spitting sound came from within, and then a small sphere of black fur rocketed out, hissing furiously, and began zooming around the room. Tirzah clicked to her, but it took a few minutes before Batcat recovered from the indignity of the carrier and deigned to land on Tirzah's shoulder.

"Aww," said Merlin, extending his hand. "Hello, cutie!"

Batcat, apparently sensing a kindred spirit in the realm of havoc-wreaking, nuzzled him and purred.

"This is a matter that concerns the entire team," Roland said. "If it's all right with you, Tirzah, I'd like them all to hear your story."

"I'm not on the team," Carter said promptly, but he made no move to leave.

"Let me rephrase that," Roland said. "A matter that concerns the entire team and Carter."

"Sure, you can all hear it," Tirzah said.

Once again, she told her story. Roland and Ransom stopped her a few times to ask questions, Carter said he was an admirer of Override's work, and Merlin let out an actual cheer when she recounted running over Jerry's toes. When she got to the part about the Apex file, she emailed it to all of their accounts, so they could open it on their laptops.

As they read it, she looked from man to man, wondering who she could quiz in return once she was done. She already knew Pete didn't want to talk about any cave bear-related issues. Much as she was dying to know if her role model could turn into something, Carter had nearly walked out the door just at the mention of flying kittens. Ransom sat in forbidding silence, the stark angles of his face as impassive as a statue's, and though she didn't know what a hellhound even was, she didn't think she wanted to meet one. Roland seemed approachable, but he hadn't been in the Apex file. That left Merlin.

Yes. Merlin would be perfect. He was friendly, he seemed less traumatized than Pete, and he could easily demonstrate his power without trashing the office. She couldn't wait to see what kind of raptor he turned into. A hawk? An eagle? Or could he become any type of bird of prey?

Tirzah had to admit, she was a bit jealous. She'd always wished she could fly…

Merlin, a fast reader, finished and looked up before the rest of them. Tirzah pounced. "Merlin, could you turn into a raptor for me? I'd really love to see it!"

"Sure!" Merlin set down his laptop and bounced up.

Out of the corner of her eye, she saw Pete hold up his hand. Even as his mouth was beginning to form the word, *"Wait,"* Merlin vanished.

Tirzah was suddenly face to face with a velociraptor.

She let out a shriek and tried to throw herself backward. Her wheelchair stayed in place, as she'd locked its wheels earlier, but rocked so hard that it nearly tipped over.

Pete grabbed her chair, steadying it, and roared, "Goddammit, Merlin!"

The dinosaur shrank to the size of a St. Bernard, then a Labrador retriever, then enlarged to St. Bernard size again. By then Tirzah had realized the nature of her error. Her panic gave way to slightly hysterical laughter.

"Sorry," she gasped. "My fault! I saw 'raptor,' and I thought 'hawk.' Not 'velociraptor!'"

"He still should've warned you," Pete said, glaring at the velociraptor. Tirzah was impressed that he could sustain a glare when faced with a dinosaur that was rapidly switching between cat and hamster sizes.

"Seriously, Pete, I asked," Tirzah said.

The velociraptor shot up to human size, then became Merlin again. "Whew. Got stuck there a moment. Sorry about that. I thought you knew. It says 'raptor' because the main difference between the raptor dinosaurs is their size, and I can change mine. The one I turned into first was actually a Utahraptor. That's the real dinosaur that *Jurassic Park* called velociraptors, I guess because it sounds cooler. Actual velociraptors are the size of a—"

"Chicken," chorused the men, as Merlin said, "Small dog."

"Okay," said Carter. "If it makes you feel better, you're the size of a Chihuahua."

As Merlin and Carter began squabbling over what animal was the size of a velociraptor, Roland turned to Pete. "What have you told her already? About everything."

"Not much. I said I'd tell her what I could. Later." Pete turned to Tirzah, wry amusement in his eyes. "Not the patient type, are you?"

"Well..." She couldn't deny it. "Would *you* rather have someone else explain it to me? So I can know, but you don't have to be the one who tells me?"

As she said it, she realized that she wanted to hear Pete's story from Pete himself. But not if it was too painful for him to talk about it.

"No. No, I'd rather tell you myself." He took a breath and went on calmly, "The short version is that me, Merlin, and Ransom were on a team of Recon Marines. We were ambushed and taken to a secret lab. The people running it made us into shifters. Just like the file says. Roland had been captured too, but separately. He was in the Army."

Pete stopped, glanced at Carter, who was giving him a *say anything and I'll murder you with my bare hands* look, and said, "Carter was part of the team that rescued us."

Pete was silent for so long that Tirzah thought he'd said all he was going to say, but then he added, "We found some animals at the lab. Flying kittens, like Batcat. Miniature dragons. Some of them got adopted by the team that came to rescue us—that was Protection, Inc., the west coast branch— but the rest disappeared before we got a good look at them. That's why I figured Batcat was either one of those or came from a different Apex lab."

Once again, Pete fell silent.

"Okay. Thanks." Tirzah could see that even saying that much hadn't been any fun for him, so she didn't press him, though it all raised far more questions than it had answered.

"Apex was the black ops agency that had started the experiments," Roland said. He glanced at Carter, then said, "That is, they'd been doing this sort of thing for a while. But by the time Pete's team and I had been captured, Apex had been taken over by something... stranger."

"Stranger how?" Tirzah asked.

The men all glanced at each other. Reluctantly, Pete said, "Lamorat called them... uh... wizard-scientists."

Tirzah felt her eyebrows shoot up. Then she remembered Batcat, not to mention the velociraptor, and they fell again. She supposed that once you were dealing with flying cats and men who turned into cave bears and dinosaurs and hellhounds, wizard-scientists fit right in.

"We'd hoped we'd seen the last of them," Roland said. "But it seems like there's at least one left. So Pete will protect you while the rest of us figure out what's going on and track them down."

A lively conversation began between the men as they started discussing the technical nitty-gritty of how to make her apartment more secure and follow up on the clues she'd given them.

Between Roland's calm confidence, Carter's technical genius, Merlin's quick wits, Ransom's aura of still waters running deep, and most of all, the way Pete stood by her like an unbreakable shield, Tirzah relaxed. She was in danger, and yet she felt safe.

Come to think of it, she'd felt safe almost from the moment Pete had broken into her apartment.

Pete, on the other hand, seemed increasingly unsettled. Finally, he got up, muttered something about having to make a phone call, and walked out.

Tirzah wondered who he was calling, that it had to be done in private. The other men were making calls to various contacts from where they were. Then she put the expression on his face together with him walking out, and knew exactly what sort of call he was making.

He's calling his girlfriend to tell her he's got a job and he's going to have to cancel their plans for the weekend.

The realization that Pete had a girlfriend struck an unexpected pang into her heart.

What did you expect? Tirzah told herself. *A hot guy like him, strong and protective and brave and considerate and funny, of course he's already taken.*

Wonder if his girlfriend knows he turns into a cave bear...?

CHAPTER 7

*P*ete took one last glance at Tirzah, making sure she looked comfortable being left alone with that bunch of weirdos, then ducked into his office and closed the soundproofed door.

First he called his mother, who didn't pick up. He left a message to let her know he had a 24-7 job and wouldn't be home until it was done.

And then came the difficult call. It was ten minutes into recess at Caro's school. He hated to upset her in the middle of school, but it would be difficult to have a private phone call later, when he'd be in Tirzah's small apartment. His team knew he had a daughter, but it wasn't because Pete had told them and he'd made sure they didn't know anything more than that. The safest thing for Caro was to keep her completely separate from his dangerous job, which meant that he didn't even discuss her *existence* with anyone involved in his job. Not even with a sweet woman like Tirzah.

Caro answered immediately. "Hey, Dad. If you were wondering if I changed my mind about cilantro, I still hate it. Bananas too."

"What?"

"For the cook-off," she said impatiently.

Something small and flickering zipped past his head. He ducked instinctively, but wasn't disturbed. Whatever the fast little thing was, he'd seen it (or rather, not quite seen it) three times now, and it didn't seem to do anything but cause a ruckus when everyone tried to catch it.

"Hang on a second," he said. "I'm putting you on speakerphone."

"Oooh," she sang out. "Am I getting to meet your team? Hi, Dad's team!"

"No. I'm alone. A… a wasp or something flew in. I'm going to open a window and try to shoo it out." Pete hit the speakerphone button and put his phone down on the table.

"Don't get stung."

At the sound of Caro's voice, the buzzing sound like the rapid flap of tiny wings stopped. Pete looked up, startled. The flittering thing had vanished.

"Never mind. It's gone." He picked up the phone again. "Listen, Lina—"

"Caro," she corrected him. Her voice had a dangerous edge to it; she'd figured out what the call was really about. "Not coming home tonight, huh?"

"No. I've got a 24-7 job."

"Will it be over by the cook-off?"

"I don't know. I wish I could tell you one way or another, but I can't. That's just how my job works."

"Funny how that's just how all your jobs always work." Caro sounded on the verge of tears. "Anyone would think you hated being home!"

Before he could reply, she hung up.

Pete caught himself pressing his knuckles into his chest. His heart ached inside. He'd missed other things she'd looked forward to because of his work before. And every time he did, the distance between them grew that much wider.

Just this once, he wished he could bring his work home with him. The one bright moment in the whole nightmare of Apex had been releasing the little creatures from their cages. Caro had always adored animals. Horses were her favorites, but she also loved all things small and fluffy. He couldn't imagine anything that would make her happier than meeting a fluffy flying kitten, other than having a fluffy flying kitten of her own.

Or a non-flying kitten of her own. But Mom was allergic to fur, and it didn't seem fair to keep a cat or dog locked in one room of the house.

Maybe he'd take Caro to the pet shop when he was done with this job, and get her a hamster or rat or guinea pig. Something like that would be content living in a cage, and she could play with it to her heart's content inside her room. It wouldn't make up for... everything else... but it'd be a start.

Pete sighed. He just wanted his little girl to be happy. This sure wasn't how he'd imagined their reunion. For one thing, those daydreams had always started with him picking her up and swinging her around, like she'd always used to beg him to do. But now she was too grown-up for that, and even if she wasn't, it'd hurt too much for him to do it for more than a few seconds...

...or would it? After all, Tirzah's touch hadn't hurt. Maybe whatever the hell was wrong with him had worn off.

Filled with hope, Pete strode out of the room, determined to find out via the first non-Tirzah person he encountered.

Unfortunately, that was Merlin. Pete stopped and stared. His weirdo teammate was leaning way out an open window, waving... something... and making strange whistling noises. Pete was strongly tempted to walk on by and pretend he hadn't seen a thing, but Merlin *had* presented him with the perfect opportunity.

"Hey," Pete said, and poked his shoulder.

A jolt of shocking agony made him yank his hand back. So it *was* just Tirzah.

Merlin twisted around, still at a precarious angle. "Yeah?"

"Uh…" Pete's mind went completely blank for a moment before he remembered his excuse. "What the hell are you doing?"

"Trying to lure the whatever-it-is," Merlin replied with a shrug.

"With what? And why?"

"With a piece of lox," Merlin replied. "And because I want a cute little pet to perch on my shoulder like Tirzah and the west coast team have, of course!"

Shaking his head in disbelief, Pete left his lunatic teammate and returned to the lobby. Tirzah was regaling Carter, Ransom, and Roland with a story of one of her exploits as Override. She made a wide gesture, and the sleeves of her loose T-shirt slid back, exposing surprisingly strong-looking shoulders. Pete supposed it was from moving her wheelchair around. Her upper arms were lightly freckled. He wanted to touch them, to feel the softness of her skin, the heat of the blood beneath, the firm swell of her muscles…

Forcing his mind back to business, he cleared his throat. "Carter? I need you to help me with the security for Tirzah's apartment. Can you come to the tech room?"

"You have a *tech room?*" Tirzah asked longingly. "Can I come too?"

"Don't see why not," Pete said.

"*You're* welcome," said Carter. "The flying menace is very much not."

Tirzah popped a loudly protesting Batcat into the carrier. They headed to the tech room, where Pete endured Carter's instructions on use and installation, all delivered with the subtext of *What sins did I commit that I have to teach* him *to use this stuff?* But Pete couldn't summon his usual level of pissed-off-ness, not while Tirzah was spinning her chair around like a kid in a candy shop, occasionally reaching out to pet some computer or gadget. He might not share her love for things with dangling wires, but her sheer delight was contagious.

She said a reluctant farewell to the tech room, and Merlin (now waving a ring of canned pineapple out the window) said a reluctant farewell to Batcat. Then, to Pete's immense relief, he extracted himself from the office and was once again alone with Tirzah.

As he drove back to her apartment, he found himself observing Refuge City with her eyes. On the way to the office, he'd mostly noticed the traffic jams, the obnoxious other drivers, the graffiti tags, and the reek of exhaust fumes and asphalt. On the way back, his attention was drawn more by a striking wall mural of some fantastical city of the future, a flash mob of classical musicians singing "O Fortuna," and a very familiar-looking man driving a pink Cadillac.

"Check out the Elvis impersonator," Pete said, jerking his head toward the man driving the Cadillac.

"You sure he's an impersonator?" Tirzah inquired. *"I* heard his death was faked. He might be the real thing."

Traffic came to an abrupt stop, trapping them beside Elvis. Pete craned his head to see what it was this time. Half a block ahead, three men had jumped out of their cars, leaving them stopped in the middle of the road, and were yelling at each other, ignoring every car in the road honking at them. Pete was tempted to go bang their heads together. But he didn't want to leave Tirzah alone in the car, so he settled back in his seat. It looked like they and Elvis might be there for a while.

"Think he'll serenade us if we ask him nice?" Pete asked.

81

"Worth a try," she replied. He'd been kidding, but Tirzah rolled down her window, leaned out, and called, "Hey, Elvis! Can we get a song?"

Elvis promptly began singing "Love Me Tender."

"I don't think he's really Elvis," Pete said in an undertone.

"I think you're right," Tirzah murmured. "But he does have a nice voice."

Love me tender, love me true...

Pete no longer hated the Refuge City traffic. As far as he was concerned, those three idiots up ahead could go on shaking their fists at each other for as long they liked. The only thing he'd enjoy more than being serenaded by an Elvis impersonator while in a car with Tirzah was being serenaded by an Elvis impersonator while in a car with Tirzah, with his hand on her thigh. Just the thought of it made him ache with longing... and desire.

A fusillade of beer cans, pizza slices, and one well-aimed tennis ball flew through the air from all the cars within throwing range of the arguing men, forcing them to retreat to their own cars. To Pete's regret, traffic started up again, ending the moment. Elvis tipped an invisible hat to them as he drove on by.

They were back at Tirzah's apartment building after what felt like a very short ride, though Pete's watch told them they'd been moving at the pace of molasses in winter. He parked, got out Tirzah's wheelchair and opened the door for her, and then hefted the big case of security equipment, his own go-bag, and Batcat's carrier/suitcase.

"Wow," she said, staring at him wide-eyed. "Just... Wow."

"What?" Pete asked. "Did I forget something?"

Tirzah chuckled. "Nope. Not a thing wrong with *that* picture. Um, it's just a lot of weight for one guy to carry."

"Nah. It's a bunch of pieces but none of them are heavy.

All of them together are forty pounds, max. In the Marines I used to carry twice that on my back every day."

Pete could almost feel her gaze, like a hot ribbon of silk, as it slid along his arms and shoulders and chest.

"Yeah," she said. "Yeah, I can see that you did."

They had to run the gauntlet of neighbors on their way in, who wanted to get all the juicy details and offer Tirzah their support. Pete told them to pass it on, and extracted him and Tirzah with the excuse of needing to install security measures immediately.

By the time they both got to her apartment, they exchanged glances of mutual relief at being away from the crowd. Tirzah unpacked Batcat, who puffed into an angry ball of fur until only her yellow eyes were visible in a black sphere.

"She looks like the soot creatures in, uh, a movie," Pete said. He could hardly say it had been Caro's favorite when she'd been younger. "*My Neighbor Totoro.*"

"They're in *Spirited Away,* too."

"Right," he said, remembering the scene. "They carry coal in the engine room."

"So, you like Miyazaki movies? What's your favorite?"

Pete resigned himself to Tirzah thinking he watched anime movies about cat buses and pig pilots all by himself. "*Princess Mononoke.* She's badass. What's yours?"

Her smile made him regret nothing but the secrets he still had to keep. "*Kiki's Delivery Service.* What can I say, I can't resist a black cat. Right, Batcat?"

Batcat spat at them both, then hid under the sofa. Pete started setting up an alarm system. Tirzah watched him work with great interest, occasionally asking questions so technical that he didn't even understand what they were.

"I can make it work," he said. "And I can tell you what it

does. But if you want to know *how* it works, you'll have to ask Carter."

"I will," she said. "I still can't believe *Carter Howe* is on your team!"

"He's not. And he'll never miss a chance to remind us of it. He just… hangs around a lot."

"So, what's up with him? Does he turn into something too?"

"Damned if I know. I sure haven't ever seen him do it."

Tirzah flung up her hands, her full lips parted in an O of astonishment. "And none of you have ever asked? You can't tell me Merlin's never asked!"

"Merlin's asked. Many, many, many times. Carter won't say." Pete finished setting up the door alarm, and moved on to the windows. Over his shoulder, he said, "I'll tell you everything I know, but it's not much. All the rest of us are ex-military. Carter's a civilian. He got kidnapped by Apex—original version, not the wizard-scientists who got me and Ransom and Merlin and Roland. That's why he was presumed dead for a while. Remember Lamorat from the file? He was the wizard-scientist we got in a fight with. He called Carter Apex's failure."

"So he doesn't turn into anything?" Tirzah sounded a little disappointed. "They experimented on him, but it didn't work?"

Pete hesitated. He had an opinion on that, but it would involve telling her some things about himself that he wasn't sure he wanted her to know. She obviously didn't mind that he could turn into a cave bear but learning that it was much more than just a physical transformation was something else entirely. Especially if she ever actually saw the raging animal within him.

Still. He *had* promised to tell her more.

"I think they did change him somehow," Pete said slowly. "I can feel it when I'm around him."

"Feel it how?"

"Hang on. Let me get this." Pete finished up the last window, taking his time on it. Then he turned to face her. He wanted to keep his eyes on her when he explained this bit, so he could know when he started scaring her and could back off. "I don't know how it is for the other guys. But I don't just turn into a bear. I *am* the bear. Or maybe the bear is me. I can hear his voice inside my head. But it's my voice, really. It's the part of me that's... a beast."

He stopped, searching her expression for fear. But he saw none, only curiosity and another emotion which it took him a moment to recognize. It was sympathy.

"Does he talk to you a lot?" she asked.

He shook his head. "But I can always feel him inside of me. That's why I think Carter does turn into... something. The beast in me recognizes the beast in him."

Even then, Tirzah didn't seem afraid. But, of course, she'd never actually seen his cave bear. And she was a city woman through and through. She probably hadn't ever seen any bear that wasn't a fat, nearly tame zoo animal. She must be imagining something big but basically harmless, like an immense St. Bernard.

He hoped he'd never have to transform in front of her. But just in case he did. He needed to warn her.

"The cave bear... It's not like Merlin's velociraptor," Pete said. "That thing looks scary—well, it does when it gets big enough—and you saw how he has a hard time getting it to turn into the right size, and turning back into a person. But he has complete control of what it *does*. I don't. When I turn into a bear, I—the part of me that can think, the part that has self-control—that goes away. All that's left is the part of me that's just..." He stopped, knowing how much this would have to scare her, but it had to be said. Quietly, he finished, "...rage."

But she *still* didn't look afraid. "So, what? You rampage around?"

"Yeah. I don't really remember it, but... Yeah."

All he saw in her eyes was the bright inquisitive sparkle she'd had in the tech room. "You ever hurt people you don't want to hurt?"

"No, but that's just luck. I know I've tried." But he could see she didn't understand. She *couldn't* understand. He gave a frustrated sigh. "Look, if you ever see that bear, and I hope to God you never do, you stay the hell away from it, all right? It's not safe."

"Got it," Tirzah said. She sounded disappointed, like she'd hoped to pet it or something.

He supposed he should be relieved that she wasn't afraid of him, since that was what he'd been worried about, but instead he had the sinking sensation that she wasn't taking it seriously enough. He consoled himself with the thought that if she ever did see it, she'd be scared enough then to keep her distance.

Pete picked up the toolkit. "I have to go set up the security cameras around the building. Would you mind staying here, so you can watch the monitors and confirm that they're working?"

"Sure. I want to set it up so I can watch the feed on my laptop and phone, too."

Pete left Tirzah busily typing. As he went around the building, setting up cameras and checking for weak points in its security, he tried to focus completely on his work. But his mind kept drifting back to Tirzah, with her clever hands and warm brown eyes, and Caro, whom he'd let down once again. It was too bad they could never meet. He had a feeling they'd like each other.

The tenants kept stopping by to say hello, thank him for protecting Tirzah, offer him baked goods, or try to pump him for gossip. And when they weren't directly interacting with him, they were often just around, chatting or knocking on doors to ask to borrow a cup of sugar. When he went round the back, he spotted a pair of girls about Caro's age perched on the fire escape, painting each other's finger and toe nails. The busy, nosy, companionable apartment building reminded him of a Marine base in the way that everyone knew and relied on each other.

It wasn't easy keeping a secret on a military base, with everyone in such close quarters and always popping in and out of each others' space. Pete wondered just how long Tirzah would be able to keep Batcat a secret from her friendly, curious neighbors.

Then, with an uneasy chill, he wondered how long he could keep his secrets from her.

CHAPTER 8

"*I*'m not coming out, and you can't make me!" Caro shouted at the locked door of her bedroom.

Abuelita's voice was distant through the door. "Just come have dinner, princesa. I made your favorite—"

"I don't want *food* as a consolation prize!" Caro said scornfully. She threw herself down on her bed and buried her face in her pillow. It immediately became damp with tears. She lifted her head long enough to yell, "Just leave me alone!" before putting it down again.

Her grandmother went on entreating her for some time, but finally Caro heard her departing footsteps. Once Caro was sure Abuelita couldn't hear her, she stopped trying to muffle her sobs.

She'd been so happy when she'd heard Dad was coming home for good, but then everything had gone wrong. Abuelita had warned her that war changes people and he might seem different. But it wasn't Dad who'd changed, it was her. She'd grown up while he'd been gone, and now she wasn't his little girl anymore. She was Caro, not Lina. And that had changed everything.

Caro had read all about parents not understanding how to deal with their kids once they became teenagers, but she'd never imagined it would happen to her. But it had. Dad had fixed fancy breakfasts for six little girls having a sleepover at Lina's place, but he'd bailed on Caro's cook-off. Lina was the one he'd hugged until *she* let go. Caro was the one he hugged for fifteen seconds, max.

She'd thought she'd cry all night. But when her tears finally dried, she was surprised to see that less than an hour had passed. She could still go down and have dinner. Abuelita would definitely have saved some for her, and she was hungry.

Caro swung her legs over the edge of the bed, then stopped. If she came down for dinner, she'd be giving in. It'd be like she didn't really care that Dad had canceled her cook-off. She had to stay in her bedroom, hungry and alone. Caro began to sniffle again.

Something flew in through her bedroom window. She gave a startled jump, then craned her head to see what it was. It was too big to be a moth or beetle. A bird? A bat? It was moving too fast to see clearly, its wings buzzing like a hummingbird's...

Of course! That must be what it was. Caro loved hummingbirds. She sat still and silent, so she wouldn't scare it, and slowly extended her hand, palm up. She didn't really believe that it would land on it, but you never knew.

The hummingbird darted in close, then landed on her hand. It let out a tiny, triumphant neigh.

Caro gasped. It wasn't a hummingbird at all, or any kind of bird. It was a winged pony small enough to stand on the palm of her hand.

Disbelieving her own eyes, she brought her hand closer. She was going to wake up from this wonderful dream at any moment, so she wanted to get a good look at it first, so she could treasure the memory.

The pony's coat was a white so bright and pure that it almost glowed, like a living piece of the moon. Its magnificent feathered wings, still outstretched, were opalescent, gleaming with all the colors of the rainbow. Its flowing mane and tail were opalescent as well, cascading like a liquid kaleidoscope. It had the perfect conformation and proud bearing of an Arabian stallion, with big, dark, intelligent eyes.

The pony snorted, then folded his wings over his back, bent down, and nuzzled her wrist. She felt the warmth of his breath and the velvet softness of his muzzle. Its hooves were hard and smooth against her palm, and her wrist ached from bearing its weight. His coat had a faint scent of rain and fresh-cut grass.

The flying pony was real.

All her sorrow was swept away in a wave of pure joy. The flying pony was *real!* She had a miniature flying pony *in her room!*

The pony tossed his head, sending his rainbow mane flying. But no, it wasn't quite a rainbow. The colors were paler and more shimmery than that. They reminded her of a photo she'd seen once of a rainbow made by moonlight rather than sunlight: a moonbow.

"My name is Carolina Alejandra Valdez," she said softly. "What's yours?"

The stallion didn't reply or seem to understand. Instead, it unfolded its wings and launched itself off her palm. It flew much more slowly this time, so she could easily see that it was heading toward the open window.

"Oh, no!" Caro cried out.

She lunged to close the window, desperate not to lose the beautiful little pony. Then she stopped herself with her hand still outstretched. Slowly, she let her hand fall to her side.

This was a magical creature, obviously. She couldn't imprison him. The winged stallion had to stay with her of his own free will or not at all.

His wings beating like living opals, the pony flew out the window. He glowed against the dark and moonless sky, flying in leisurely swoops and circles and figure-eights, while Caro watched with her heart in her mouth.

And then, at last, he flew back into her room, landed on her bed beside her, settled down, whickered softly, and laid its head down on her bare foot.

"You don't talk, do you?"

The pony made no reply. From all her experience with horses, which admittedly consisted of riding lessons for one wonderful summer and reading about a million books about them, she felt sure that he was a regular... miniature winged pony... as opposed to a human-level intelligent miniature winged pony.

"I'm naming you Moonbow." she said. Even if he couldn't understand her words, he'd understand her tone. Even regular ponies were very smart. "I promise to take good care of you, and feed you and groom you, and keep you secret. Make sure no one but me sees you when you go flying, okay? They'd lock you up and keep you in a lab or a zoo or something. But don't worry, Moonbow. I'll protect you!"

Moonbow gave another little whicker. She stroked his velvet-soft coat and silk-smooth feathers, and he turned his head to nuzzle her fingers. Her heart swelled with love and happiness.

It was too bad she couldn't tell Dad. He loved animals too, and he'd always bought her horse books and toy horses, and paid for her riding lessons. And he'd be amazed to see the pony. But he was a bodyguard, and before that he'd been a Marine, and before that he'd been a cop. He believed in law and order and rules and institutions.

He'd think Moonbow was an important discovery that the government ought to know about—much too important to keep for herself. And then men in black would arrive and show him their badges and say they'd take good care of Moonbow, and Dad would believe them. And Caro would never see Moonbow again.

"You'll be my secret," whispered Caro, stroking him. "I'll just stay up till Abuelita's asleep, and then I'll sneak out and collect some grass clippings and rolled oats and chopped carrots for you to eat."

Who cared about some stupid cook-off when she had a tiny magic flying stallion?

CHAPTER 9

irzah had always been a homebody, content to stay in her apartment and have the world come to her. She could easily go a week without ever leaving, and not even notice till some neighbor knocked on her door and asked her if she wanted to go somewhere with them. But after less than a week in her apartment with Pete and Batcat, she was going stir-crazy.

Batcat wasn't the problem. Tirzah had worried that she'd never be able to have neighbors over again, but she'd found that she could stash Batcat in the carrier with a slab of lox and then stick the carrier back in the closet, and she'd be happily and silently occupied until Tirzah took her out.

The problem was Pete. She'd never lived with anyone once she'd moved out of her college dorm, and had worried that she was too introverted to be able to stand having someone else in the apartment with her. But he was quiet and self-contained enough that she didn't feel intruded upon, and she could always retreat to her bedroom if she wanted more privacy. And when she wanted company, she had someone interesting and funny and smart to chat or watch movies with.

She also had someone *who could turn into a cave bear* and who had a teammate *who turned into a velociraptor* alternately neatly dodging her attempts to inquire about that little matter, or looking so troubled at the prospect of talking about it that she felt guilty and dropped it. Override's burning curiosity was going unsatisfied and literally keeping her awake at night.

And then there was that other thing keeping her awake at night, which was that she had someone extremely hot sleeping on her sofa (while she lay in bed imagining him lying beside her), borrowing her shower (while she sat in her living room imagining him naked and dripping wet), having daily private phone calls in whatever room she wasn't in, presumably with his girlfriend since he didn't leave the room to talk to his teammates (while she sat in the other room seething with jealousy), and just generally being *there* (while she was in his presence imagining what he'd be doing with his girlfriend as soon as he finished being her bodyguard.)

And since there hadn't been the slightest hint of anyone trying to come after her, and Pete's team hadn't yet found any leads, there was no distraction. There was just Pete, being secretive and sweet and sexy, right there with her all of the time. Being with him was wonderful and frustrating and also pre-emptively heartbreaking, because eventually he or his teammates would track down Jerry. She'd be safe then, but Pete would be out of her life for good.

Enjoy what you have while you have it, she told herself.

It was hard to do when she was pretending to work on her computer while Pete sat at the table drawing up a blueprint for a superhero obstacle course, complete with adorable sketches of Batman brooding atop a wall that

94

Spiderman was climbing while drill sergeant Wolverine yelled at them from the sidelines.

The knock at her door came as a welcome distraction. Both she and Pete glanced at the camera feed, but it was only Esther with a cup measure in her hand, her white hair in a neat bun. Pete went to the fridge and got out a slab of lox. Batcat, by now used to the routine, flew straight into her carrier, purring loudly.

Tirzah waited till the closet door was shut, then went to open the front door. "Hi, Esther. Need something for your baking?"

"Snickerdoodles," Esther said. "I thought I had enough sugar, but I'm a quarter cup short."

"Could you reach it down, Pete?" Tirzah asked. "It's on the far left top shelf."

He headed for the kitchen. Tirzah, still in the open doorway with Esther, watched him go. The rear view was very fine indeed—

WHACK!

Something hard smacked into Tirzah's head. More startled than hurt, she let out a yelp and looked up, just in time to see Esther, her wrinkled face twisted with fury, take another swing at her with the plastic cup measure.

Tirzah ducked, and the cup measure shattered against the doorframe. Bewildered, she spun her chair backward. "Esther! What are you—hey!"

With a scream of animalistic rage, Esther lunged at her, stabbing with the tiny stub of the plastic handle.

Pete jumped in front of Tirzah and caught Esther's arms. The elderly woman shrieked and kicked at him, but he easily held her at arm's length.

Past Pete and through the still-open door, Tirzah saw more neighbors rush from their apartments and toward hers. All of them had the same look of feral rage as Esther. Miriam brandished a coffee mug with coffee slopping out of it, Ali held a thick college textbook as if he was going to slam it down on someone's head, and Jamal had a can of spray paint which he was madly spraying in all directions.

"Pete!" Tirzah yelled. "Shut the door! The neighbors have all gone crazy!"

Pete twisted around and took in the situation at a glance. He scooped up the thrashing, shrieking Esther, ran to the door, placed her down in the hallway, and shut the door. A second after he did, the ravening neighbors slammed into it, nearly breaking through. Pete braced his entire weight against it and locked it.

Thuds and howls of rage sounded in the corridor. The doorframe shook as the neighbors whacked it with whatever they had in their hands.

"Apex!" Tirzah gasped. "The file said you all had powers— Could they—"

"Yeah, the Apex guys do too," Pete said. "This has got to be Jerry."

"That asshole! He's putting everyone in the building in danger just to get to me. Can you call your team?"

Pete shook his head, his expression grim. "The last thing we need right now is an enraged velociraptor."

"Oh." Tirzah swallowed. "Good point. Then what?"

Pete spoke with calm decisiveness. "We leave. I'm sure he's doing this to force you out, so once we're gone, your neighbors should be safe. And I'll keep *you* safe."

"But Batcat—"

Pete was already striding toward the closet. Over his shoulder, he said, "I need my hands free. You hold her."

He extracted the kitten from her carrier and thrust her into Tirzah's arms. She yanked out her collar and stuffed Batcat down the front of her blouse. Pete's eyes widened.

"I need *my* hands free for my wheelchair," she reminded him.

"Right. Right," he muttered. "Okay, let's go."

"Don't hurt them!" Tirzah said.

"I won't. And I won't let them hurt you, either."

CHAPTER 10

*P*ete fetched some supplies from the closet. Then, shielding Tirzah with his body, he opened the door.

The mob of enraged neighbors had gotten even bigger. But whatever power was compelling them obviously couldn't control their individual actions beyond "grab something and attack." Pete redirected the blow of another tiny white-haired grandma, this one swinging a cast iron frying pan, into the wall instead of his head. A necktie wielded like a whip by a middle-aged man in a suit slapped him across the back of his neck.

Then, with them all nicely bunched up, Pete flung the quilt he'd gotten from the closet over the entire pack of them. He and Tirzah bolted for the elevator. He'd intended to push her chair, but her shoulder muscles bunched as her hands flew, and she easily kept pace with him.

The elevator chimed, and the door slid open. The teenage girl inside hurled a bottle of nail polish at Tirzah. Pete batted it out of the air, grabbed the girl firmly by the shoulders, and held her off while Tirzah went inside. Then he dropped a pillowcase over her head, gave her a gentle shove toward the heaving, amoeba-like quilt, and stepped inside. The doors closed and the elevator began to head down.

Tirzah's eyes were wide, her mostly-exposed cleavage moving up and down as she panted for breath. A mist of sweat made her skin almost seem to glow. Pete looked aside, to keep his mind on his job rather than where it wanted to go, which was straight into the gutter.

The elevator chimed and stopped... on the fourth floor.

"Goddammit." Pete made sure he stood between Tirzah and the door. It opened, revealing an angry ten-year-old with both hands clutched full of Legos. Pete let the hurled Legos bounce off his chest and fall through the space between the floor of the hallway and the elevator until the doors closed again.

"Poor Maricela," Tirzah said. "Those were her favorites. I'll have to buy her another set."

"You ever think of having kids?" Pete asked. The question just slipped out. She was so good with them and liked them so much that he was surprised she didn't have any already. She didn't seem to have a significant other, but she was so independent that he couldn't see that stopping her.

"I might adopt some day."

"Why adoption?" Then, realizing that she might have fertility issues, he said, "Forget it, that was way personal."

She waved him off. "Not at all. It's just that I'm not big on babies. I start liking kids when they're old enough to have conversations with."

The elevator chimed again. To Pete's relief, it was on the ground floor. But that only meant that the real danger was fast approaching. As he escorted her along the corridor, fending off neighbors left and right, he quietly warned her, "This is all a set-up for an ambush, you know. Whatever I tell you to do, you do, okay? I tell you to get away, you get away. I tell you to freeze, you freeze."

"Got it," Tirzah replied. She sounded brave, but he could hear the shakiness underneath.

Pete swallowed. He wanted to lay a comforting hand on her shoulder, but touching her was just too intense for him. It would distract him when he needed to be most alert. So he had to make do with words. "I'll protect you. I promise."

Outside the apartment building, the city was strangely quiet. Too quiet. He'd worried about attacks from mind-controlled bystanders who were less harmless than Tirzah's neighbors, but he instantly realized that he'd been barking up the wrong path. Jerry wasn't planning to sic armed cops or gun collector civilians on them. He was clearing a path to attack them himself.

"Hold tight. I'm going to push you." Pete grabbed the push handles and began to run toward his car, which was parked a block away. Tirzah's hair streamed back like a banner in the wind. They approached an intersection. To get to their car, they needed to make a left turn. Very softly, he repeated, "Hold *tight*."

Her hands gripped the armrests so hard that knuckles went white. Pete swerved into an alley on their right. The wheelchair tried to throw her out, but she held fast.

Pete hadn't been running as fast as he could. Now he did. If they could get to the end of the alley before Jerry realized they weren't headed for the car and tried to intercept them, they'd make it to the subway stop. By the time Jerry arrived, they'd be long gone. A couple quick subway switches, and they'd lose him.

Sunlight glinted off the subway sign up ahead. Two more minutes, and Tirzah would be safe.

The ground heaved beneath his feet. Pete staggered, nearly losing his footing, then stumbled to a halt.

"Earthquake?" Tirzah gasped.

Ahead of them, the ground rippled, then rose upward in a wall of shiny black stone. He spun around, ready to snatch Tirzah up and carry her out of the alley, but he was too late. Another wall of stone was rising up to block off the other end of the alley. And Jerry stood in front of it, smirking, empty hands upraised.

Pete didn't hesitate. Leaping in front of Tirzah, he drew his gun and leveled it at Jerry.

Jerry gave a casual wave of one hand. The familiar heft of Pete's gun was suddenly a heavy weight, pulling down his hand. It had turned to stone.

For the first time in his entire life, he dropped his gun. It hit the pavement with a sharp crack, and shattered into fragments of glassy black stone.

"My teammates are already on their way," Pete bluffed. "You can't turn them *all* to stone."

"Sure I could," Jerry retorted. "If they showed up. But they won't, because you haven't called them yet. And if you were thinking of hitting some kind of panic button, forget about it."

Jerry waved his hand again. A weight tugged at Pete's hip, then tore through his pocket. He had just enough time to see a cell phone-shaped piece of black rock before it too smashed like a dropped glass.

Inside his head, his cave bear snarled. Pete had to give him a mental shove to keep him in his place; now wasn't the time to shift, when he didn't know if Jerry could also turn living beings to stone. The bear pushed back, ferocious and filled with the urge to fight.

Want to leave Tirzah caught in a trap, alone with an enemy and a bear statue? Pete asked.

With a resentful snarl, the bear subsided.

"Let's talk," said Jerry.

101

"Yeah, let's," said Tirzah.

She wheeled her chair out from behind Pete, so she sat at his side. Pete started to step in front of her, then restrained himself. He could shield her if Jerry made any sudden moves. And if she had a plan, he wanted to let her try it and give her whatever backup she needed. She wasn't trained, of course, but she was smart, resourceful, and cool-headed. And if her plan was to stall Jerry until Pete could make *his* move, he could certainly work with that.

"What do you want?" Tirzah asked.

"Same as before," Jerry replied. "The file, any copies you made of it, and your promise to never say a word about it."

"If I do, will you promise to leave me alone? And leave my neighbors alone?"

"Absolutely." A contemptuous look crossed Jerry's face as he said, with the slightest mocking edge, "My word of honor."

"Deal. I've got it here in my purse." Tirzah patted the purse she'd slung over her wheelchair.

Pete had hoped that she'd succeed in luring Jerry close enough that he could tackle him before their enemy could use his stone powers, but he didn't have high hopes that it would work.

Sure enough, Jerry shot a hate-filled glare at the wheels and said, "Lay it down on the ground."

With an irritated huff of breath, Tirzah did so. Pete had been keeping quiet in the hope that Jerry would pay less attention to him and more to Tirzah, creating an opening for Pete to make his move.

Then Jerry looked straight at Pete. "You. Valdez. I have an offer for you."

Suppressing his impulse to tell Jerry where he could put his offer, Pete said, "Yeah?"

"How's your power working?"

"Fine. Want a demo?"

Jerry seemed briefly confused, and then his face cleared. "Oh. Yes, your cave bear's inability to feel pain or be affected by drugs." As if Pete was a not-too-bright child, he said, "All you Apex subjects have two powers, not including shapeshifting. I meant your other one."

That was the first Pete had ever heard about that. As far as he knew, apart from shapeshifting they all had one power each. Unless you counted finding human touch excruciatingly painful, which he sure didn't. But he kept his expression blank as he said, "That's fine too."

Jerry smirked. "I don't think so. I think you're having some problems with it. But we can fix that for you. Just pick up Override's purse and come with me."

There's my chance. If he could just get a little closer to Jerry, he could knock him unconscious before he had a chance to do any of his rock stuff. Pete tried to sound as if he was hoping against hope as he said, "Seriously? You can fix it?"

Jerry nodded. "Absolutely."

"It *better* work," Pete said menacingly.

He turned his back on his enemy and caught Tirzah's eyes. In that brief exchange of glances, he knew that she understood.

"What?" Tirzah burst out. "No! Hey! You can't do that! I *hired* you to *protect* me!"

With a callous shrug, Pete said, "Put a stop payment on your card."

Tirzah bent and made a grab for her purse, but Pete snatched it up. Her fingers closed on empty air.

As he started walking toward Jerry, he heard her increasingly frantic yells of, "Hey! Hey, get back here! That's my purse, you thief! You can't—"

Jerry gave a wave of his hand. Tirzah's voice cut off in mid-yell.

Pete whirled around. Tirzah was gone, with only a round hill of stone where she had been. She had been buried in solid rock.

His cave bear roared in grief and rage. A red haze clouded Pete's vision as his body became bigger, heavier, stronger.

Pete tried to fight the shift. The cave bear would immediately try to kill the enemy; that was what he always did. But he needed to rescue Tirzah, not attack Jerry—

And then Pete was gone. Only the bear remained. Throwing back his shaggy head, he roared his fury to the skies. And charged.

CHAPTER 11

"*P*ete! PETE!" Tirzah yelled.

Her words fell into a smothering silence and dark. The bubble of stone had encased her so quickly that she hadn't even had time to scream. Batcat huddled inside her blouse, mewing piteously.

"It's okay, baby," Tirzah whispered, petting her. "We'll get out."

She wished she felt confident in her words. Tirzah couldn't see a thing, so she stretched out her arms and felt around. The walls were glassy and smooth, like the shards of Pete's shattered gun. With a sudden burst of hope, she wondered if they were equally fragile. She couldn't break out from the inside, but maybe Pete—

CRASH!

Light flooded her eyes as the walls of her prison smashed like a dropped egg. She flung up her forearm, shielding her face, then cautiously lowered it.

An enormous bear loomed over her, one massive paw still upraised, snarling and ferocious. Its glittering black eyes were half-hidden within its shaggy brown fur. Its teeth were white and very sharp, its claws big as daggers.

Tirzah had imagined a cave bear as just a larger grizzly. But now that she was looking at it, she knew that it was something else entirely: a prehistoric beast from another, fiercer time. She knew it had to be Pete, but she still shrank back nervously.

The cave bear swung its heavy head away from her. It gave vent to a terrifying roar, then charged Jerry in a shambling run, unstoppable as an avalanche.

Jerry stared at the bear, his eyes wide in a suddenly pale face.

How's it feel to be the one getting threatened instead of making the threats? Tirzah thought with vengeful satisfaction. *Serves him right for messing with my neighbors!*

She expected him to take down the stone walls he'd created and run like hell. But Jerry's weasely eyes narrowed. The air around him darkened and blurred, making him hard to see. Tirzah blinked, thinking it was her own vision that had gone wrong.

But when she opened her eyes again, Jerry had changed. His skin had gone a glassy black, like the stone he wielded, and looked hard. The planes of his face had become sharpened, even faceted, and his features were grotesque and demonic. His limbs had lengthened, and his hands were now clawed. He had a long, whiplike tail ending in an arrowhead. Instead of the shirt and pants he'd worn, he was now wrapped in a long black cloak.

The cave bear didn't flinch or hesitate, but continued its charge. It roared as it came, a sound so primal and ferocious that Tirzah couldn't believe that Jerry was still standing his ground.

Then Jerry's cloak unfurled and spread out. Tirzah realized that it was actually a pair of membranous wings. With a harsh, hawklike scream, he leaped into the air. The gargoyle that Jerry had become circled above their heads like a hideous man-sized bat.

The cave bear was unable to instantly halt its momentum. It was so big and heavy that if it had, it would have gone tumbling head over heels. And while it was trying to dig in its paws to come to a lumbering stop, the gargoyle plummeted down from the sky with a bloodthirsty screech, claws outstretched.

"Look out!" Tirzah shouted.

The cave bear reared up, its massive paws swatting at the air. But the gargoyle was quicker and more agile. It veered out of the way and landed atop the bear's back, slashing with all four sets of claws.

The bear threw itself down and rolled. Tirzah hoped with all her might that he'd crush the gargoyle. But the winged monster launched itself upward, unharmed. And when the bear regained its feet, there was blood on the pavement where it had lain, and blood matting its shaggy fur.

The bear roared. The gargoyle screeched and circled, then descended once again. This time the bear was waiting for it to try to land on its back, and lunged to intercept it. But again the gargoyle was far quicker. It swerved aside untouched, and slashed at the bear with its vicious black claws. Once again, it was the bear's blood that dripped down.

Tirzah grabbed the closest thing to hand, which was the lid from a nearby trash can, and flung it at the gargoyle. It evaded her throw with contemptuous ease, and let out a mocking shriek. Then it circled in a leisurely manner, preparing for its next strike.

Furious and helpless, she wished there was something, anything she could do to help. But what could she do from her chair? What could she do even if it wasn't for the chair? Even the cave bear was outmatched against that flying horror. The only way she'd be useful would be if she had wings.

Twenty needle-sharp claws dug into her chest. "Ow!"

Batcat scrambled out from Tirzah's blouse. Before Tirzah could grab her, she launched herself off Tirzah's shoulder, hissing and spitting. The little winged kitten flew straight at the gargoyle.

"Batcat, no!" Tirzah yelled. "Come back! It'll kill you!"

Her words were drowned out in an equally frantic roar from the cave bear. But Batcat didn't falter from her path as she darted toward a monster twenty times her size. The gargoyle hovered, batlike wings beating hard, clawed arms ready to grab its tiny foe.

Then the gargoyle shrieked in pain as it was hit in the belly by a fusillade of needle-like green spines. When Tirzah craned her head to see where the attack had come from, she spotted a creature crouched atop the wall Jerry had created. It was a winged kitten with spiky green fur. As she watched, it arched its back and spread its wings. The kitten hissed, and green needles shot out from its fur and struck the gargoyle.

The gargoyle shrieked and dove down toward it, its long tail trailing behind it. The green kitten leaped down off the wall, landed neatly on its feet, and dashed toward the cave bear, with the gargoyle in hot pursuit. Batcat, deprived of her fight, also flew low, chasing the gargoyle. She put on a burst of speed, caught the gargoyle's tail-tip, and bit it hard.

The gargoyle let out a pained screech and lashed its tail. Batcat clung to it with all four paws and her teeth. Tirzah abruptly realized that there *was* something she could do, now that the monster was distracted. She started scooping up the black stone remnants of Pete's gun and her prison, and flinging them at the gargoyle. Some missed, but more struck home. The gargoyle dipped down even lower, trying to evade

Tirzah's rock shards while also trying to dislodge the stubborn Batcat and catch the green kitten.

And then the cave bear struck. It had been crouching close to the ground, its great head held low. But now it reared up on its hind legs, striking out with a huge paw. It struck the gargoyle square in the chest with massive force.

The gargoyle shattered. Tirzah watched, dumbstruck, as fragments of glassy black stone rained down to the ground.

A moment later, the stone walls began to crumble away, collapsing on themselves in slow motion.

Batcat spat out an arrowhead-shaped piece with a "Ptui!" sound, then flew down to land in front of the green kitten. They circled each other warily, sniffing. Batcat put out an exploratory paw, and the green kitten gave a warning growl and puffed out its spines. Batcat backed off, then extended her paw again.

The cave bear had sunk back down to a crouch. Blood matted its shaggy fur, and more blood dripped down to the pavement. Its dark eyes were half-closed.

Tirzah had kept her distance from the bear before. It was so huge and fierce, she couldn't help feeling wary of it. But it wasn't "the bear." It—*he*—was Pete. And he was hurt. He needed help.

She went to his side. "Pete? Hey, Pete?"

She laid her hand on his massive head. In the blink of an eye, the bear was gone. Pete crouched on all fours, palms braced on the ground, blood soaking through his clothes. Her hand was still on his head. His short-clipped hair was surprisingly soft, even velvety.

He struggled to get up, muttering something she couldn't catch, then sank back down.

"Hey. Hey. Take it easy." Tirzah leaned down and put her arms around him.

Pete was shaking, his skin damp with sweat and blood.

He took a deep, shuddering breath, then another. "You... you okay?"

"Yeah. I'm fine, Pete. Don't worry about me."

"I don't..." His voice trailed off.

He tried again to get up, this time using the arm rests of her chair to pull himself up. He ended up kneeling with his head against her side, partly in her lap. Tirzah held him close, stroking his hair and trying not to panic. She couldn't tell how badly he was hurt, but he was covered in blood and seemed disoriented.

"I know I was the bear. But after that..." He shook his head slowly. "I hit something... and it broke...? Where's Jerry?"

"Oh, boy," Tirzah said. "That's a lot. Short version is Jerry's dead, so we don't have to worry about him any more. I'll explain the rest later. For now, you rest, and I'll call 911."

"No!" He almost jerked out of her embrace.

"You're hurt, Pete. You need help."

He gritted his teeth, then carefully articulated, "I can't go to a hospital. They'll notice I'm... different. "

"Right, right. Sorry, I should've known better. But we can't stay here."

Tirzah looked around. The kittens were still warily circling each other. The stone walls were still slowly disintegrating, as were the scattered stone fragments. It seemed like Jerry's powers were dissolving with his death. Which also meant that very soon now, all the people who he'd ordered to keep away from the area would start coming back. And then she'd have to explain a bleeding man and a pair of flying kittens.

CHAPTER 12

*P*ete struggled to orient himself. His memories of being the cave bear were dreamlike and fragmented. The only part he remembered with any degree of clarity was Tirzah shrinking back from him in fear. Just as he'd dreaded, she'd seen the part of him that was a beast, and she'd been horrified and afraid.

And yet she hadn't left him. Even now, she was holding him. He could feel his wounds as slashes of pain across his back and shoulders and sides, but they faded into insignificance beside the touch of her body against his, and the steady thud of her heartbeat.

She was alive. She was safe. She was unharmed. However it had happened and whatever she thought about him, he'd protected her.

"You have to see someone, Pete," she was saying. "There must be, I don't know, some shady veterinarian who patches up criminals? Or a shapeshifter doctor? Ah-ha! Let's call your team, one of them must know—"

"No!" The word burst from his mouth. If his team found him wounded, they'd check him over and give him first aid, then find some doctor. And as weak as he was, he might not be able to hide how much their touch hurt him. They'd know his secrets—see him vulnerable— "No. Don't call them."

"Why not? Jerry's dead. He can't control them anymore."

"I know. But…" Pete searched for an explanation that would satisfy her, but nothing came to mind. He couldn't seem to think straight. "No."

A meow startled them both. Batcat flew to Tirzah's shoulder. And something else rubbed against his ankle. Pete looked down. He was being nuzzled by a winged kitten a little bigger than Batcat with spiky olive-green fur.

"What…?"

"Got me," Tirzah said with a shrug. "It helped us in the fight."

"Hey, little buddy." He reached down and petted the kitten. It purred and arched its back into his hand. Its fur felt stiff, like hair with way too much gel. "Its fur feels funny."

"It's got spines. It fired some of them into the gargoyle."

"Oh." Pete's mind was beginning to clear, and he managed a smile. "It's a cactus cat."

Tirzah gave him a suspicious look. "Is that a real thing, or are you pulling my leg?"

"It's real folklore, like Bigfoot or chupacabras. They slash open cactuses and drink the sap, and then they get drunk and dance under the light of the moon—" Pete realized that *he* probably sounded drunk, and cut himself off. "My mom told me stories about them."

He took a moment to concentrate on the cactus kitten's spiky fur and vibrating body, and on Tirzah's soft body and human warmth. The solid reality of them both made him feel stronger and more grounded. Then, gritting his teeth, he gripped the arm rests of the wheelchair and used them to haul himself to his feet.

Black spots danced across his field of vision. His legs

threatened to give out, and he held himself up with his upper body strength alone.

Tirzah was looking up at him, her alarm plain on her face. "Pete, I really think we should call your team. You can't—"

The image of his entire team, no doubt plus Carter, showing up and seeing him in this state flashed across his mind, followed by exactly how it would feel when they picked him up. And cut off his shirt. And... "No! Just brace me."

With an irritated huff of breath, Tirzah helped steady him. As he'd noticed before, she was strong enough to do so; she looked soft, but her upper body had a lot of muscle beneath the luscious curves. With her support, he managed to step behind her chair and take hold of the handles.

Realizing his plan, she said, "You use those to hold your-self up, I actually move the chair?"

"Uh-huh."

She scooped up Batcat and stuffed her down the front of her blouse. The cactus kitten climbed Pete like a tree, then dove inside his shirt.

"Huh," Tirzah said. "Guess it's yours."

The last thing Pete needed right now was a pet, let alone an impossible-to-explain magical one. But the kitten's warm body and prickly fur felt oddly comforting, and he had no desire to kick it out of the refuge it had found.

"I'll name him Spike," Pete said.

He glanced around. The stone walls that Jerry had raised had crumbled completely into dust, as had the stone frag-ments scattered across the ground, and it was already starting to blow away in a light breeze. Pete could now see the streets at either end of the alley. To his immense relief, he didn't see any people. But if Jerry's powers were fading with his death, they could start showing up at any moment.

Tirzah stooped to snag her purse from the ground. "Since Jerry's dead, it's safe to go to my apartment, right?"

"No," Pete said. "Not yet. We don't know exactly how long it takes for his powers to wear off."

"Then...?"

There was an obvious answer, but Pete hesitated. He'd never broken his rule about separating his work from his family. But Jerry *was* dead. There was no one left to endanger his family by following Tirzah. In fact, under normal circumstances, his job would be over. A pang twisted his heart at the idea of never seeing her again.

"We'll go to my place," he said.

The car was only a block away, but it took all of Pete's strength to make it there. Once he did, he half-fell against it, gasping for breath and soaked in sweat.

"I... I can't drive." Tirzah's voice shook in a way he'd never heard before, and when he looked down at her, he saw that she looked both afraid and ashamed.

Pete felt terrible. He'd made that embarrassing display of his own weakness, and now she not only believed he couldn't drive, she was blaming herself for being disabled! He rushed to reassure her. "I know. Don't worry about it. I can drive."

She shot him an extremely dubious glance.

"I'm fine," he said. "I was just catching my breath."

Tirzah looked even more doubtful, but opened the driver's door for him. "Sit down. I can handle my chair."

Pete collapsed more than sat into the driver's seat, then watched Tirzah balance on one foot to fold her chair and cram it into the back seat. She grabbed the roof and swung herself into the front seat with a lovely agility and grace.

"You sure you can drive?" she asked.

He straightened, gathering his strength. "Yeah. Don't worry. I won't crash."

People were starting to come back on to the streets, and were going about normal activities like nothing had happened. Pete was relieved that Jerry apparently hadn't done anything permanent or even noticeable to them, but even more relieved that the temporary break in traffic enabled him to get to the freeway entrance much faster than usual. He felt dizzy and weak, and his wounds hurt badly. The drive to his house was manageable—probably—but he wasn't sure he could handle being stuck in traffic for hours. And it wasn't as if Tirzah could take over if he passed out over the wheel.

To keep himself awake and distract himself from how absolutely terrible he felt, he said, "The fight. Tell me what happened."

"Right. Well, you—cave bear you—broke me out of this sort of stone bubble. And then Jerry turned into a—a sort of bat thing, like the gargoyles on old buildings—and attacked you. And then Batcat attacked it—"

Batcat meowed at the sound of her name and scrambled out of Tirzah's shirt and on to her shoulder. The cactus kitten poked its head out of Pete's shirt at the sound of Batcat's meow and clambered out to perch on Pete's shoulder. Both kittens puffed up and hissed at each other.

"There better not be a catfight on top of me right now," Pete said.

Tirzah plucked Batcat off her shoulder and deposited her in the backseat, then, much more gingerly, did the same to the green kitten. Ominous hissing and growling rose up, but Tirzah resolutely ignored it. "And then the cactus kitten appeared out of nowhere and it, um, it shot its needles at the gargoyle. The kittens distracted it until you got it. You hit it with your paw, and it smashed into a million little pieces of stone."

"And you...?"

"I was totally useless," Tirzah muttered. "Well—I chucked some rocks at it."

Pete had to work hard just to drive safely, so he didn't dare take his eyes off the road or his hands off the wheel. He tried to put the equivalent of a comforting touch into his voice alone. "Hey. Don't talk like that. You fought, just like I did. You got me out of there when I couldn't even stand up by myself. Don't put yourself down, okay?"

"Okay." Her voice trembled.

"Say it like you mean it. We're all alive, right? The enemy's dead. We won."

"Yeah, we did win," she said, and this time she did sound like she meant it. "We were a good team."

"No grandmas or gargoyles can stand against us."

Tirzah started to chuckle, then frowned. "I wish I knew how the grandmas are doing—Oh! I forgot, I've got the camera feeds on my cell phone."

As Pete exited the freeway, she fished her phone out of her purse. When they stopped at a red light, he glanced over at the video feeds on her phone, and was relieved to see that everything seemed back to normal. A couple people were scratching their heads and studying ordinary objects, apparently trying to figure out what had happened to them or what they'd been doing with them, like Esther with the broken cup measure.

"It looks like they don't remember any of it," Tirzah said. "We could go back now, if you'd rather."

Pete weighed the odds of passing out over the wheel if he tried to turn around and drive all the way back, and didn't like them. Rather than scare her by saying so, he just said, "We're almost here. This is my neighborhood."

"This is where you live?" Tirzah asked.

The astonishment in her voice made him see his neighborhood through her eyes. All the houses were identical except for their paint jobs, which were excitingly varied between blue with white trim, white with blue trim, blue with gray trim, and gray with blue trim. Everyone in sight had white hair, gray hair, or no hair.

"Sorry," she added. "It's, uh, I'm sure it's very safe. And quiet. It just looks like you having a house here is single-handedly pulling down the average age of the residents from 70 to 69.5."

"It's actually my mom's house."

"You live with your *mom?"*

"Yeah." He clicked open the garage behind their house and pulled into it. Once the garage door had closed behind them, he took a deep breath. He'd already made the decision to bring Tirzah to his home, so it couldn't delay the revelation any longer. "And my daughter. Caro. She's thirteen. My mother took care of her while I was overseas."

Tirzah stared at him. "You have a daughter? You never mentioned a daughter!"

"I know. I—" A wave of intense dizziness swept over him, blurring his vision. He gritted his teeth, trying to ride it out. He decided to cut to the chase, just in case he passed out within the next few minutes. "Mom will have just left to pick her up from school, so they'll both be back in an hour. And they don't know about Apex, or the cave bear, or—or anything."

She groaned. "Or adorable flying kittens, right?"

"Right. I don't want my family involved in any of that stuff, okay? Jerry's gone, so as long as all they know is that you're the client I just finished protecting, they'll be fine. As long as they don't know anything else. And I don't want them knowing I was hurt in a fight. Tell them I'm... sick."

"You're covered in blood!"

"I'll clean up before they get here."

"What about seeing a doctor?" she demanded. "You can barely even stand up!"

"I don't need a doctor. Shifters heal fast."

Tirzah looked exasperated. "Let me get this straight. You're asking me to hide two flying kittens in your mom's house, conceal your gargoyle fight injuries, and dispose of your blood-soaked clothes, not to mention *my* blood-soaked clothes. In one hour. And then explain to your mother and daughter, who I'll be meeting for the first time, who I am, why I'm here, and what was wrong with you, without ever mentioning that we got run out of my apartment by my mind-controlled neighbors and you got hurt in a fight with a gargoyle.'"

"It wouldn't just be you doing all that," Pete protested. "I'd help."

"Pete, this is *impossible*." She took her cell phone out of her purse. "Forget it. I'm calling your team."

"NO!" He sat bolt upright, twisting in his seat to make a grab for the phone.

Everything went black.

CHAPTER 13

*P*ete lunged for Tirzah's cell phone, and collapsed across her lap. His shoulder knocked the phone out of her hand, and it fell into narrow space between the seat and the gearshift.

"Pete!" Tirzah bent over him anxiously. She could hear him breathing, but his skin was ashen and he felt clammy. She stroked his hair, which was wet with sweat and blood, then patted his cheeks. "Come on, Pete. You have to wake up. Come on…"

His eyelids fluttered. He mumbled, "Don't… Don't call…"

"I won't. I promise." Under her breath, she said, "Can't reach the phone anyway." Then, pitching her voice for his ears, she said, "Just wake up, Pete, please? You don't want to be sitting here when your daughter gets home."

That got him going. He struggled out of her lap, fumbled to undo his seatbelt, and opened his door.

"Wait, wait!" Tirzah called. "I can help—"

To her total lack of surprise, he tried to get out, and more-or-less fell out instead.

"This is ridiculous," Tirzah muttered. "Why did I promise not to call? I shouldn't have promised."

Swearing under her breath, she opened her own door, slung her purse across her chest, hopped out of the car, and opened the back seat. Spike and Batcat had reached some sort of wary détente, glaring at each other from opposite ends of the shelf behind the seats. When Tirzah dragged out her wheelchair, Batcat flew out and perched on her shoulder, and Spike flew out and then over the car. Tirzah used a combination of hopping and hanging on to the car to haul her chair to the other side, where she found Pete sitting on the floor, head in hands, with Spike on his shoulder and chewing on his ear.

She braced herself and the chair against the car. "Get in."

"I can stand—"

Remembering what had worked to motivate him before, she said, "You want your daughter to come home from school and find you bleeding on the garage floor?"

That did it. Pete reluctantly levered himself into the chair. "What about you?"

"I'll hang on to the back and hop. Just don't go fast."

Pete glanced up at her with a glint of humor. "I don't think that'll be a problem."

What she really wanted to do was quiz him about the daughter he'd never bothered to mention. What was she like? Were her mother and Pete still a couple, or was his girlfriend someone else? If he was still with the mother of his child, why was he living with *his* mother?

Tirzah forced herself to save the questions for later. Pete didn't seem in any shape to answer them, and she had her hands full just trying to escape the garage. You had to go up a step to even get into the house. Pete had to get out of the chair, lean against the doorframe, drag the chair up the step, sit back in it, and then help Tirzah up.

She used a wheelchair for a reason; though she could use her left leg to stand on, it wasn't strong. A wheelchair allowed her to get around far more easily than crutches would, and without exhausting herself in the process. She'd tossed her crutches into a closet almost a year ago, and barely taken them out since. Now, as she hopped along at the back of the wheelchair, trying not to skid on carpets, bang into furniture, or knock Pete into anything, she wished she had them with her.

She was so busy concentrating on just making it through that she got only the vaguest impression of the house, mostly consisting of "not accessible," "*really* not accessible," and "way too much furniture." By the time they made it into Pete's bedroom and then the connected bathroom, they were both tired and sweating. Once they stopped there, the kittens flew off their shoulders and perched on opposite ends of the bathroom, Batcat atop the half-open door and Spike on the ceiling light.

Pete slid out of the chair and sat down on the floor. He leaned against the bathtub with his head tilted back and throat exposed, breathing heavily, eyes half-closed.

Tirzah sat down beside him and put her hand on his shoulder. "How're you doing?"

He made an indistinct sound that did not suggest anything along the lines of "Just fine," then said, "I have to get out of these clothes."

"Do you know if you have a pair of—" Before she could say "scissors," Pete put his hands on either side of his collar. His biceps bulged as his shirt ripped in half. A pair of bloody rags dropped to the floor.

His muscular chest and back were scored with painful-looking slashes. To Tirzah's relief, they'd stopped bleeding, but he'd lost plenty of blood already if he couldn't even walk. She once again wished she could take him to a doctor.

Pete, looking down at himself, apparently came to the opposite conclusion. With a mind-boggling degree of casualness, he remarked, "I knew I didn't need a hospital. Shallow cuts like these always bleed a lot. I'll be fine if I rehydrate and rest a bit."

"Rest, rehydrate, and eat a steak," Tirzah suggested. "That's what you're supposed to do when you give blood, right?"

He smiled faintly. "That's the kind of prescription I like."

"Let's start with rest and rehydrate. Unless you have a steak in here."

"I wish."

She filled a glass with water from the sink and handed it to him. His hands shook, spilling some water over the rim. She put hers over his, steadying him as he drank. When she refilled the glass, he was able to hold it himself.

"I should clean those cuts," she said. "They might have gargoyle germs. Where's your first-aid kit?"

"In the cabinet in the kitchen, over the sink."

"I'll get it. Let me just make sure I'm not tracking blood all over your house." Tirzah wetted a washcloth and cleaned all the blood off her chair, then used another to dry it. She tossed the gory washcloths into the pile with his shirt-halves, then looked down at her own clothes, which were very noticeably stained with Pete's blood. "I am not going to greet your family looking like Lizzie Borden."

"Borrow something of my mom's. It'd be a bit big on you, but—"

Tirzah could not even begin to express her horror at the idea of meeting Pete's mother for the first time while wearing some outfit of hers which Tirzah had borrowed without asking permission. "Pete, I am not just helping myself to your mom's clothes!"

Pete frowned. "I'm not sure Caro would be okay with you borrowing hers."

"*I* wouldn't be okay with that, either!" Tirzah was still processing the fact that Pete even had a daughter. She was dying to meet Caro, but she knew teenagers, not to mention having been one herself, and if there was one thing she was sure of, it was that no teenage girl appreciated some random adult borrowing her clothes.

"Take that, then." Pete pointed to a shirt on a hanger on a hook on the door. "That's mine."

Tirzah hung on to the door handle, stood on tip-toes, and dragged the shirt off the hanger. Once she had it in her hand, she was instantly extremely conscious that she'd have to undress to put it on, and that if she left the bathroom to do so, she'd get blood on the carpet or bed or something. And also, that Pete was bare-chested already, and enough blood had gotten on his pants that he'd have to take them off even if he didn't have any below-the-belt injuries. She looked away, and caught her own face in the bathroom mirror, blushing fiery red.

"I'm turning my back," Pete said. "Let me know when it's okay to turn around."

"Thanks," Tirzah muttered. Her ears and cheeks still felt like they were on fire. She stripped off her clothes (to her intense relief, her bra and panties were fine) and yanked on Pete's shirt in record time. It said WORLD'S BEST DAD in huge letters across the front and hung almost to her knees, becoming a sort of embarrassingly short shirt-dress. She sat down in her chair, pressed her legs tight together, then wedged some of the fabric between her thighs for good measure.

"Done!" Tirzah spun the chair around. And got a good look at Pete kneeling with his back to her, wearing nothing but a pair of boxer shorts.

She tried not to stare too hard at him. But she was still staring when he turned around, and then she caught *him* staring. They both dropped their gaze to the floor, then looked up and away.

"I'll go get the first aid kit," Tirzah said hurriedly.

"Thanks. Hey, where'd the kittens go?"

"They're perched..." Tirzah's voice trailed off as she saw that they were no longer perched where she'd last seen them, or anywhere else. "Somewhere in the house, I guess. I'll collect them on my way back."

She fled the bathroom and the mostly-naked Pete as fast as she could, which was not very fast as his bedroom had thick carpeting that made her feel like she was pushing her chair through deep water. While she was huffing and puffing and trying not to think too hard about the impending meeting with his family or how she was dressed for it, she did a quick flying kitten check. They were nowhere in sight.

The hallway was hardwood, which was great for thirty seconds. Then she encountered a throw rug that bunched up under her wheels and stopped her cold until she rolled it up and shoved it to the side. Then she reached a huge china vase decorated with painted cacti, resting on a delicately balanced pedestal that she had to maneuver around with about one inch of clearance.

The kittens weren't in the hallway either, which was initially a relief as they at least weren't about to knock over the cactus vase, and then was much less of one when she contemplated searching the house for them. From what she'd seen of it on her way in, it was an obstacle course of random pieces of furniture, each decorated with a minimum of three breakable objects.

And also cacti, which someone, presumably Pete's mom, seemed to collect. Everywhere she looked, there was a cactus. The living room had more cacti than she could count. There were cacti on the windowsills, cacti on tables, cacti on pedestals, cacti in hanging baskets; fat cacti, skinny cacti, flowering cacti, smooth cacti, prickly cacti, furry-looking cacti. And that wasn't even counting the decorative cacti sculptures and dishcloths with cactus prints.

Tirzah dodged an elegant table holding a collection of blown glass cacti and went into the kitchen. It had a little round cactus on either side of the sink, a tiny potted cactus glued to a refrigerator magnet, and an entire lovingly tended cactus garden atop an inconveniently located table.

What it did not have: a cactus kitten. Nor did she see Batcat.

"Batcat?" Tirzah called, venturing further into the kitchen. "Spike?"

Tentacles brushed against the back of her neck.

"Augh!" She recoiled, shoving herself backward and looking around wildly.

A cactus in a hanging basket lurked before her, with a cascade of spiny tendrils trailing down to the exact nape-of-neck level of a seated Tirzah.

"You all right?" Pete called from the bathroom.

"Fine, fine!" Tirzah called back.

After checking very carefully for 1) cacti, 2) rugs, 3) things shaped like cacti, 4) flying kittens, Tirzah retrieved the first aid kit. She'd expected a tiny thing bought in a supermarket with a few Band-Aids and bee sting tweezers, totally inadequate for her task, but what she found was a large military surplus kit. Which was unsurprising upon reflection, as it had no doubt been bought by Pete.

Since she'd already used up the washcloths in the bathroom, she filled a bowl with warm water, rummaged around until she found some clean folded washcloths, dipped and wrung them out, and draped them atop the first aid kit.

Taking a final incredulous look at the sink cacti, she piled everything in her lap and started to turn around to go back. Then she remembered something odd. Hadn't there been one cactus to the right of the sink and one to the left when she'd come into the kitchen? Now there was one to the right and two to the left...

The second cactus on the left leaped into the air with a hiss.

"Augh!" Tirzah jerked back, then had to snatch at the kit and washcloths before they fell off her lap.

"Everything okay?" Pete called.

"Fine, fine!" Tirzah yelled back.

Spike, who had been curled up in a ball beside the left-hand sink cactus, was now flying around the kitchen hissing at Batcat, who had been lurking behind the coffee canisters. Batcat also took to the air. Before Tirzah could even try to coax them to come to her, the kittens flapped out of the kitchen and were lost from view. An angry yowl sounded from an indeterminate direction, and then there was silence.

Once again, Pete's voice rose up. "You *sure* you're okay?"

"Yes!"

Clutching the kit and washcloths, she made her way back through the hallway and bedroom.

"Tirzah?" Pete called from the bathroom. "I have pajamas in the bottom shelf of my dresser drawer."

She half-expected them to be printed with cacti, but they were all plain, navy blue or black. Impersonal, like the rest of his room. Unlike the rest of the house, it contained no cacti or even excessive furniture. Though she was glad to not have to maneuver through an obstacle course, the room felt oddly sterile: a hotel room rather than a home.

In the bathroom, she found Pete was still sitting on the floor, but his color was better and he seemed more alert. He'd taken the washcloths and used them to scrub the bloodstains off the floor and bathtub, and was stuffing them, along with their discarded clothes, into the cabinet under the sink.

Tirzah slid out of her chair, sat on the floor beside him, and began cleaning his cuts. He didn't wince at the sting of the antiseptic.

"What was going on out there?" he asked.

"Got attacked by a cactus," she said. "That weird tentacle thing in the kitchen."

"It's a rat tail cactus. I keep thinking it's a fly on my back and slapping it."

"Your mom is sure into cactuses."

Pete chuckled. "She and my dad had their honeymoon in Arizona. He bought her a cactus, and she liked it so much that he bought her another one for her anniversary. And her birthday. And Christmas. It got to be a tradition. And then other people in the family decided she collected cacti, so they started giving them to her. Dad died ten years ago, but everyone else kept it up. This house is basically the display case for forty years of gift cacti."

"Does she even like cacti anymore?"

"We're all afraid to ask."

"From the striking lack of cacti in your bedroom, I'm guessing you're not a fan."

"Not especially," Pete admitted. "I stick myself on Mom's all the time. It gets a bit old."

"You need to get out your own tchotchkes."

"My own what?"

"Tchotchkes," Tirzah repeated. "It's Yiddish for knick-knacks. Like your action figures."

"You speak Yiddish?" Pete asked.

"Nah. I know a couple words, but they're all words people use who don't really speak it. I don't think anyone's actually spoken it in my family since maybe my great-great grandparents. Sometimes I think about learning it—there's a woman in my apartment building who's offered to teach me—but, well, time flies."

"Yeah, I keep meaning to brush up on my Spanish, and Mom would teach me, but like you said..." With pride, he added, "Caro's nearly fluent, though."

"Did the three of you always live together? I mean, when you were in the US."

"Uh-huh."

"Here, in the cactus house?"

He chuckled. "Nah. Different cactus house. Mom bought this one when she retired, so I never really lived in it. I thought me and Caro would get our own place when I was done with the Marines, but..."

"But what?" Tirzah asked when he didn't finish the sentence.

"But I got a lot going on." And that was clearly all he was going to say about that.

She tried not to grind her teeth with frustrated curiosity. Did he mean the cave bear? His bodyguard job? The fact that his team were a bunch of magical shapeshifters? All of the above?

Well, she'd at least get to meet his mother and daughter. She was dying to see him as a dad. She had the feeling he was a good one. It must drive him nuts that he couldn't talk about his own daughter in order to keep her safe. All the parents she knew would whip out photos of their kids at the slightest provocation.

"So, Caro's mother," Tirzah ventured. "Are you divorced? A widower?"

Pete gave her a long look, allowing plenty of time for her to take back the question, but she just stared right back. If he was going to stonewall her on that one, at least he could own it. At last, he said, "We never married. Ana's never been in the picture."

"She got pregnant, and *you* kept the kid?" Then she calculated Pete's probable age against Caro's age, and said, "Oh, wait. You both must've been in high school."

"Yeah. We were madly in love for about three months. You know how it goes at that age. By the time she realized she'd gotten pregnant, we'd already broken up. She was headed for college and she wasn't ready to be a parent. I wasn't either, or at least I thought I wasn't. We agreed to give the baby up for adoption. Then I went to see Ana in the hospital, and I held our daughter. She was so small, I could cup her in my hands." His face softened as he re-lived that moment of joyous, unexpected love. "And that was that," he concluded. "I was a teenage idiot, so my mom and dad did most of the parenting at first. But I grew up fast."

"I bet. That must've been hard."

"It *was* hard." He smiled. "It was wonderful."

Tirzah felt oddly jealous. She still didn't want a baby, but if she'd gotten pregnant at 18, she too would have a 13-year-old now. "And, um, your girlfriend...?"

"What girlfriend?"

"The one you talk to on the phone every day?"

Pete's eyebrows flew up, then he chuckled. "That was Caro. And my mom, sometimes."

"Oh." Tirzah lowered her face to hide any pleasure that might have shown at *that* revelation. No wife, no girlfriend. Well, well, well.

"When he's bleeding on the bathroom floor" was probably number one on the list of "when to not hit on a man." But maybe later...

Pete pulled on his pajamas, buttoning up the top to make sure the bandages were concealed. "Thanks. That's better. I'll help you catch the kittens now."

"I don't think that's a good—"

Pete stood up, swayed, and clutched at the sink for support.

Tirzah scrambled into her chair and backed it up to the sink. "Hang on to the back."

Pete gingerly transferred his hold on the sink to the chair handles, and leaned heavily on it as she steered him to his bed. He collapsed as much as lay down on it.

She pulled the covers over him. "And stay in!"

"I will. And thanks." Pete's dark gaze caught and held her. "I know I backed you into this. I just wanted to say how much I appreciate it."

His intensity caught her like a butterfly in amber. Her earlier thought about "when not to hit on a man" came back to her. "When he's telling you how much he appreciates you" was probably *not* on that list.

She opened her mouth, then closed it, suddenly unsure of what she wanted to say. They'd gone through so much already, she was afraid to ruin it by coming on too strong. Wouldn't Pete have asked her himself if he was into her?

That extremely important issue aside, what did she want from him? He obviously was a serious relationship kind of guy. He had a family already. If she asked him on a date, it wouldn't be a simple date, it would be the start of something big. She hadn't even met his daughter yet. There was so much she didn't know about him. There was so much he didn't know about her...

She was rescued from her indecision by the sight of the clock by his bed. "I have to go. I have fourteen minutes to clean your blood off the garage floor and catch two flying kittens."

She found Spike happily splashing around in the bowl of water she'd left in the kitchen sink, his green fur as sleek as the succulents lining the window. She scooped him up and took him to Pete's bedroom, where he flew from her hands to Pete's pillow and started licking his face with a startlingly pink tongue.

Tirzah shut the door behind her, figuring she could lure both kittens into a closet once she had them in the same room, collected a wad of damp paper towels, and made her way to the garage. There she was once again confronted by the step. Trying to get over it in her chair was liable to dump her out, and there was nothing she could hang on to between the step and car.

"So much for dignity," she muttered. Tirzah slid out of the chair and slithered on her belly to the bloodstained floor, which she scrubbed maniacally. She wiped down the car seats and handle, assured herself that the garage no longer looked like a murder scene, crawled to a trash can and buried the paper towels beneath the rest of the trash, then slithered back to her chair and clambered in.

Now for Batcat. Where *was* she? It wasn't like the winged terror to be this quiet.

"Batcat? Heeeeere kitty kitty kitty!" Tirzah called.

No one came, but she heard a faint flapping sound. She followed it down the hall until she reached a closed door. Puzzled, she leaned over and put her ear to the door. Yep. Flapping.

Well, she definitely wouldn't put it past Batcat to figure out how to open a door and then close it behind her. Tirzah opened the door and looked in.

It was Caro's room; Tirzah realized that at once. For one thing, it was completely and utterly cactus-free. For another, it was unmistakably the room of a teenage girl, split between remnants of childhood and new interests. The bed piled with homework pages and bottles of nail polish and video games and a few much-loved stuffed animals, all atop a faded patchwork quilt. Posters of horses and kittens adorned the walls, interspersed with the occasional rock star. A beautifully made pegasus figurine stood on the bedside table beside a teetering stack of library books.

The furniture was sturdily constructed out of unpainted, honey-colored wood. The posts of the bunk bed were carved into the heads and tossing manes of horses, each with individual personality, and engraved horses galloped and pranced and reared across the table and desk and chairs. It was beautiful and constructed with love, but was just a little bit small for a teenager. Pete must have made it for her when she was younger.

Tirzah still hadn't met Caro, but seeing the room made her feel like she knew the girl a little already. Like Tirzah, she had her own tastes and hobbies... and she loved animals.

Unfortunately, there were no visible animals in the suddenly-silent room, unless you counted the stuffed ones and the pegasus figurine. "Batcat? Here kitty kitty kitty."

She waited, listening, but there was no response. Tirzah hated to further intrude into Caro's private space, but she had to get the kitten—and soon. She decided to split the difference. Tirzah stood up, bracing herself with both hands on the doorframe, and leaned in, trying to spot the kitten.

"HEY!"

The yell behind her made her jump. Tirzah's left hand slipped off the doorframe, and she grabbed out wildly for support. She caught the edge of the carved table, which tipped over. Tirzah fell headlong into the room. The WORLD'S BEST DAD shirt flew upward, and something small and light fell on her head and cracked open, showering her with what looked and smelled like lawn clippings.

"ABUELA!" a girl's voice yelled behind her. "I CAUGHT A BURGLAR! CALL THE POLICE AND TELL THEM I CAUGHT A NAKED WHEELCHAIR BURGLAR!"

Tirzah, horrified, levered herself to a sitting position and yanked down Pete's shirt. "No, no, I—"

The teenage girl in the hallway, who had to be Pete's daughter Caro, yelled, "A HALF-NAKED WHEELCHAIR BURGLAR WEARING DAD'S SHIRT!"

"She's not a burglar!" Pete shouted from the bedroom. "She's my client!"

A white-haired woman hurried up behind Caro and peered down at Tirzah. "Are you all right?"

"Yes, fine."

And that had to be Pete's mom. Great. Tirzah felt incredibly conscious of her sweaty, grubby, half-naked state. She had to be making the worst impression ever, even if you didn't count the part where she'd just appeared in their house with neither invitation nor explanation. She had been so busy frantically cleaning up and searching for flying kittens that she had completely failed to come up with a cover story for why she was in the house, let alone why she was currently in—

"What are you doing in my room?!" Caro demanded.

Tirzah's mind went utterly blank, at least as far as an explanation for that was concerned. There apparently wasn't room for any thoughts other than *help* and also *Batcat is somewhere in this room*. She looked around frantically, as if she could find a plausible excuse somewhere inside Caro's room, and spotted the lovely little pegasus figurine.

"What a beautiful pegasus," Tirzah said. "I can't see from here—is it porcelain?"

Caro lunged past her, nearly knocking her over, then whipped around and stood as if she was shielding the figurine with her body. "This is MY ROOM! What are you doing in MY ROOM?!"

Tirzah could remember being a teenage girl who hated people intruding into her space and touching her things, so she was more sympathetic than defensive. On the other hand, there was Batcat to worry about. Maybe the best thing to do was to deflect suspicion and get all of them out of the room.

"Sorry! Sorry! I was looking for... pants!" She scrambled back into her wheelchair, shedding bits of grass as she went, and backed it out of the room.

The white-haired woman picked up a blade of grass. "Caro, why do you have a box of lawn clippings in your room?"

Caro looked as furtive as Tirzah felt. "It's for... school! For, um, an art project."

The white-haired woman split a skeptical glance between them both, then called out, "Pete? Mijo? Where are you?"

"In my bedroom!" Pete called. "I'm sick!"

Pete's mom gave them a final dubious stare, then turned around and headed for his bedroom. Tirzah was torn between trying to get ahead of her to warn Pete to hide Spike, and staying to try to find Batcat. She fiddled with her wheelchair brakes, hoping Caro would go ahead, but the girl stayed where she was, eyeing Tirzah suspiciously.

Tirzah gave up and followed Pete's mom. Behind her, she heard Caro's footsteps. At least Caro wasn't staying in the room with Batcat. If Batcat was even in that room. For all Tirzah knew, the flapping had been some bird outside the window.

Though if Batcat wasn't in Caro's room, where *was* she?

CHAPTER 14

*Y*ou didn't get to be a wizard-scientist by giving up at the first sign of adversity. But that knowledge gave him little comfort as he stood in the alley and surveyed the black dust that was all that remained of his gargoyle minion.

"That fool," he muttered to himself.

He should never have allowed the gargoyle a second chance after his failure to secure the computer file. Now the crippled hacker was still free, the file was still undeleted and may have even been shared, and his chosen Dark Knight had once again slipped from his grasp.

He wished he could pursue at once, but using his power to enrage so many people and then make them all forget what had happened had left him drained. The wizard council had a strict policy of covering up their tracks, even at the price of letting their quarry escape for a while. Their plans were far too important to risk premature discovery.

He gave the dust an irritated kick with the tip of a polished shoe, then stopped in surprise. Bending down, he plucked a green spine from the ground.

"So that's where the cactus cat went," he said softly. "Well, well, well."

So many of the magical creatures had been lost to their enemies already, it would be quite a feather in his cap if he became not only the first of the wizard council to secure his Dark Knight, but the first to recapture one of the magical beasts.

He smiled as he strode from the alley, black dust drifting in his wake. So the Dark Knight had fled with the hacker female. No matter. That would only make it more convenient for him to catch them both—and the cactus cat too!

As he emerged from the alley, he had to step around a couple enthusiastically kissing as they leaned against the graffitied wall. How repulsive.

Worse, the sight of them gave him a disquieting idea. At the laboratory and base the wizard council had taken over from Apex, they'd severed their prospective Dark Knights' ability to recognize and bond with their mates. At least, they thought they had. But they hadn't had the chance to test the severing. And the longer the Dark Knights were free, the greater the chance was that they would meet their mate. And if the severing had been incomplete, who knew what might happen?

For all he knew, that hacker female might be the Dark Knight's mate!

He scowled so darkly at that thought that a pedestrian who caught his eye edged backward and bumped into a fruit cart, sending a cascade of oranges rolling down the street.

Mortals, he thought with scorn as everyone in the vicinity scrambled to pick them up. *Scurrying like the ants that they are.*

Well, even if that troublesome female was his Dark Knight's mate, it would make no difference. Once he had rested and recovered his power, he would track them down. The female was a helpless cripple, and he knew the key to making the Dark Knight his own. They would not escape again.

And once all the Dark Knights were assembled, the wizards' plan, which had been so long in the making, would finally become a reality.

CHAPTER 15

*P*ete felt pretty guilty over not helping Tirzah with the cleanup and kitten catching, but if the last hour had demonstrated one thing, it was that any attempts to help that involved standing up would only make things worse. So he stayed in bed, letting Spike lick him with his rasping tongue, and tried to think of where Batcat might be hiding.

The mystery was solved a minute before the shouting began, when he heard a gnawing sound from under his bed. Pete rolled over and peered under it. A pair of disembodied yellow demon eyes stared back at him, and then Batcat went back to trying to eat one of his sneakers.

Pete reached under the bed and extracted Batcat. The kitten squeaked in protest, but he kept a firm grip on her. If he let her go, there was no telling where she'd go. He'd just hold her till Tirzah came back.

He was about to yell that he'd caught her when he heard the front door open. A moment later, there was a shout and a crash. Spike tensed to fly, so Pete grabbed him too. An instant later, both kittens were flapping and struggling in his hands as Caro started yelling about naked wheelchair burglars.

"She's not a burglar!" Pete shouted. "She's my client!"

He wasn't sure anyone had even heard him. Pete was debating trying to hide the kittens in the closet (likely to end with him on the floor and them circling the ceiling) when his mother called, "Pete? Mijo? Where are you?"

"In my bedroom!" Pete called. "I'm sick!"

Footsteps approached rapidly. In desperation, he crammed both kittens into his pillowcase, then sat up so he was leaning against the headboard rather than on them, but his body hid any visible squirming. He hoped.

He wasn't a moment too soon. His door opened and in marched his mother, followed by Caro and a very disheveled (but, to his guilty disappointment, not actually half-naked) Tirzah with what looked like lawn clippings in her hair. A moment later, Mom and Caro were standing over him, and Tirzah was... sitting... over him. She *did* have grass in her hair.

Two furry lumps squirmed against his back, and one began worrying at his shirt. He suspected Batcat. He'd recognize those needle teeth anywhere.

"Mijo!" His mother put her hand to his forehead. Pete braced himself against the pain, which was far worse than that of the cuts, until she lifted it. "You don't look good. What's the matter?"

"I... uh..." Pete considered and rejected "a cold" (not serious enough to keep him in bed), "the flu" (contagious, which wouldn't work as he wanted to get his mom and Caro out of the room but keep Tirzah in it), and "heatstroke" (too serious, Mom would insist on a doctor.) Then it came to him. "Food poisoning. I must've eaten a bad burger."

A kitten hurled itself into his back, and another one tried to climb up it. He leaned back a little harder, blocking its access.

"Why's *she* here?" Caro asked suspiciously. "Why's she wearing the shirt *I* gave you?"

"I threw up on her dress."

"EWWWWWWW!" Caro shrieked. Out of the corner of his eye, he caught Tirzah stifling a grin.

"And I think I'm about to throw up again, so if you could all..." He waved a hand toward the door.

Caro fled, but his mother wasn't so easily grossed out.

"Do you need help getting to the bathroom?" Mom asked. "A bucket?"

"I can manage—"

One of the kittens squeaked, which Pete covered with a loud gagging noise. And apparently not a very convincing one, because Mom's eyebrows shot up.

"Mijo..." she began, then sneezed.

"Bless you," Pete and Tirzah said simultaneously.

"Thank you." Mom sneezed again, then wiped at watery eyes. "I feel just like there's a cat in here. Hmm. I wonder if Caro smuggled one into her room. Maybe the lawn clippings were to make a nest for it. Or makeshift kitty litter."

Pete felt completely at sea. "The lawn clippings were from Caro's room?"

"I have a cat," Tirzah volunteered. "I'm probably covered in cat hair. Sorry."

"Not in Pete's shirt, you're not," Mom said.

"Cat saliva," Tirzah said. "She licks me all the time. People who're allergic to cat fur are usually allergic to their spit too. And she likes to climb on my head, so my hair's bound to have fur all over it. I'll take a shower... Um..."

"You can use mine," Pete said.

Mom's eyes seemed to bore into him. Just like the forty kitten claws currently boring into his back. "I see. Well, you certainly don't look well. I'll make you some soup. Tirzah, I'll bring you something from my closet for you to wear."

"Thank you, Mrs. Valdez," Tirzah said.

"Please," Mom said. "Call me Lola."

"Thank you, Lola."

"Thanks, Mom."

Mom sneezed again, shot a suspicious glance at Pete and an incredulous one at Tirzah's hair, then went out. To Pete's relief, she closed the door behind her.

"I couldn't find Batcat," Tirzah whispered.

"I've got her," Pete said. "Spike too."

"You do? Where are they, in the closet?"

He shook his head. "In my pillow."

"What?!" Tirzah burst into giggles.

There was a knock at the door.

"Come in!" Pete called.

Mom came in with clothes draped over one hand and a plastic bucket in the other. With a twinkle in her eye, she deposited the bucket by the bed and handed the clothes to Tirzah. "Here you go. I'll have soup ready in half an hour."

As soon as she closed the door behind her, Pete said, "I think Mom thinks we... uh... have something going on. She never knocks."

Tirzah flushed a pretty pink. Avoiding his eyes, she said, "I guess that saves us having to come up with a more convincing explanation."

Both kittens bit Pete hard, saving *him* from having to respond to Tirzah's implication that they should go ahead and fake-date by default. "Ow!"

He leaned forward and handed her the kittens, pillow and all. "Can you put them in the bathroom? It's got a pretty thick door, so if it's closed, hopefully no one can hear them. And they can drink out of the sink."

"Hope they can use the toilet, too," she muttered.

"Or we could lay down some newspaper. I could get today's from the living room." With an exasperated sigh, he said, "I mean, you could get it."

"Hey, tough guy." Tirzah's voice was gentle. "It's okay. You got hurt saving my life. I'll get the newspaper, and hide the kittens, and say... whatever... to your family. You rest. You earned it."

Pete opened his mouth to say he was fine, then closed it again. Sure, he'd be better soon—the one thing he liked about being a shifter was the speed with which he recovered from injuries—but he wasn't now. And it didn't make her think less of him, any more than it made him think less of her because she couldn't walk.

You don't need to hide from her, his cave bear rumbled unexpectedly.

Pete wasn't so sure about that. But maybe he could hide... less.

"Okay." His voice came out thick, and he swallowed. "Hey, I'm really tired. If I'm asleep when Mom comes in with the soup, can you tell her to wake me up?"

"Yeah. Yeah, Pete. You get some sleep."

Pete lay back down, turned over, and settled his head against the other pillow. He expected Tirzah to leave, but instead she leaned over the kitten pillow and put her hand on his shoulder. He'd gotten used to her touch, a little bit; the pleasure of it no longer came as such a shock, but it was no less of a pleasure for that. She stroked the bare skin at the nape of his neck, then worked her way farther down, easing her hand under his collar. He drew in a deep breath, relaxing into it, as she rubbed the unbandaged parts of his back.

His cave bear made that deep rumbling sound that was almost a purr.

I can't fall asleep now, Pete thought. *I don't want to miss a single second of this.*

But he did.

CHAPTER 16

Caro pushed a piece of acorn squash around her plate, then reluctantly ate the part that had melted butter on it. Abuelita would get on her case if she didn't eat *some* vegetables. "Can I have some more soup to take to Dad?"

"He's sleeping now," Abuelita said. "He can have the rest later, when he wakes up on his own."

"That might be tomorrow morning. Nobody wants soup for breakfast!"

"He will if he's still sick," Abuelita said firmly. "Eat your squash."

Caro shot a pointed look at Tirzah, who was also poking at her squash. "She's not eating hers."

In a very soft voice, Tirzah said, "You're a smart cookie, Caro. Very observant." Then she shoved a bite of squash in her mouth and spoke for Abuelita's ears. "'S'delish."

Caro couldn't help being pleased that Dad's client thought she was smart, which annoyed her because she wanted to keep on being mad at Tirzah for barging into her room. But more than any of those feelings, she was curious over Tirzah's extremely short and unsatisfactory explanation of why she'd hired Dad and what she was doing in their house. "So why did you have a stalker? Like, how did he find you?"

"Princesa, let's not talk about stalkers at the dinner table." Abuelita offered her a dish. "Green beans?"

Caro ignored the disgusting beans. "But I'm really curious. Dad *never* talks about his job!"

"Yes, well, that's the problem," Tirzah said. "Your father's job involves a lot of private stuff. I probably shouldn't have even said it was a stalker without checking with him first. So sorry, Caro, but I shouldn't say anything more until I get a chance to ask him what it's all right for me to tell you."

"He'll say, 'nothing,'" Caro said. "Just like how he used to take off and we'd never know if the next time we'd hear from him would be next week or in six months, and then when he came back, all he'd ever say was 'Sorry, Lina, I'm not allowed to talk about it.' And when we went swimming, he'd have new scars."

A silence fell. Both her grandmother and Tirzah were eyeing her like they thought they understood and felt sorry for her. Caro hated being pitied, and they *didn't* understand.

She pushed back her chair. "I'm done! Good night!"

Caro fled before Abuelita could stop her, running into her bedroom and slamming the door. She clicked the lock behind her and turned on some music on her phone, and only then allowed herself to look for Moonbow.

Her beautiful, brilliant, magnificent, magical stallion stood on her bedroom floor, grazing on lawn clippings. Her breath caught in her throat as she knelt to gaze at him.

So the rest of her life sucked. So her dad didn't trust her with secrets and could barely stand to hug her, so everyone in her neighborhood was a hundred and twelve, so she wasn't allowed to go anywhere by herself, so she was in danger of flunking computer science, so she had some weird woman in a wheelchair snooping around her room, so Abuelita still hadn't figured out that she hated green beans—none of that mattered, because she had a *tiny flying pony*, and that made up for everything else.

"You're so smart," she whispered, softly enough that no one outside her room could hear her over the music. "You held so still that you tricked the half-naked wheelchair burglar into thinking you were a toy!"

Moonbow playfully froze again, making her laugh. Then he went back to grazing.

Caro watched him, hugging her knees to her chest and her secret to her heart. Thank goodness she'd come home in time! That snoopy Tirzah might've picked him up if Caro hadn't been there to stop her, and then stolen him or sold him to a lab or kept him for herself. Tirzah had claimed that she was going into Caro's room to look for pants that would fit her, and Caro wasn't sure whether to be mad because Tirzah might've been lying, or mad because she might've been telling the truth. Borrowing other people's clothes without their permission was not okay.

Moonbow finished his meal, pranced around the floor for a while, then trotted to her and nuzzled her. She stroked his silken coat and sleek feathers, and used a doll's hairbrush to comb out his mane and tail. The stallion seemed restless and fidgety, often stamping and breaking away from her to fly near the window, only to come back.

"What's so interesting outside, huh?" she asked. All she could see was the moon as a half-circle of silver outside her window.

The little stallion followed Caro's gaze. His ears pricked up, he stamped again, and he flew to the closed window and landed on the ledge.

Caro smiled. He'd never seen the moon this big before, at

least not from her window; when he'd arrived, it had been a mere crescent. "Pretty, isn't it? Want to go flying in the moonlight?"

Moonbow whinnied eagerly, and tapped one hoof against the window. It made a sharp chime against the glass.

She hurried to open the window before anyone heard the sound. "Here you go!"

Moonbow flew out into the night. When the moon bathed him in its silvery light, it grew brighter, surrounding him in a glittering, opalescent halo. And as the halo expanded, so did he. In the blink of an eye, he went from being small enough for Caro to hold in her hand and hovering outside her window to a full-size pony like the ones she used to ride and standing on the lawn outside.

Caro gasped in amazement and wonder. The pale moonlight turned his coat and feathers to purest silver, and his mane and tail to living opals. He was the horse of her dreams, gazing at her with huge dark eyes that reflected the waxing moon.

She reached out to stroke his velvet nose. He nuzzled her, then tossed his head, sending his mane flying. Moonbow extended a wingtip and batted her shoulder with it, then gave an impatient stamp.

Caro suddenly understood the message he was trying to convey. He wanted to fly. And he wanted her to ride.

She climbed out her window and slid on to his back. There was a hollow in his back, just in front of his great wings, that she fitted into perfectly. His hide was sleek and warm, and she could feel the power of his muscles held in check. She'd never ridden bareback before, let alone ridden anything that flew. But she knew Moonbow would never let her fall.

She gripped tight with her legs, took his mane in both hands, and whispered, "Fly."

The winged stallion sprang aloft, his powerful white wings beating. Caro's heart soared with him as he flew up and up, then circled high above her house. The whole world seemed spread out below her. She could see the lights of the city like a dragon's hoard of diamonds, and above her the winking stars. The air was chilly, but Moonbow was very warm.

She gave a gentle tug on his mane with her left hand, as if it was a rein. Obediently, he flew to the left. Caro made him turn and circle, fly up and down and even, after some experimentation, figured out how to make him hover by giving a rapid flip of his mane with both hands.

Caro had no idea how long they flew. Moonbow was so responsive that it was as if she and the winged stallion were a single being. Nothing had ever been more glorious, and she didn't want it to end.

But after what felt like far too short a time, Moonbow stopped obeying her commands and began to fly in a single direction. Soon she saw a familiar set of identical buildings, and realized he was returning home.

"Tired, huh?" she asked him, suppressing a yawn. "Me too."

Moonbow began flying down. She supposed it was toward her house, though it was harder to see now. The moon was setting, its silvery light growing dim...

"Oh!" Caro exclaimed. "Can you only get big by the light of the moon?"

He beat his wings faster, hurrying downward in a tightening spiral. She held tight, sensing his urgency. A sliver of cold fear pierced her chest as she imagined him becoming small again in mid-air, imagined herself falling...

Moonbow gave a snort, as if to tell her she was being silly. The house and lawn grew bigger and bigger, until she knew she wouldn't be hurt even if she did fall. And then he was landing in the backyard, light as a feather. He folded his wings and snorted again. Caro scrambled off him.

A moment after her feet touched the ground, the moon set. And Moonbow was once again small enough that the grass reached his belly.

Caro crouched down, smiling. "I should've trusted you, huh? Should've known you'd get me safely home."

He gave a soft nicker. She held out her hand, palm stiff, and he trotted on to it.

A door-slam and a thud made her whirl around. There on the porch was Tirzah, clutching an umbrella which she seemed to be using as a cane. "Caro? What're you doing?"

CHAPTER 17

*C*aro leaped to her feet and whipped her hand behind her back. "Nothing! Nothing!"

Well, that certainly wasn't suspicious. Tirzah debated whether to ignore it—after all, Caro wasn't *her* kid—and yet, she felt somehow responsible. Caro's father and grandmother weren't there, and Tirzah was. She didn't care that Caro had to be up way past her bedtime, given that it was midnight, but she was obviously up to something more than just that. Tirzah vividly remembered being thirteen, and knew that kids that age did all sorts of wild and even dangerous things.

On the other hand, thirteen-year-olds were also painfully sensitive and private. Caro was obviously going through a lot, and Tirzah didn't want to be yet another adult getting all up in her business.

Also, her leg was killing her. So was her hand that clutched the umbrella. Tirzah leaned against the porch railing and slid down until she was sitting on the wooden porch with her legs resting on the steps. "The stars are beautiful tonight."

Caro's furtive expression melted into happiness. "They sure are."

Tirzah put down the umbrella and the purse that concealed the Ziploc bag of used newspaper, which had been easier to obtain to create a makeshift litter box than lawn clippings. She patted the step next to her. "Look at them with me?"

"Um, I have to get back to my room." Caro tried to sneak past Tirzah, still keeping her hand behind her back.

Nope nope nope, Tirzah thought. She wasn't letting the girl leave before she found out what she was hiding, even if she had to take shameless advantage of her disability to do it.

She tried to stand, staggered, and grabbed Caro's arm for support, yanking it out from behind her back. Caro was holding the beautiful pegasus figurine from her room, posed with one hoof upraised.

"Sorry!" Tirzah exclaimed. "Oh, it's your little pegasus. I love it! Where'd you get it?"

Caro looked acutely uncomfortable and mumbled, "I don't remember."

"If you help me sit down, I'll show you something."

Caro helped Tirzah sit back down, then reluctantly sat, holding the pegasus well out of Tirzah's reach. Tirzah pretended not to notice that. She slipped her hand into her purse, pulled out her phone, opened the album of dollhouse photos, and held them out to Caro. "These are in my bedroom."

"What?!" Caro looked from the dollhouses to Tirzah, amazed. "You have dollhouses?!"

"Uh-huh. I play with them, too. See, here's the Victorian dollhouse with all my ninjas living in it... And here's the ninjas attacking it and the dogs defending it..." Tirzah was pleased to hear Caro's delighted laugh.

Caro turned adoring eyes up to Tirzah. "You're so cool!"

"That's nice to hear. Most people think I'm a giant nerd."

Earnestly, Caro said, "Don't let anyone peer-pressure you into being boring and ordinary. All the best people are non-conformists."

"I totally agree," Tirzah replied. "Listen, I can't say anything about any rules about how late you're supposed to be up, because that's up to your dad and grandma. But when you're my age, you can stay up as late as you want. And if you still have that pegasus, I hope you take him out whenever you like, no matter what anyone else thinks. Like you say, all the best people are non-conformists."

"Like you!" Caro carefully put down the pegasus and took Tirzah's phone, flipping through the dollhouse photos. "Now I want a dollhouse too. Or maybe a little barn."

"Ask your dad to build you one," Tirzah suggested.

To Tirzah's dismay, Caro's face unexpectedly crumpled. In a voice on the edge of tears, she said, "I can't! Everything I do is wrong! Ever since he moved in, he's acting weird and he's gone all the time and he won't talk to me and he won't talk to Abuelita and he hates hugs! I don't think he even *likes* me anymore!"

Tirzah gave Caro a hug herself. The girl buried her face in Tirzah's shoulder and sniffled, then pulled back, muttering, "Sorry."

"What's to be sorry about? Being a person who has feelings?" Tirzah tried to choose her next words carefully. This was a far more difficult situation than she'd realized when she'd thought Caro was just embarrassed to be a teenager who still loved playing with her little animals. "Look, I haven't known your dad for very long. And you're right, he has a real problem with talking sometimes. But there's one thing I'm sure about, and that's that he loves you. He's been through a lot—"

"And war changes people, I know." Caro sounded like she

was quoting something she'd heard a lot. "But he was a Marine before. And now he's different."

Tirzah chose her words carefully. "Maybe something happened to him this time that hadn't happened before. But I promise you, he loves you more than anything on this Earth. If you and he had a talk—"

"Yeah, right!"

"If you and he had a talk," Tirzah repeated, "Would you tell him how you felt?"

"Of course I would." Caro gave a bravado-filled shrug, but Tirzah saw the uncertainty beneath it.

"Would you mind if I asked him to talk to you?"

"Abuelita's asked him to talk to me," Caro sighed.

"Sometimes things come across differently when someone who's not your mom asks you," Tirzah pointed out, carefully not mentioning the even more important factor, which was that they might come across differently when the person asking already knew about certain pertinent facts such as cave bears and wizard-scientists. "So, would you mind?"

"What're you going to tell him?"

"Whatever you want me to. If you like, I could repeat this conversation—sometimes it's easier to start talking when you know the other person already knows about the stuff that's hard for you to say. But if you don't want me to, I won't say a word about it. I'll just say I think the two of you need to have a heart-to-heart."

Caro took a moment to think about it, then nodded decisively. "Tell him everything I said, please. And thanks for asking me what I want instead of treating me like a little kid. And for showing me your ninja house. And—Uh-oh, Moo—uh, *I'm* tired! Goodnight!"

She snatched up her pegasus statuette and fled, her long black hair whipping out behind her.

Tirzah waited until she was sure Caro wouldn't come back, then hobbled around the side of the house and dumped the baggie of used newspaper in the trash. The umbrella-cane was both painful and precarious, but there was no way she could get her wheelchair to the trash can without someone volunteering to throw out her trash for her.

Once she was back inside, she gratefully sat down in the chair she'd left by the door, then went to Pete's room. She opened the door slowly, not wanting to risk waking him with a knock, and peered in. The bathroom door was safely shut, and all was quiet within. All she could see of Pete was the shape of his body under the covers and his head on the pillow. He lay so still that she couldn't see him breathing.

He's fine, Tirzah told herself. *His own mother thought it was safe to leave him alone in his room.*

Of course, Pete had gone to great lengths to make sure his own mother believed there was nothing wrong with him but an upset stomach. And Tirzah hadn't figured out any way to suggest that she keep an eye on him without either wrecking his cover story or outright saying they were involved. She wished she could do the latter, since Lola obviously suspected as much anyway. But there was no way she was going to drop a bomb like that on Caro without Pete's consent, which she already knew he'd never give, so that was that. Lola had made up the sofa bed in the living room for Tirzah, and Pete was in his room with no one there if he needed something or got worse or...

Tirzah went into his room. The thick carpet made her sweat just turning the wheels, but it also muffled the sound of her entrance. She closed the door behind her, then went up to his bed. By the time she got there, her eyes had adjusted to the light and she could see the slow rise and fall of his chest as he breathed.

On the one hand, he didn't seem to be having any trouble

breathing. On the other hand, she'd never been able to sneak up on him when he'd slept in her apartment. He was always, *always* awake by the time she got into the living room, even when she went in at 3:00 AM on the pretext of getting a midnight snack, but actually to see if he was a light sleeper or just an early riser. And the carpet didn't muffle *all* sounds. Based on her previous experience, he should've woken up just from her turning the doorknob.

She sat and watched him until she started falling asleep in the chair. Tirzah didn't want to end up suddenly crashing to the floor of Lola Valdez's house *again*. She considered the sofa bed, then Pete's bed. Her whole body flushed with heat at the thought of Pete waking up to find her climbing into bed with him. That was a whole world of nope. And the carpet *was* thick.

Tirzah slithered out of her chair and on to the floor. She'd just take a tiny nap, to refresh herself enough to watch Pete until she could plausibly claim that she'd woken up in the morning and gone to check on him.

Her eyes closed.

CHAPTER 18

S   *he needs you.*
      The rumbling voice of the cave bear awoke Pete
as instantly as if a gun had gone off next to his head. He sat
up before he could decide to do so. His half-healed cuts
screamed in protest, but he ignored them, searching for the
source of the alert.

His room was dark, but he could make out the glitter of
metal beside his bed. As his eyes adjusted, he realized that it
was Tirzah's wheelchair. Empty. What in the world...?

Then he heard the sound of breathing from beside his
bed. He leaned over, adrenaline coursing through his veins,
and saw Tirzah curled up on the floor.

For a terrible moment, he thought she'd somehow fallen
from her chair and was unconscious. Then he realized that
she was asleep and dreaming. Sweat gleamed on her face, her
muscles were tensed, and she was breathing in ragged gasps.
Pete had seen enough people having nightmares, from Caro
when she was a little girl who'd seen a poster for a horror
movie to Marines dreaming of combat, to recognize the
signs.

He also knew that waking up from a nightmare could be almost as terrifying and disorienting as being in one. He had to make the transition as gentle as possible.

Pete turned on the reading lamp by his bed, casting a golden light across the room. He hoped that would wake her, but if it penetrated into her nightmare, all it did was make it worse. She gave a stifled moan that made his heart twist with sympathy—and guilt. She had to be dreaming about the gargoyle.

Or, worse, his cave bear.

Pete sat down on the floor beside her, praying that she wouldn't recoil in fear from him, as she had from his bear. Much as he longed to touch her, to hold her safe in his arms, he held himself back. He'd nearly gotten his nose broken by a Marine whom he'd tried to shake awake once. And though he didn't care if she hit him, he didn't want to scare her even more.

"Tirzah?"

She woke with a strangled gasp, her eyes flying open and her hands flailing at nothing.

"Hey, hey, it's okay," Pete said. "You're safe. Everything's all right. You were just dreaming."

She stared at him, wild-eyed, breathing so fast that he was afraid she was going to hyperventilate and pass out. He could tell that she was having a panic attack and wasn't taking in a word he was saying.

You need to touch her, rumbled his cave bear.

Pete *wanted* to touch her, but it was 50-50 whether doing so would just scare her more. The terror in her eyes made his heart hurt. Hoping he was doing the right thing, he leaned over and gathered her into his arms.

The touch of her skin to his came as a staggering shock, as intense as when they'd touched for the very first time. He'd seen and heard and understood that she was terrified

157

and confused and overwhelmed, but now he *felt* it. Her emotions were as open to him as if he could physically touch them, all razor-sharp edges and sandpaper roughness.

And not just emotions, but sensations: some remembered, some happening now.

He was falling through open space, his body tensed for the impact that would kill him.

He was dragging himself upward, his lower body in agony, his fingers raw, his muscles on fire.

He couldn't breathe. He couldn't *breathe!*

Pete forced himself not to flinch away from her. Still holding Tirzah close in his arms, he visualized a pane of bullet-proof glass between him and her feelings. At that, the onslaught stopped. But then he couldn't do anything to help her. And while he didn't really understand what was happening, he had an instinctive sense that he *could* help.

Hold her, rumbled his cave bear.

I am holding... Pete began, then realized what the bear meant.

He dissolved the glass and stood fast against the storm. Pete found Tirzah in the middle of it. He couldn't see her, but he could feel the essence of her: strong and brave and funny, smart and sensual and quirky, a lover of justice, a defender of the defenseless, her own unique self and unafraid to just *be* herself.

He felt her, and he loved her. There, in that inward realm of emotion, he could no longer deny his own heart.

It was the most natural thing in the world to reach out and enfold her in his love and caring, loaning her his own strength and calm.

You can have everything, he thought. *Whatever you need from me. I'm yours.*

A roar sounded from deep within his heart and soul, from

158

the most primal part of his being. The voice of his cave bear shook him like an earthquake as it said, *MINE.*

And then Pete was out of that inner realm and back in his body, holding Tirzah in his arms. Her breathing slowed and steadied, and she looked up at him without fear.

"I was having a nightmare," she said. "When I woke up, it was like I was half awake and half still there, and that was just as awful and scary as the nightmare was. And then you... What *did* you do?"

"I don't know." Pete hesitated, knowing that what he was going to say would sound bizarre... but then again, no more bizarre than getting your cell phone turned to stone. "I could feel your emotions. And I... I did something. What did it feel like to you?"

She tilted her head, and her curly hair brushed against his throat. "Like you gave me a shoulder to lean on. Like you were holding me, but inside my mind. Thanks, Pete. I don't know exactly what happened, but I really appreciate... whatever it was."

She doesn't know, Pete realized, his heart sinking. His realization that he was in love with her hadn't been shared, but had occurred only in his own mind. He'd stopped her panic attack, but that was it. She was grateful, but that was all. She didn't love him back.

Why would she? Pete asked himself fiercely. *Who are you to her, anyway? You're her bodyguard who turns into a terrifying, out of control, prehistoric* animal. *You're the guy who* is *that animal.*

And as if that wasn't enough, he was a single dad with a daughter—who lived with his mom, no less. He already had a family and responsibilities.

Tirzah was a world-class hacker, and even thirteen-year-old Caro, who was barely surviving her computer science class, understood computers better than Pete did.

When you really got down to it, Pete had to be the opposite of what Tirzah wanted in a man.

No, growled his cave bear. *She is ours. Our mate!*

What does that even mean? Pete asked silently.

She's the one we love and protect and rip the heads off anyone who tries to harm her. His bear sounded distinctly satisfied.

"Hey. Earth to Pete." Tirzah snapped her fingers.

"Sorry, what?" Pete asked.

"I said, did you know you could do that?"

"No. No idea. But Jerry did say that I had two powers, and I hadn't figured out the other one yet. I guess that's it. I'm not even sure what to call it."

"Emotional comforting?" Tirzah suggested. "Man, what a great power!"

"Really?" Pete asked doubtfully. "It doesn't sound very... uh..."

"You could call it the Shoulder of Strength if you want it to sound more like some manly, manly superhero in spandex," Tirzah teased. Then, with a self-deprecating edge in her voice that he didn't like at all, she said, "I'm sure *you've* never had a panic attack, but trust me, they're horrible."

"I haven't, but I've had... other things."

"Oh?"

Pete saw that Override gleam in her eyes, and rushed to satisfy it before she could dig any deeper. "Nightmares. Comes with being in combat. Hey, how'd you end up on the floor? You're not hurt, are you? I mean physically."

"No, I'm fine." Casting her gaze down, she said, "I was worried about you. I thought you should have someone keep an eye on you. How are you feeling?"

Pete had completely forgotten about his injuries. Now that she mentioned them, he did feel battered and bruised, but no more than that. "A lot better. I told you, I just needed a little rest. And soup. So what *did* happen? You fell out of your chair?"

"I don't fall out of my chair any more than you'd fall out of yours," Tirzah said with great dignity. "I just didn't want to risk falling asleep in it in case I..."

"Fell out?"

"Okay, fine. Anyway, I decided to take a nap on the floor. I guess I was more tired than I realized."

"Didn't Mom make up a bed for you?!"

"Of course she did! But it's in the living room. Like I said, I was worried about you."

That when Pete finally understood what had actually happened: Tirzah had sat by his side for so long that she'd started falling asleep, and slept on the floor rather than leave him. He knew how sweet and caring she was, but it was still hard for him to believe that she'd do that for a man she didn't even love. That she'd do that for *him*.

"Hey..." His throat felt thick, and he cleared it. "You want to get off the floor?"

"Sure."

"Can I lift you?" She hesitated so long that he added, "I can. Really."

"Oh, I believe you." She lightly touched his arm, sending a shiver of desire down his spine. "But you're hurt. And I can get up on my own. And...What the hell. Go ahead."

He scooped her up and stood up. Hot pain ran along the half-healed cuts and slashes, but it was nothing to the satisfaction of holding her in his arms. Pete got back into bed and settled Tirzah down next to him.

She leaned against him, her side against his, making his breath catch. He was in pajamas and she was in sweat pants and a long-sleeved T-shirt. None of their skin was touching. But for the effect on him, they might as well both have been naked.

"I'm sorry," he said.

"Sorry? For what?"

"For not protecting you better. For losing control of my bear. I'm sorry as hell that you're having nightmares about that."

"About *that?*" Tirzah gave an unexpected laugh. "Pete, you think my nightmare was about *you?*"

"Wasn't it?"

"No! It had nothing to do with you!"

"Oh." Pete felt like an idiot. "I guess I'm so vain, I think the song's about me."

"Don't sweat it. Maybe I'll have gargoyle nightmares later. But no, that was about… something else."

"You want to talk about it?" Pete asked.

"I wish. I wouldn't mind if you knew. I'd *like* you to know. But whenever I've tried, I… I…" She was sitting so close that he could feel her muscles tense and her breath come faster. "Goddammit. Just *thinking* about talking about it is making me feel like I'm about to have a panic attack."

"Maybe I could help." Pete offered her his hand, palm up. He expected her to hesitate, but she seized it without taking so much as a second to think. At the touch of her skin, he again felt her rising panic like a cresting wave. He reached inside and pushed it back down.

Tirzah gave a deep sigh, her tension easing. "Thanks. That's better. Normally I have to try not to even *think* about it, or I start feeling like I'm back there."

Her panic threatened to spill over again as she spoke, but Pete kept a firm grip on it. "Don't worry about that. I won't let it happen. But you don't *have* to talk about it."

"I want to. I like to talk, you know? I don't tell people I know in real life about Override. But I talk to other people *as* Override, who don't know about Tirzah." She added, "By 'talk,' I mean I email."

Pete couldn't help being amused by that. "I didn't think you were meeting them for coffee."

Tirzah smiled too, but quickly grew serious again. "But this... It's something nobody really knows about. I mean, I can tell them what happened in a couple sentences. But what I can't talk about isn't just what happened, it's how it felt." She swallowed hard. "That's what my nightmares are about. That wasn't the first one, you see. Ever since..."

Once again, he had to shove down her fear. "It's okay. I've got you."

"I know." She turned her eyes up to his, brown and beautiful and trusting. "You've never asked why I use a wheelchair."

"It was none of my business."

"You weren't curious at all?" She sounded disappointed.

"Yeah, okay, I was. But you didn't say, so I figured I shouldn't pry."

"I guess I do enough prying for the both of us."

Pete squeezed her hand, then put his arm around her shoulders. She snuggled in close. He'd missed this kind of intimacy so much: not only physical touch, but holding someone, being held, talking late into the night about things that might be too hard to speak in the light of day.

She swallowed. "Okay. Enough putting it off. You'll catch me if I start falling, right?"

"Yes," he said. "I'll be there."

TIRZAH'S STORY

I love Refuge City, but sometimes it gets to be a bit much. All the noise. All the people. And I love my neighbors, but sometimes they get to be a bit much, too. So I have a place I go to take a break, be alone, and recharge. It's a little cabin in the woods, in the mountains north of the city. You take the freeway out of town, then go up this mountain road, then up a dirt road.

It has internet, of course, but no cell phone service. Sometimes I go there to concentrate on some really difficult hacking, sometimes I just go to relax. I like—I used to like the drive up there. It's very green. Very quiet. If you're on the road at twilight, you have to watch out for deer and wild turkeys.

A year ago I drove up there to take a week or so to relax. Though actually, I ended up doing some hacking too. It was late fall and the autumn leaves were absolutely gorgeous. When I hit the time I'd meant to go back, I decided to stay for one more week. But I'd only bought enough groceries for two weeks—there's a supermarket in the town at the base of the mountain, about an hour's drive away—so I drove down to stock up.

What I didn't know was that there'd been a cold snap overnight. And there had been some water spilled on the road. It turned into a very thin, very slick sheet of black ice, and it didn't melt because it was in the shade.

That's what I was told afterward. I never saw it.

I'd just gone around a hairpin curve when my car hit something slippery and skidded. It seemed like everything was happening in slow motion. It was a narrow road along a cliff without a shoulder or guardrails or even a tree—nothing to stop me from going over the edge. I knew that if I couldn't get control of my car back, I was going to die.

I remembered not to slam on the brakes. I braked slowly and tried to steer around the corner. But the car just kept on sliding straight ahead. I remember thinking, "This isn't a nightmare. This is real. I'm really going to die."

And then the car went over. It tumbled in mid-air. Everything inside the car was flying around and hitting me. I was listening to an audiobook, and it kept playing. To this day, if I ever see its title mentioned, I feel like I'm going to be sick.

The car smashed into the ground, flipped over a few times, and then it slammed into something and stopped.

I don't know how long it was before I realized that I was still alive. The audiobook had stopped. At first I thought I'd been blinded, but then I realized that there was something over my face. I pulled it off—it was part of the seat cushion—and I could see again.

The car was completely destroyed. All the windows were shattered, and big parts of it were just crumpled metal. The driver's side door had been ripped off, and my legs were both out of the car. I knew as soon as I saw them that I'd never walk again.

The car was in this dense thicket at the bottom of the

165

cliff. There was no way anyone would've been able to see it from the top. And I'd emailed my neighbor who was watering a plant I had that I was going to stay another week, so no one would expect me back.

My legs hadn't hurt as long as I stayed still, but once I moved, they hurt so badly that I screamed. And then I started screaming and yelling at the top of my lungs, hoping someone would hear me.

I screamed until my voice wore out. But I didn't hear an answer. I hadn't really expected one. There was no one living there—it's just forest—and a car goes by maybe once every hour. The chances of anyone in that car being able to hear me were slim to none. I could either stay where I was and die there, or try to get back up to the road.

So I crawled out of the car. It hurt like—I can't even describe how much it hurt. I had to pull myself up a muddy slope with my hands. I'm stronger now than I was then—I actually get more exercise using the wheelchair than I used to do walking—but back then, I basically sat in a chair and typed all day. Trying to crawl on my belly up a steep hillside was excruciating and exhausting and awful. I think I cried the entire time, I was so sure I couldn't do it.

But I did.

It took me all day and part of the night. Most of my clothes were ripped off by thorns and rocks and sharp bits of metal. I was hypothermic and dehydrated, and I'd lost a lot of blood. But I made it. I lay down by the side of the road and waited for help to come.

When I saw the headlights, I tried to flag down the car. But I was too weak and exhausted to sit up. It drove right by me—never saw me. So did the next, and the next. There were no streetlights, and I was covered in mud.

I finally dragged myself into the middle of the road. I figured the next car would either hit me or see me, and either way it'd be over. My guess was it'd hit me. Lying there in the road felt like lying on the train tracks. It was even more terrifying than falling had been, and it went on and on. Every time I heard a noise, I'd try to wave in case it was a car coming, but it never was.

Eventually I got so weak that when I heard a noise, I couldn't move at all. I thought, "This is it. All that work and pain, and it was all for nothing. I should have stayed with the car."

That's the last thing I remember. The next car did see me and stop, but by then I was unconscious. I woke up in a hospital a week later. I was so glad to be alive and between clean sheets and be able to lie down and not have to *try* any more, I can't even tell you.

The doctors told me I'd never be able to use my right leg again, and they weren't sure about the left. They brought in a counselor to talk to me, but that didn't go so well. See, she thought I'd be angry and grieving and all that stuff over being disabled. When I said I thought I'd deal with that just fine, she said I was in denial. I told her I knew myself better than she knew me, and she could kindly fuck off. Out she flounced.

But I was right. I mean, adjusting to being disabled is no walk in the park—ha, it's literally not a walk! I had to do a lot of hard, painful physical therapy to get any use of my left leg back, using a wheelchair is physically hard work and there's a steep learning curve, once you can use it strangers treat you differently, and a lot of normal stuff is about 500% harder if you can't walk.

But the thing is, I already spent most of my time sitting down at home. I wasn't an athlete or a hiker or anything like that. You can get almost anything delivered. I stayed with my family for a while and they helped me out, and when they started getting on my nerves I went back to my apartment and my neighbors helped me out.

I tried going to another therapist once, but the exact same thing happened: he thought I was in denial over how upset I was about being disabled, and wouldn't believe me when I said it was mostly just an big inconvenience. And when I tried to explain what *was* bothering me, I got a few words out before I started crying and hyperventilating, and he took that as proof that he was right and I was much more traumatized than I was admitting. So I walked out. Excuse me. I *wheeled* out.

He wasn't wrong that I'm traumatized. But he was wrong about why. Being disabled is just a thing I deal with. It's not traumatic or horrible. What was traumatic and horrible was the crash. And getting up to the road. And watching the cars go by without them seeing me. And lying down in the middle of the road, knowing I might get run over, because I'd die for sure if I stayed where I was.

That's why I don't drive. I physically could. I could drive with my left foot in a pinch, though it's too weak for me to go long distances. So I bought a car with hand controls. And it's been gathering dust in the garage under my building for almost a year, because every time I even *think* about driving, I feel like I'm falling.

Oh, it's great being a computer genius! I can earn whatever money I need any time I want to. So I own a car I can't drive and a cabin in the country I can't get to and a fantastic antique bed to have nightmares in, when I'm not staying up all night hacking because I'm afraid to go to sleep.

CHAPTER 19

$\mathcal{I}$t wasn't an easy story to tell, even with Pete lending her his strength: inwardly keeping her from panicking or flashing back, and outwardly in his steady regard and the solid warmth of his body. But nor was it as hard or terrible as she'd always imagined it would be. Once she was done, she felt that a burden had been lifted from her. She was still scarred, but she no longer staggered under the weight of the unspoken.

His face had begun to darken with anger when she'd recounted her visit with the counselor. And when she finished, he burst out with, "I can't believe those asshole counselors!"

Tirzah was gratified to see his anger on her behalf. "So you believe me?"

"Of course I believe you!" He still looked royally pissed off. "What gets to people isn't always what you expect. I've seen guys go through shit in combat like you wouldn't believe, but what wrecks them is that their girlfriend broke up with them while they were gone. And I've seen them get told they're in denial, too. People can be such assholes."

"Don't I know it. You should see some of the stuff Override digs up. But I have to tell you… Thanks again. I feel so much better just having told someone this story."

"I'm honored that I was the one you told it to," Pete said. "If you ever want to tell anyone else, I could… sit next to you, I guess. Like a therapy dog."

Tirzah giggled. She didn't just feel better, she felt lighter. Free. "I could also take another crack at therapy. Call them up and ask them straight up if they believe what people say even if it sounds weird."

"And if they get on your case for asking, hang up on them."

"Good idea. The first time, I just made an appointment and marched on in." She chuckled. "Really, the hardest thing about using a wheelchair is trying to figure out if I can still say words like 'marched' and 'walked.'"

Pete remained serious. With the utmost sincerity, he said, "You are one of the toughest, bravest people I've ever met. Crawling all the way up that hill, and then deciding to lie down in the middle of the road—that took a lot of guts, and it must've been absolute hell. I'm not surprised it left a mark on you. Think of your nightmares and panic attacks and being afraid to drive as battle scars, okay?"

"But…" Tirzah knew he meant it, but on some level it was hard to believe. He was a combat veteran, and she was just a hacker who'd been in a car crash.

"But nothing. Look." Pete pulled up his shirt. Tirzah obediently examined his brown skin, his black hair, his six-pack abs, the swell of muscle beneath the bandages…

He tapped a jagged white scar, and she guiltily forced her attention away from his body, or at least away from the sexy parts of his body. Not that the scar wasn't sexy…

"Night patrol," Pete said. "Someone set up a low-tech booby trap with barbed wire, and I walked right into it."

"Ouch."

He bent his head, showing her the back of his neck. There were a few flecks like pale freckles. "Shrapnel. Anyway, my point is, I'm like you. The scars you can see aren't the ones that bother me. Like you not being able to walk doesn't bother you. It's the ones on the inside that did the real damage."

She bit back the question that rose to her lips. He didn't want to talk about it. Or did he? They were sitting together, side by side, in bed. He'd held her the whole time she'd told her story. He'd showed her his scars. He'd literally been inside her mind. It didn't get more intimate than that.

Maybe she should stop trying to sneak around and break through his walls. Maybe if she could get him to take a good look at them and think about why they were there, he'd take them down himself.

"You know, Pete, you keep dropping hints that something really bad happened to you. When I ask you about it, you shut down. And then I feel guilty for asking."

"I don't mean to make you feel guilty. There's just stuff I don't like to talk about."

"Yeah, I've noticed. And I know you've been in combat, and you were kidnapped and experimented on. I don't know if it's like me, where I could say what happened but not how it felt, or if there's other things I don't know about at all. But if you really don't want to tell me, why do you keep hinting? Are you hoping if I pry hard enough, eventually I'll break through?"

Pete looked taken aback. He was silent for a long while, then said, "Maybe I was. But if I tell you, I don't know what you'll think about me."

"You care what I think about you?" Tirzah blurted out. "Sorry, that came out wrong. Me and my big mouth."

But he took no notice of the awkward way she'd phrased it. "Yeah. I care."

The golden glow from the reading lamp was the only light in the dark room. It made her feel like they were sitting around a camp fire. Like they were the only people in the world, huddled together against the cold.

"I care too, Pete. I care about *you*. I hate to see you weighed down by all this stuff you feel like you can't talk about. I can't give you the Shoulder of Strength, but I'll give you my real shoulder."

She took his hand, and felt a shiver go through his body.

"Okay." His voice was husky, his head bent so his face was in shadow. "I'll lean on you."

PETE'S STORY

started working as soon as I graduated from high school. I wouldn't have even bothered to graduate, except high school dropouts have bad job prospects, and I had a family to support. I spent a couple years doing odd jobs, messengering, handyman stuff. My parents were both working, so me not having a 9-5 schedule was better for Lina —that's what Caro went by then.

Once she was old enough for preschool, I went into the police academy. I liked being a cop. Mostly. There was a lot of paperwork. But I liked being on the beat. This was in a pretty rough part of Los Angeles, so there was always a lot going on.

I was working Narcotics when I noticed something weird. On some of the drug busts I'd done, the quantities of drugs I'd turned in that had gotten recorded in the file didn't match with what I thought they were. And the recorded weight was always lower, not higher.

I got suspicious. I got myself a scale and the next bust I did, I weighed the drugs myself before I turned them in. When I checked the file later, sure enough, the weight recorded was lower. Someone was falsifying how much had been turned in so they could skim off some of the drugs themselves, but nothing would seem to be missing from the evidence room. Like, ten pounds of coke was recorded as confiscated, and ten pounds of coke was in the lockup. Only it had really been thirteen pounds confiscated.

I was furious, and I didn't know who I could trust. So I did my own investigation, and it was so much bigger than I'd realized. It was a whole ring of corrupt cops in my division. Including my own watch commander. I'd really respected him, too.

I was young and stupid then. I should've said nothing, and gone straight to Internal Affairs. Instead, I went into his office and told him what I knew. I said he should talk to everyone involved, and have them all come clean on their own. I said I understood how they could've been tempted, but it was wrong and they needed to do the honorable thing and come forward voluntarily, or I'd do it for them.

Man, he was a smooth customer. He listened to me and said everything I wanted to hear. He said they had families they needed to provide for and they'd just gotten so tempted and then it had taken on a life of its own, but a lot of them had been feeling guilty for a while and if he was honest, he was glad I'd found out. He said to give him some time talk to everyone, so they could make arrangements to keep their families safe and provided for once it all came out.

It was complete bullshit. They were greedy and didn't care who they hurt. Their money wasn't going to their kid's college fund, it was going for sports cars and shit like that. And they spent the time I gave them covering their tracks and figuring out what to do with me.

The watch commander walked me to my car. Said he wanted to talk. I went, and he leaned on the car and told me he'd planted drugs in it, and it had all been documented already. He said if I talked, he'd turn *me* in. Or I could resign and he'd document a fake on-the-job injury for me so I could get my pension and provide for my family.

I was completely blindsided. I realized that no one was going to believe my wild story against his photo proof and however many cops he'd get to vouch for him and against me. And I couldn't risk going to prison and letting Lina grow up without a father.

I grew up about ten years in the next ten seconds. I realized that the only reason he was threatening me instead of killing me was that he didn't want the sort of investigation that would happen if a cop turned up dead. And I also realized that if I threatened him enough, he'd do it anyway. So I told him I'd keep my mouth shut, and I'd resign for personal reasons. I said I was thinking of joining the Marines and I didn't want an injury on my record.

Then I went home and told Mom what had happened—Dad had died by then—and I said we had to move across the country. She was pretty upset, but she said I'd done the right thing, and she understood why we had to go. So we packed up and left. We didn't tell Lina because she was too young to understand, let alone keep it a secret. I'll tell her someday. Maybe when she's in college.

Here's what I've never told anyone. When I'd investigated the drug ring, I found the warehouse where they were keeping the drugs they stole. Once Mom and Lina were safe on the other side of the country, I went back to LA to pick up the rest of our stuff. I also picked up some plastic explosive and blew up that warehouse. And then I used a burner cell phone to call the papers and tell them it was full of drugs and had been used by crooked cops. I pretended I was a drug dealer who'd figured it out and was mad as hell.

Like I said, I was young and stupid. I was just betting that those cops either wouldn't realize it was me, or would have their hands way too full with their own problems to try to figure out where I went and come after me. They didn't, but it wasn't a smart risk to take. I was just so furious over the whole thing, I couldn't stand the thought of doing nothing.

It worked out, though. The whole thing got blown wide open—so to speak—and they all went to prison. But while all that was going on, there we were, in a new state with no jobs. I thought back about what I'd said to my watch commander about joining the Marines. It was an excuse—I didn't want to take his dirty money, and I didn't want to make him suspicious if I said so. But my own dad had been a Marine, and I'd thought of it, which was why it came to mind. And now that I'd trashed my career as a cop, I thought of it again. I wasn't crazy about being gone all the time, but I could provide for my family and I never wanted to get involved in any kind of criminal conspiracy again.

So what did I get mixed up in? A military criminal conspiracy!

I was on a fire team in Afghanistan with Merlin and Ransom and another guy, Ethan. He's with west coast Protection, Inc. now. It was a new team and I didn't know them very well. We were on patrol at the ass end of nowhere when I got stung by a bee—I thought. Ransom yelled, "Ambush!" And I passed out. That "bee" had been a tranquilizer dart.

I woke up in a chair like you get in a doctor's office. In fact the whole room looked kind of like that. It was painted white and there were instruments in trays, and this guy was leaning over me. For a second I thought I was in a military hospital and he was a doctor.

Then I realized that I was handcuffed to the chair. And the guy stepped back, and I could see that he was wearing a white coat like a doctor's, but it was covered with these weird black symbols. Then I didn't know what to think. It didn't seem like a prisoner of war setup, but it sure as hell wasn't an American military base.

I said, "Where am I? Who are you?"

He said, "You may call me Gorlois. I'm here to offer you an opportunity beyond your wildest dreams."

"Why don't you uncuff me, and then we'll talk," I said.

I wasn't expecting him to do it, and he didn't. In fact he didn't even respond to it at all. He said, "I'm looking for a man with special talents. A fighting man, the best of the best. Valdez, you are the man—"

I interrupted him. "Where's the other guys on my team?"

Gorlois obviously didn't like being interrupted. He glared at me, then went on with his canned speech. "A new world is waiting to be born. You can be a part of that new world, with strength and powers that you never—"

I interrupted him again. "Fuck that shit. Where's my buddies?"

He got all huffy. Said I'd better address him with respect.

I thought he was stalling me because they were dead. I thought this fucking asshole had killed them and taken me prisoner, and he had the nerve to be lecturing me about my manners. And then I thought about my watch commander, and how I'd respected him and he'd probably been laughing at me the whole time for actually believing in things like honor and honesty and the law. I thought about me, what I'd done blowing up that warehouse and risking my family to get revenge.

I was so angry, I literally saw red. His lips were moving, but I couldn't hear a word he was saying. It was drowned out by this sound rising up inside of me, like a roar.

I only remember fragments of what happened after that. I saw bits of metal and chain exploding off a huge shaggy paw —my paw. I knew where my teammates were, because I could smell them. But I could smell other people, too.

177

Enemies. And I wanted to kill them. I wanted to kill them all, and smash the building. I wanted to destroy everything that got in my way.

I remember breaking things. I remember people screaming. At one point I charged through a sort of hospital room and saw a man handcuffed to a bed.

All of a sudden, I was a man again, standing in the doorway of a storage room. Ethan was there. He put his hand on my shoulder, and it felt like he'd stabbed me. I jerked away, and then I saw that Merlin was there too, and Ransom —he looked really fucked up—and a woman I didn't recognize. That was Destiny, from Protection, Inc. Ethan had gotten away from the ambush, and he and Destiny had come to rescue us.

We went to get the prisoner I'd seen—that was Roland— but we got attacked while we were trying to set him free. That was the first time my cave bear spoke to me. He said, *Kill them. Kill them all.*

I was supposed to be guarding a door. But this fury just rose up in me. I heard that roar again...

The next thing I knew, I was somewhere else in the base. All the guys were standing around me. I was kneeling next to a dead saber tooth tiger. I was bleeding. I guess it had attacked me, and I'd killed it. I didn't remember anything.

Roland tried to shake my hand, and it hurt so bad I thought I'd smashed every bone in it. But as soon as he let go, it seemed fine.

I didn't have much time to think about that, or about why it had hurt when Ethan touched me. We got attacked by monsters and shifters and finally Lamorat. He was dressed the same as Gorlois, so I guess Gorlois was a wizard-scientist too. No idea what they planned to do with us. It didn't get that far.

I don't know what happened to Gorlois. Maybe I killed

him when I shifted that first time, maybe he got away. But Lamorat got killed in the final battle, and we blew up the base.

I thought it was all over then. But it wasn't. Every time I touch a person, it hurts worse than anything's ever hurt in my entire life. Even when I try to hug my own daughter. I just want her to have a normal, happy, safe life. But whatever they did to me fucked me up somehow. She can tell something's wrong, but I can't explain what it is, because I can't tell her about any of this shit. It's creating this distance between us that keeps getting wider and wider. It's tearing me up inside.

Everything I did, I did for my family. And everything I did screwed things up for them.

And now I can't even touch anyone.

Except you.

CHAPTER 20

*T*here were points in Pete's story when Tirzah really wished she had his power, because he sure looked like he could use some comfort. But since she didn't, she offered him what she did have, which was her attention and her touch. He'd held her hand, so the moment he started audibly struggling to talk, she took his. He gripped it like it was a lifeline. When it grew damp with sweat, she put her arm around his shoulders. Soon they were in a side-by-side embrace. His short hair was velvety against her cheek. She breathed in his scent of clean sweat and woodsiness and, beneath them, a faint iron tang of blood.

The last thing he said astonished her. "Me? You can touch me? But not anyone else?"

"Yeah."

"Why just me?"

Pete shrugged.

"Man, Pete," Tirzah said. "That sounds awful. All of it. Though I have to say, I approve of the whistle-blowing and drug exploding. No wonder you weren't shocked by Override!"

"No, I get it. You did your whistle-blowing in a much smarter way than I did, though."

"You just let me know the next time you want some powerful bad guy to go under. Give me their info, and I'll take care of it for you."

He chuckled.

"I'm serious," Tirzah said, poking him in the ribs. "You've got a semi-famous, very successful hacker in bed—" Realizing what that sounded like, she broke off with a cough that sounded even faker than him trying to convince his mom he was about to throw up. "Uh, *with* you." Even worse! "I mean, on your side."

"Thanks. You let *me* know the next time you want something blown up."

"Or clawed up!" The moment she said it, she wished she'd bitten her tongue. He was much too wary of the cave bear to think that was funny.

Sure enough, he muttered, "Not a good idea."

He'd assumed she was having nightmares about seeing him as a bear, she remembered. Knowing that, plus what he'd just told her, plus having actually seen the bear made a whole lot of things click into place.

"Why are you so scared of what you might do as a bear?" she asked. "I was there when you were the bear—"

"And it scared you half to death!"

"What? What are you talking about?"

Pete sat up straight, pulling out of the embrace. "I don't remember much of that fight. But here's the part I do remember: you recoiling from it—*me*—looking terrified."

"Whoa, whoa!" Tirzah held up her hand. "Pete, I got trapped inside a magical rock bubble, then it was smashed to bits right over my head, and then I suddenly had a cave bear in my face. I was *momentarily alarmed*."

He looked vastly unconvinced.

181

"Do you remember what I did when I suddenly had a velociraptor in my face?" she asked. "Well?"

"You screamed," he admitted.

"*And* recoiled in terror."

"Yeah, but—"

"No but. I was exactly as terrified of Merlin as I was of you. Which was for about five seconds, before I processed who the scary-looking critter actually was."

"*Critter?*" Pete repeated with wounded dignity.

"Oh, right," Tirzah said, nodding. "You prefer 'beast.' Sounds more macho. Well, let me tell you, as far as I'm concerned it's a big old fluffy... cuddly... *critter*. And I know, because I cuddled it."

Pete looked so torn between dismay and relief that Tirzah had to bite her tongue to not laugh. "I don't remember that... Wait. My bear just said *he* remembers."

"And?"

"He says he'd never hurt you." But he didn't sound as satisfied as that should have warranted.

"Pete, you told me the bear is *you*. Would *you* ever hurt me?"

He looked straight into her eyes, and she knew he was telling the absolute truth when he said, "I'd die first."

"Then why are so afraid of what your bear might do?"

He spoke so quietly that she had to lean in to hear him. "*Because* he's me. When I was a boy, I got in fights a couple times. Someone tried to bully me, or I saw someone getting bullied. I remember stepping in, and that's all I remember until someone was pulling me off and the bully was on the ground bleeding. When I was fifteen, I got kicked out of school for breaking someone's arm. I don't remember doing it. I just remember seeing him threatening another boy with a switchblade."

"*He* should've gotten expelled, not you!" Tirzah said indignantly.

"He claimed it was mine. My parents believed me, but..." Pete gave a little wave of his hand, brushing off the injustice that made Tirzah burn with anger for the sake of the boy he'd been. "I didn't grow out of that sort of thing, either. I got mad at the crooked cops in my department, and I blew up a building!"

"You ever hurt anyone who wasn't trying to hurt you or someone else?"

"No! But..." He shook his head, slowly, reminding her of the bear. "You don't understand what it's like to have that kind of rage inside you."

"Oh, don't I? Why do you think Override exists?"

"Because you're a good person. You believe in justice, and you make it happen."

"Because I'm an angry person," Tirzah corrected him. "I used to read the news and seethe all day. It was burning me up inside. And then I decided to do something about it. Oh, sure, I don't have rage blackouts. When I get mad, I don't break anyone's arm. I sit down and figure out how to destroy their company. Put them in jail. Ruin their life."

"That's different."

"Not as much as you think. Are you worried that I might broadcast your home address on the internet?"

"Of course not."

Tirzah put her hand on his shoulder. He was so tense that he was trembling, like a stretched wire. "Right. Because I don't want to. You don't want to hurt anyone except in self-defense or to protect someone else. And you won't. Because you don't want to. Even if you don't remember afterward, you're always you."

She felt him slowly relax under her hand. He swallowed, then said, "Okay."

The darkness outside the windows was lightening into gray. They'd talked away the night, or at least as much as was left of it once he'd woken her up. "Want to go back to sleep? Or shall I bring you some coffee?"

Pete got out of bed. He was moving a little stiffly, but he was steady on his feet. "*I'll* bring *you* coffee. Or maybe we should both get up, to avoid awkward explanations. Mom's an early riser."

"Good idea."

They traded off using Pete's bathroom to shower, get dressed, and pet their kittens. When they convened in the kitchen, he made coffee while she quietly recounted the conversation she'd had with Caro.

He looked like he'd been stabbed in the heart. "I don't know what to say to her. I can't explain what's going on."

"Sure, you can't explain the details. So tell her that, and then talk to her about everything else." Teasingly, she said. "You know. *Feelings.*"

"Right." Pete poured her out a mug of coffee. "I'm glad you talked to her. I think it's good for her to have a woman to talk to who's not her grandma."

"She can talk to me any time," Tirzah promised. "I'm like the aunt for all the kids in my building."

"Speaking of that..." Pete began, then broke off when his mother came into the kitchen, followed by a yawning Caro.

They both exclaimed over how much better he looked, then hustled him and Tirzah to the table so he could sit down and they could make breakfast. Tirzah saw, her heart aching, how both his mother and daughter took care not to touch him. They might not understand exactly what was going on, but they'd sure figured out that something was.

Soon they were sitting down to pancakes plus a bowl of soup that Lola insisted Pete have as a sort of curative side dish.

Caro tapped her spoon on the table. "I have an important announcement! Tirzah, Dad and Abuelita and I planned a cook-off a while back. I wasn't sure it was going to happen because first Dad was gone and then he was sick, but he's obviously fine now. So let's do it next week!"

Pete was about to ask why they needed to wait a week, then remembered the call he'd gotten from Mom a couple days ago. Her sister in Phoenix had broken her foot, and her husband was on a business trip he couldn't cut short. So Mom had arranged to have her friend Nancy take in Caro while she flew to Phoenix to help her sister. If Pete recalled correctly, her flight was in a couple hours.

"Tirzah, do you cook?"

"A bit," she said.

"Then cook with us! We need a third vote as a tie-breaker."

Tirzah glanced at Pete, trying to telepathically inquire, *Do you want me to get out of the way of your father-daughter bonding, or would you like me to stay as a buffer?*

He gave her a quick nod, which she interpreted as *YES PLEASE be my buffer.*

"If nobody else minds, I'd love to," she said.

"Excellent!" Caro proclaimed. "And since Dad is now both fine and home, we can cancel Nancy."

"Princesa, your father has to work," Lola said firmly.

"No! I want to stay!" Caro sounded almost panicky.

Poor kid, Tirzah thought. *She must have really been looking forward to that heart-to-heart with Pete. What a shame that it's going to be delayed—when you're thirteen, a few days can feel like forever.*

"Caro..." Lola began.

Pete held up his hand. "Mom. She can stay if she likes. Tirzah was just, uh, giving me a hand. My job with her is

185

done. I can tell my boss not to assign me anything new until you get back."

A brilliant smile lit up Caro's face. "Yay! Thanks, Dad. Tell your boss not to assign you anything till a day after Abuelita gets back. We can have the cook-off then!"

"Sure," Pete said. "Sounds good."

Tirzah saw Pete and Lola exchange pleased glances. She too was glad Pete and Caro were going to get some father-daughter time, but she had to work hard to keep her own feelings off her face.

"My job with her is done."

Was that it for everything she and Pete had shared together? Would they stay in touch afterward as friends, at least? Or had all the intimacy they'd shared just been a matter of two damaged people connecting because they'd been thrown together by circumstance, who would drift apart now that the circumstances had changed?

Lola called her friend Nancy and canceled the babysitting, then went off to fetch her suitcase.

"I should get back to my apartment," Tirzah said. Pete and Caro were obviously dying to have their much-delayed talk, and she felt like a third wheel. Not to mention that Batcat was probably sick of being locked in a bathroom with her arch enemy Spike. "I can take a taxi."

"No, no," Pete said. "I'll drive you. Caro, do you mind taking a ride into the city? After we drop Tirzah off, we could explore a bit."

"I'd *love* to go to the city!" Caro's eyes gleamed. "Can we have lunch at 3.14159?"

Pete looked completely blank for a moment, then chuckled. "I get it. It's the value of pi. And no, we're not having pie for lunch. We could go there for dessert."

"It's got lunch-type pies too," Caro said. "Chicken pot pie, steak pie, spinach pie..."

Pete glanced at Tirzah. "Have you heard of this place?"

"A restaurant whose name is a math joke?" she replied. "Of course I have. I recommend the steak pie for lunch and the Snickers pie for dessert."

"Great idea!" Caro said enthusiastically. "Dad, I'll get the Snickers pie, and you get a different one, and we can split them."

"Sounds good," Pete said.

Lola came out with her suitcase. She and Pete and Caro said their good-byes, Caro with big hug and Pete with a wave.

"Caro, go grab your purse," Pete said. "I'll help Tirzah pack her stuff."

Caro ran off to her bedroom. Once her door slammed shut, Pete said to his mother, "I don't need details, but I hope you had a good time at your date—I mean, Shakespeare in the Park."

"The play was excellent," Lola said. "We didn't have much in common." She shrugged. "Maybe next time."

"You're giving him another chance?" Pete asked.

Lola, in a 'oh you sweet summer child' tone, said, "I meant my next time with someone else." She took a step toward Pete, then frowned, took a step back, and waved, which broke Tirzah's heart a little. "Love you, mijo. Have fun with Caro... and Tirzah!" She winked and went out the door.

Pete seemed thunderstruck. Tirzah nudged him. "We better get two pairs of flappy wings safely in the suitcase before Caro comes out."

He opened the refrigerator and grabbed a package of sliced ham, and she followed him to his bedroom.

Once the door had closed behind them, he held up the ham and whispered, "Think this'll keep Batcat quiet in a suitcase until we get to your apartment?"

"I sure hope so," Tirzah whispered back. "I've never fed

her ham before, though. I don't eat pork. Let's see if she likes it."

They opened the bathroom door and were immediately greeted, or possibly ambushed, by their kittens. Batcat flew to Tirzah, landed on her shoulder, and began loudly purring and kneading and chewing on her hair. Spike flew to Pete, landed on his shoulder, scrabbled briefly, then dove into his shirt.

"What're you going to do with Spike?" Tirzah asked.

"For now, he stays in the bathroom. But as soon as I can get away, I'll move him to the Defenders office."

"Oh, good idea. You could set up an automatic feeder for weekends."

"I will as a backup, but there's usually someone there. Roland practically lives in the office. I admire how hard-working he is, but he ought to take a break some time. Go to a ball game or something."

"Invite him to one," Tirzah suggested.

"I don't go to games anymore. They're too crowded. People brushing up against you all the time." Pete spoke without self-pity, but Tirzah's heart ached for him. She put her hand on his shoulder, instinctively offering him the touch he could only get from her and wondering once again why that was.

He gave a deep sigh and closed his eyes briefly, leaning into her touch. Batcat gave a warning hiss, which was answered from deep within Pete's shirt.

"Weirdo cats," Tirzah said.

"Let's see if she likes ham." Pete tore open the package and held out a slice. Batcat hissed, sniffed, then snatched it from his fingers and began greedily gulping it down.

"Guess that's solved," Tirzah said.

Spike suddenly emerged from Pete's shirt, nipped another slice from the package, and flew with it to the toilet tank, where he began to eat it in neat little bites in contrast to Batcat's messy gobbling.

They watched the kittens for a while, then glanced at each other. Pete's brown eyes were wells of some intense emotion that Tirzah couldn't identify. She had the sudden, vivid sense memory of him holding her in his arms.

The silence stretched out, reminding her of the moment after a date when you're not sure whether or not there's going to be kissing. Normally Tirzah would have broken the silence—she knew Pete well enough to be sure that *he* wouldn't—but she felt at a loss for what to say.

"You'll come to the cook-off, won't you?" Pete said abruptly. "I can pick you up. I don't want you to feel like I'm ditching you—"

"I don't at all," she replied. "You and Caro need to talk. By yourselves. But yeah, I'd love to come to the cook-off."

Inside, she was doing a little happy dance. Maybe that wasn't exactly a date. Or maybe it was. But either way, it was Pete wanting to spend some more time with her. And she sure wanted to spend some more with him.

"Good. Let me go find a kitten-sized suitcase." Pete went into his bedroom and extracted a suitcase from the closet.

Tirzah stuffed Batcat and half the package of ham inside. Just as she was latching it, the doorbell rang.

Pete froze. Very quietly, he said, "Stay here. If you hear anything, lock the door."

He stepped out, feet silent as a stalking cat, every movement filled with deadly grace. Tirzah, who doubted that an assassin would ring the doorbell, felt sorry for whatever hapless delivery man was about to face an over-protective Pete defending his home.

"You!" Pete's exclamation was outraged, not alarmed. "What are *you* doing at my *house*?!"

A familiar voice said, "Whatever happened to 'Come on in, have a seat?'"

Leaving the Batcat case on the floor, Tirzah emerged from Pete's bedroom. She'd gotten accustomed enough to the obstacle course that she only bumped into one thing, a pedestal displaying a blown-glass cactus. It wobbled dangerously. Merlin leaped forward and steadied it.

"Hi, Tirzah," he said cheerfully. He wore a black T-shirt with a ghostly blue dinosaur and, in *Harry Potter* lettering, MY PATRONUS IS A VELOCIRAPTOR.

Pete's face was dark as a thundercloud. "What are you doing here?!"

Caro came out of her room. "What's going on?"

"Hi, I'm Merlin Merrick, one of your dad's co-workers," Merlin said. "Pleased to meet you."

"I'm Caro," she said, examining him curiously as she shook his hand. "I love your shirt! Are you a bodyguard too?"

"I am. And if you'll excuse us for a moment, I have to talk to Pete about some private work stuff."

"Sure." With a final fascinated stare, Caro returned to her room.

Merlin lowered his voice. "Nice to meet your daughter. Finally. Quick question: does she know you're a cave bear?"

Pete also spoke quietly, but the suppressed rage in his voice could have powered Tirzah's apartment building for a year. "No, she does not! She doesn't know anything about anything, for her own safety. Which you've just risked by coming here, so you better have a damn good reason. How did you even find me?"

"Ransom gave me your address," Merlin replied.

"How did he get it?" Pete demanded.

"Same way as everything: he just knew. Listen, Pete, that's why I'm here. Ransom says the gargoyle you fought wasn't the one who can drive people into a rage. He says that was the gargoyle's boss. By the way, why didn't you call in to say you fought a gargoyle?"

"Because he turned my cell phone to stone," Pete snapped.

"Oh. No wonder it kept saying it was out of service. Anyway, Ransom says the boss is still after you and Tirzah. And he knows where you live."

The angry flush drained from Pete's face, leaving it pale. "Caro. We have to get her out of here."

"Yeah. I figured we could take her to—"

"The office, right." Pete shouted, "Caro! Has Abuelita texted you?"

"Yeah, she did a couple minutes ago," Caro called back. "She said she'd just boarded the plane."

"Okay, good. She's safe, then." To Merlin, he said, "Warn everyone in the office that we're coming, and not to let *anything* slip to Caro."

"About that," Merlin said. "Ransom—"

Pete interrupted, "Tell him especially that if he can't say anything normal, he needs to keep his mouth shut!"

"But—"

"Caro!" Pete yelled. "Come back in here!" In a much lower voice, he said, "Merlin, help Tirzah get Spike."

"Who's Spike?" Merlin asked.

"Um." Tirzah felt like everything was moving way too fast, leaving her scrambling to catch up. "Easier to show you than to explain. Follow me."

Tirzah and Merlin hurried into Pete's bathroom, where they found Spike bathing under a dripping shower head, his wings spread out and his wet fur glistening green.

"Aww," said Merlin. "What a cute little cactus kitten. Is he yours or Pete's?"

"Pete's," Tirzah said. "It's a long story. Can you check the closet for another suitcase?"

"Can't you put him in that one?" Merlin asked, nodding at

191

the one Batcat was locked in. "We really need to hurry. You can get clothes later."

"Batcat's in there," Tirzah said. "And they don't get along."

"Gotcha." Merlin rummaged around the closet and extracted a backpack. "Best I can find. It's waterproof!"

Tirzah scooped up Spike and deposited him and the rest of the ham in the backpack. Merlin hefted it and the suitcase and returned to the living room, with Tirzah following. She'd heard Pete and Caro talking with increasingly raised voices, which escalated to outright yelling as Tirzah came in.

"Just give me ten minutes to pack!" Caro shouted.

"We don't have ten minutes!" Pete yelled back.

Caro whirled around, pointing dramatically to Merlin's suitcase. "You're taking *your* stuff!"

"Pete," Tirzah interrupted. "Give her five minutes, okay? She can throw a change of clothes and a toothbrush in a backpack."

"Okay, fi—" Before Pete could finish, Caro had bolted into her room and slammed the door. "FIVE MINUTES! THAT'S ALL!"

"YEAH, YEAH!" Caro yelled from behind the door.

"What did you tell her?" Tirzah whispered.

Pete gave an exasperated sigh. "What Merlin told me. Minus the part about me fighting a gargoyle and that the reason I know we're in danger is because my psychic team-mate had a vision of the mind-controlling big boss." He checked his watch. "Caro! Hurry up!"

"I'm coming!" she yelled.

There was a clattering sound like a box of nails dumped out on the floor, then several loud bangs like she was hammering the nails into something.

"Maybe I can help her get organized," Tirzah suggested. "She might take it better from someone who's not her parent."

192

"Yeah, good idea," Pete said, then bellowed, "Caro! Open the door! Tirzah's going to help you pack!"

"No!" Caro shrieked. "I'm almost done!"

"Just open the door!" Pete shouted. He glanced at his watch again, and said, "You've got one minute!"

There was a huge crash and a yelp from the room.

"Are you okay?" all the adults yelled simultaneously.

The door opened. Caro stood in the doorway, her hair all over her face, clutching a battered pink jewelry box in her arms. Tirzah recognized it as the type that plays a tune when you open it, while a little ballerina twirls. She'd gotten one as a Hanukkah gift when she was eight.

"You packed your *jewelry*?" Pete said incredulously. "Leave that box and grab some clothes!"

"No!" Caro shouted, hunching over the box protectively. "Abuelita gave me a necklace every birthday and they're all in here and they're the most precious things I own!"

"Guys," Merlin interrupted. "Can I be the voice of reason for a moment? We need to stop arguing and get out of here!"

"She can order clothes online and get them delivered to the office," Tirzah said. "A toothbrush too."

A faint meow came from the suitcase, which Tirzah covered with a loud coughing fit. But there was no way she could cover that all the way to the office. "Merlin, how about you take the luggage?"

Merlin grinned. "Will do! If you can just stay for a moment, Tirzah, I want to borrow some of your Advil you said was in a secret pocket in the backpack, but I can't seem to find it."

"Oh, right!" Tirzah said. "You guys go on to the car. I'll get Merlin his Advil and then I'll be right there."

"I have some in my medicine cabinet," Caro offered.

"Come on, Caro. Tirzah will catch up." Pete hustled her out toward the garage. As she passed, Tirzah noticed that her jewelry box wasn't just old and beat-up, but had actual holes in it, ringed with splintered wood. It was funny—and sweet, too—what kids found precious. Tirzah bet Pete or her grandmother had given her that box, and that was why Caro clung to it so desperately.

Once the garage door was closed, Merlin murmured, "Any special kitten instructions?"

"They each have half a package of ham, so they should be fine. If you get to the office before us, just stash them in a room somewhere. IN their carriers. Once they get out, it's really hard to recapture them."

"Gotcha. In that case, I won't let them out in the car."

"You'd really want to drive with two kittens flying around in the car?"

Merlin shrugged. "I've driven in more challenging situations. When I was with the circus—I was raised in a circus, you see—I once had to drive a clown car completely filled with clowns, ahead of a raging forest fire..."

CHAPTER 21

*P*ete was right behind Caro as she stepped into the garage, holding her jewelry box so carefully that it didn't even jingle. A flicker of warmth lit up the darkness of his protective fear for her and fury at anyone who might harm her. He hadn't seen her wear a single piece of jewelry since he'd come back, but when she had to do the equivalent of saving one thing from a burning house, what did she prioritize? The old jewelry box he'd given her for her tenth birthday (after consulting with Mom). He wondered if it still played a tune.

He flipped on the garage light and closed the door behind them, then remote-unlocked his car. "Go on in. I'll just wait here so I can help Tirzah down the step."

"Oh, I'll help too," Caro said. "Hang on."

She trotted to the car, placed her jewelry box in the back seat, and returned to Pete's side. He tried to examine her face without looking like he was staring at her.

"Dad!" Caro said instantly. "You're staring."

"Sorry. I just wanted to know if you were all right. If you're scared."

"You *could* ask." She waited, then made a "go on" gesture.

The lack of shakiness in her voice and her willingness to tease him gave him the answer, but he asked, "Are you all right? Are you scared?"

She gave a toss of her long black hair. "Not really. I'm excited, mostly. You always keep everything so secret. You won't tell me about your jobs, you won't let me visit your office, you never even told me you had a cool co-worker who likes Harry Potter and Jurassic Park. Well, now I'm finding out all your secrets whether you like it or not!"

Pete was taken aback. Had his secrets bothered Caro so much that she was willing to accept that much risk if it meant she'd get to find some of them out? Or was she not taking the danger seriously? "Aren't you worried about being in danger?"

"No, Dad." She rolled her eyes at him like he was missing something incredibly obvious. "I know you'll protect me."

She threw her arms around him and gave him a hug. Instinctively, he hugged her back. Only then did he remember that he couldn't touch her, couldn't touch anyone but Tirzah. He started to brace himself to endure the pain...

...but there was none. There was just his daughter hugging him and him hugging her back, like they'd always used to do. The shock of joy and relief made his eyes sting.

Suddenly, Caro stiffened in his arms. "Hey!"

Before Pete could react, she'd yanked down his collar, exposing the bandage taped to his chest.

"What's that?" she demanded. She didn't give him a chance to reply—not that there was any explanation he could think of anyway. Her voice rose in a fury. "You lied to me! You said you had food poisoning! Did your *bad burger* shoot you in the chest?!"

"Okay, first of all, it's not a gunshot wound."

"What is it, then?" she demanded.

Pete took a deep breath. "I can't tell you that. I'm sorry I lied to you. I should've just said I couldn't talk about it."

"I'm sick of you not being able to talk about it!" Caro shouted. "You never tell me anything! I'm not a little kid anymore!"

"Then stop yelling like one!"

"You're the one who's yelling!" she yelled.

Tirzah pushed the door open. "Hey guys—whoa, sorry, awkward—but we should probably get going, right?"

"Right." Pete had never been so relieved to be interrupted in his life. He lifted her chair down the step.

"You can take the front seat," Tirzah said to Caro.

Sulkily, she said, "I'll sit in the back."

Pete decided not to make an issue of it. He loaded Tirzah's wheelchair, checked to make sure no one was waiting to ambush them outside, and peeled out of the garage.

As he got on the freeway, a small voice rose from the back seat. "Dad? Are you all right?"

"Sure," he said automatically, then realized what she was talking about. "Yeah, mija. I'm fine. Just a few cuts."

"A few cuts wouldn't make you not be able to get out of bed!"

Pete glanced at Tirzah, who seemed to be trying to make herself invisible. He couldn't blame her. There was nothing worse than being trapped in the middle of a family argument when you weren't part of the family.

She is family, his cave bear rumbled unexpectedly. *She is our mate.*

And there was that mate thing again. He was watching the road, making sure they weren't being followed, but all these questions were bubbling at the back of his mind.

What did being a mate really mean?

Was Tirzah really his?

What happened if your mate didn't love you?

Why had he only been able to touch Tirzah before?

Why could he suddenly hug Caro now?

Who was the gargoyle's boss, and where was he now?

Tirzah softly cleared her throat, catching his attention. She indicated herself with a flick of her hand, then raised her eyebrows questioningly: *Want me to talk to her?*

Pete nodded. Caro, who was very selective about who she liked, adored her already; if he hadn't already noticed, he would have when Caro actually invited her to the cook-off.

"I wish I could tell you everything," Tirzah said. "I hate being curious and not knowing what's really going on, so believe me, I get it. But I'll tell what I can, and I promise it's the truth. Okay?"

"Okay," Caro said warily.

"First off, Pete really is fine. And he really does just have a few cuts. They bled a lot and he was exhausted, and that's why he needed to rest for a while."

"So why didn't he say that?" Caro asked.

Pete started to open his mouth, but Tirzah gave her head a small warning shake. He closed his mouth again.

"Because he couldn't tell you how he got hurt, and he knew how frustrating that would be," Tirzah said. "He thought it would be simpler if you didn't know there was more *to* know. And because he was afraid that if he told the truth, you'd worry about him and it would upset you."

Pete wouldn't have put it in those words, but it was the truth. It was almost scary how well Tirzah understood him.

"Okay," Caro said. He could hear from her tone that she accepted the truth of the explanation. "But isn't there anything you *can* tell me? I'm old enough to understand, I promise. And I won't tell anyone else if it has to be a secret."

"It's not safe," Pete said firmly. "The less you know, the safer you are."

"We just had to flee our own house!" Caro said. "How would I be any *less* safe if I knew why? Maybe I'd be *more* safe if I knew what was going on."

For his ears only, Tirzah murmured, "She has a point."

Pete gave her a quick headshake. For all of her brilliance, there were things she just couldn't understand, not being a parent herself. Not to mention not having been experimented on and turned into a shapeshifter. To Caro, he said, "No, you wouldn't. There's things you just can't know. And that's that."

Sulkily, Caro said, "I wish I'd gone with Abuelita. Maybe you should put me on a plane to Phoenix!"

Tirzah glanced at him, eyebrows raised to signal, *Should you?*

"I'm not putting you on a plane alone," he said. "And don't call your Abuelita and tell her to come get you. She's safe where she is. If she comes here, she may not be. Understand?"

"I would never put Abuelita in danger!"

"I know you wouldn't, mija. I just wanted to make sure you understood—"

"I'm not *stupid*," she snapped.

Pete was so relieved that there was no chance of Caro texting Mom to come get her that he let that slide. The rest of the ride to the office occurred in an uncomfortable silence. On the positive side, nothing attacked them on the way, nor did he catch anyone following them. When he pulled into the Defenders parking lot, he saw that Merlin had beaten them there, and Roland and Ransom's cars were also there.

At least Carter's not around, he thought with relief. The last thing he needed right now was dealing with that arrogant billionaire who wasn't even on the team.

Caro perked up once they parked, jumping out of the car

199

and looking around curiously, still clutching her jewelry box. "Ah-ha! So this is the Bat Cave!"

Pete, imagining Batcat flapping around the parking lot, couldn't help grinning. Tirzah gave a sudden laugh, loud enough to echo in the cavernous space.

"You can leave your jewelry box in the car," Pete said.

Caro hugged it to her chest. "No! Where I go, it goes!"

"It's completely safe in the parking lot," Pete began, then broke off when Tirzah again jabbed him in the ribs. He had no idea what had gotten into Caro, but there was no point wasting time squabbling and it wouldn't do her any harm to walk around cradling the box like it was her pet cat. Maybe she was so stressed out that she was using it as a sort of lovie for teenagers.

On the other hand, other than clinging to her jewelry box for dear life, she sure didn't seem stressed. She seemed excited and curious.

"Are the rest of the bodyguards as cool as Merlin?" she inquired. "Are any of them women?"

"No women yet," Pete said resignedly, since the cat was sure out of the bag as far as telling her *nothing* about his job was concerned. "But there's only four of us total. You think Merlin is cool?"

"His T-shirt had a Harry Potter joke," she pointed out. "Well? Are they?"

The elevator dinged and opened, saving him from having to answer that. As it carried them upward, he mentally crossed his fingers that it wouldn't open to some scene of craziness like the last time he'd come in. For that matter, he *really* hoped the flittering creature wouldn't decide to make an encore appearance, just for his daughter.

Merlin was waiting for them in the lobby, alone. At first Pete was relieved. Then he realized that given what was going on, all three of the guys ought to be waiting for them.

This feeling was only bolstered when Merlin began speaking, a bit too loudly and rapidly. "Hi, Pete, Tirzah! I put your luggage *safely* away. Hi, Caro! Want a tour of the office? We have some rooms in case you end up staying overnight— want to put your jewelry box in one of them? Let me show you around while Pete and Tirzah have a talk with our boss! He's in his office."

Caro glanced at Pete, who nodded, then back at Merlin. "Who's your favorite Harry Potter character?"

"Luna Lovegood," Merlin said instantly. "Who's yours?"

"Harry," she said. "I think I'd be in Gryffindor too."

"Oh, you'd definitely be in Gryffindor," he said. "Just like your dad."

"What about you?" Caro asked.

"Well, that's hard to say…"

They were still discussing Harry Potter as they vanished down a corridor. Once Pete could no longer hear them, he and Tirzah exchanged glances.

"What was that about?" she asked. "One of the kittens is loose in Roland's office and he and Ransom are trying to catch it?"

"Got me," Pete said. "I hope that's all."

She touched his shoulder. "Hey—I hope it didn't come across like I was second-guessing your parenting. You're a great dad."

Her thoughtfulness warmed him as much as the touch of her fingers. He could feel the outline of each one like a brand, if fire could burn without pain. "I'm trying. There's been so much of her life I wasn't there for."

"Well, she really loves you, so you were obviously there enough. And, Pete—you're here now." She gave his shoulder a squeeze, then released it as they went to Roland's office.

The door was closed. Given what Tirzah had said about

the kitten, Pete knocked. "Roland? It's me and Tirzah. Caro's getting an office tour from Merlin."

Roland opened the door. His usually-neat clothes were rumpled, and he looked worried. "Come in."

They went in, and he closed the door behind them.

"Where's—" Pete started to ask. Then he saw Ransom. His teammate was sitting on the floor in the corner, knees up, face down, arms wrapped around his head. Lowering his voice, Pete asked, "What's the matter with him?"

"He saw... knew...I don't quite understand how his power works, but it somehow showed him that you and Tirzah were in danger. We tried calling you both, but we couldn't reach either of you. I asked Ransom if he could get some specifics, like where you were now and who was after you. He said he'd try. He closed his eyes, and then he told us what I'd asked for. And then..." Roland gestured toward Ransom. "He's been like that ever since. Something obviously went wrong, but he can't seem to explain what it is."

"Pete," Tirzah said. "Maybe you could do for him what you did for me. You know, the Shoulder of Strength."

"What's that?" Roland asked.

"Tirzah had a nightmare, and I calmed her down. I mean, inside her mind. I didn't know I could do it until I did. So maybe I could do that for Ransom. I don't know, though. I might only be able to do it for Tirzah."

Roland looked puzzled. "What makes you think it might only work on her?"

"Well..." Pete didn't want to give his boss the entire story. Not now, anyway. Instead, he said, "Can you shake my hand?"

Pete held it out. Roland looked into his eyes, startled, and Pete realized that Roland had guessed far more of his secret than Pete had ever known. Then he reached out and gravely took Pete's hand.

He felt nothing more than Roland's grip, solid and strong. "Okay," Pete said. "I'll try."

He knelt down in front of Ransom. His teammate didn't move, but Pete could hear his shaky breathing. "Hey. Hey, buddy. Can you hear me?"

Ransom lifted his head and looked at Pete with bleak, haunted eyes. Or rather, Pete realized with a chill, he was looking *through* him, as if he wasn't even there.

"I opened the door," Ransom said in a barely audible voice. "I opened it, and I can't close it."

"What door?"

Ransom went on talking over Pete, as if he hadn't heard him. "It'll never close again."

Stepping inside the storm of Tirzah's emotions had been strange enough, and there was nothing in her mind or soul that he didn't love. For all that Ransom was his teammate, he'd never felt that he'd known the man well. And the way he was talking now sent a chill down Pete's spine. He wasn't sure he wanted to get inside Ransom's head.

He's still your buddy, Pete reminded himself. *And he's in pain. He needs you.*

His bear agreed, *You are pack.*

Pete put his hand on Ransom's shoulder.

Tirzah had been a storm, but Ransom was chaos. He was battered by a million voices shouting different things at the top of their lungs and a million images flashing too fast for him to see.

Is this what it's like for him all the time? Pete wondered.

Ropes of guilt wrapped around his throat, choking him. He was drowning in a cold black well of despair.

A few voices rose about the ear-shredding cacophony:

"Why don't you try it on yourself?"

"There's nothing wrong with the lights."

"What card am I holding?"

"You're a born betrayer."

Pete recognized the last one. He even remembered those exact words. They'd been spoken by the wizard-scientist Lamorat at the base where they'd all been changed, who'd taunted them all before they'd managed to turn the tables on him.

That memory—his own memory, not Ransom's—enabled Pete to find himself again within the chaos inside his teammate's mind. And once he had done that, he searched for Ransom himself: the essence of him. He was harder to find than Tirzah had been, but Pete located him at last: brilliant and brittle, wounded and enduring, self-sacrificing and fearless. And, small and alone within the enveloping darkness, a spark of hope burned bright.

Pete offered Ransom strength and calm and steadiness, support and clarity and friendship.

Let me be your rock, Pete thought to him, trying to make his voice heard above all the rest. *You can lean on me.*

And then he was abruptly back in the real world and his own body, kneeling on the floor of Roland's office, with his hand on Ransom's shoulder and Tirzah's hand on his.

Ransom jerked away, then scrambled to his feet. The shutters had come down over his face again, showing none of what Pete had seen within. "Don't ever do that to me again."

If Pete hadn't felt what he'd felt, he might have been angry. But he was still shaken by what he had experienced, and moved by the knowledge that Ransom had endured that willingly to protect him—and more importantly, to protect Tirzah. And now that he'd met the Ransom who lived behind that closed-off interior, he couldn't help liking him.

"Thank *you*," Pete said. "Me and Tirzah and my daughter are safe here because of what you did."

"Oh." Ransom glanced around. "Where is she?"

Pete was about to say, "With Merlin," but he saw then that Merlin was in the room but Caro wasn't.

"In a client room. Shopping. She left without packing any clothes, so I gave her my laptop and an Amazon gift card," Merlin said. "Couldn't you just X-Ray vision her, Ransom?"

"No. Finding Pete took everything I had." Ransom blinked, then looked from Pete to Tirzah to Merlin. "Wait. Pete's daughter is here, in the office? When Pete and Tirzah are here too?"

"Is there something wrong with that?" Pete asked.

"Your enemy can track you," Ransom said. "You *and* Tirzah. And he can drive people into a rage. Anyone near you will be pulled into the fight once he catches up with you."

The cave bear roared in protective fury.

Pete felt the blood drain out of his face. Then his gut-wrenching fear transmuted into anger. "Merlin! Why the hell didn't you tell me that?"

"That's the first I heard," Merlin protested.

"My fault," Ransom said. "I think I got... lost... before I said everything I knew. But your daughter needs to be somewhere else, if you're staying here."

"You know where he is right now?" Pete asked. "Or how close behind us he is?"

Ransom shook his head. "Sorry, no idea."

"I have to get out of here," Pete said. His mind was in a whirl of *protect Caro* and *protect Tirzah*, and his cave bear was roaring out the same things. It was hard to think straight. "Or get her out. Or—"

Roland held up his hand. "Pete. Wait. You weren't attacked at your house, and that would have been a good time to do it. I think we can assume that it takes your enemy some time to recharge, so to speak. Let's not rush off half-cocked."

"Then Tirzah and I need to leave before he does recharge," Pete said.

"Should all three of you split up?" Merlin asked. "If you go together, couldn't he turn the two of you against each other?"

A bone-chilling horror came over Pete at the thought of being forced to hurt Tirzah.

Never, snarled his cave bear. *We would die before we harmed our mate!*

Pete wasn't sure if the bear actually knew something or if he'd just *rather* die than turn on Tirzah, but something deep inside him believed that what his bear said was true. And though he couldn't logically justify it, staying with Tirzah felt right. "Well, I can't leave her alone if someone's after her!"

"I don't think he'll turn us on each other," Tirzah said calmly. "If he'd wanted to do that, he'd have done it already, instead of using the neighbors to drive us out. He wants to get that file from me and he wants... something... from Pete, and he can't get it if either of us is in a blind rage."

Pete nearly blurted out, *"That's what I love about you."* But though he couldn't express it, he was immensely relieved that she had pinpointed the reasons for what he'd instinctively felt. "Yeah. We should stick together. But not here."

"I have a cabin in the mountains," Tirzah said. "It's isolated, so no one else is going to get pulled into a fight. And I have a lot of my hacking equipment there. If Pete and I go there, he can protect me while I try to get some info on our enemy."

"I don't like to send you to face an enemy alone," Roland said. "I could go with the two of you while Merlin and Ransom stay here to guard Caro."

Pete forced himself to calm down and think. "Thanks, Roland. But the last thing we need is a mind-controlled phoenix setting fire to Tirzah's cabin."

Incredulously, Tirzah said, "Roland's a *phoenix*?!"

Merlin nodded enthusiastically. "He burned a six-headed dragon to ash once!"

While Tirzah was eyeing Merlin, visibly trying to figure out whether he was pulling her leg, Pete thought fast. He'd brought Caro here to protect her, and weird as his team were, he still couldn't think of anyone he trusted more to do that. And if he was gone, their enemy would follow him and leave his daughter alone.

"Tirzah's plan is good," Pete said. "I can protect her, she can do her thing, and you can guard Caro while I'm gone."

"I'll protect her with my life," Roland said.

"This may be burned out for now." Ransom tapped his temple. "But this is still good." He touched his chest, leaving Pete wondering whether he meant his fighting spirit or a concealed weapon.

"I'll stick to her like Harry Potter chasing after a Golden Snitch!" Merlin assured him.

"You can be in charge of entertaining her while she's stuck here," Pete said.

"Where's Carter?" Tirzah asked. "He could stay here, so he's not a danger to us, and I could coordinate with him over email."

"No idea, sorry," Merlin said with a shrug. "He took off. He does that."

Roland said, "If he turns up, I'll have him email you immediately."

"I'll talk to Caro now," Pete said. "Remember, guys, she doesn't know anything about any of the weird shit. And she's a very bright girl. No subtle talking over her head—she'll get it. And absolutely no shifting, Merlin!"

"Why are you singling me out?" Merlin protested.

Exasperated, Pete snapped, "Because Ransom hates his shift form and Roland doesn't want to burn down the office!"

It was only after the words left his mouth that he realized

that Ransom had never said a word about hating his hell-hound. Pete just knew it, now that he'd been inside Ransom's mind.

The muscles around Ransom's jaw tightened, but he said nothing.

Pete wished he could apologize, but that would just call more attention to it. Meanwhile, Tirzah looked like her wish was to sink into the floor. "Tirzah, want to come with me?"

"Sure!"

They fled more than left the office. Once they were outside, Tirzah said, "Thanks for the rescue. But I don't have to sit in on your talk with Caro unless you actually want me to."

"I'd like you to," Pete said. "But you don't have to. I don't want to pull you out of the frying pan and into the fire."

She smiled that irresistible smile of hers. "I don't mind. I like her."

And that was when Pete realized that *he* was the one going out of the frying pan and into the fire. Being pitched into the dark chaos of Ransom's mind was nothing compared to having to tell his daughter he was leaving her behind. Again.

CHAPTER 22

*T*irzah could tell that Pete was shaken from whatever it had been like to calm Ransom, worried about Caro, and not looking forward to the talk they were about to have with her. She couldn't give him the Shoulder of Strength, so she put her hand on his arm. On him, a simple touch seemed to work like magic: she could actually feel him relax.

"Caro's going to hate this, isn't she?" Tirzah asked.

"Yeah. But it's for her own protection."

She glanced up at his set face. There *was* something about him that reminded her of the bear: powerful, fierce, protective, and stubborn as hell. Crashing through obstacles, moving forward with such momentum that he couldn't turn aside or stop. Who'd be willing to step in front of a charging cave bear?

Me, Tirzah thought glumly. *Oh, he's going to hate* this...

But she'd never been able to stop herself from saying what she believed was the truth.

"Pete? Have you thought of telling her what's actually going on?"

"You mean that I'm leaving to draw the danger away from her?" He shook his head. "I can't. She'd be scared. She'd worry about me. Maybe she'd even feel guilty."

"Yeah, she might. But she'd also understand why you're doing it, and she wouldn't feel abandoned."

He shook his head dismissively. "I'll explain that I don't have any choice."

"You do have a choice, though," she said. Pete gave her a look like she was suddenly speaking a language he didn't understand, but she went on. "And also, everything else. Being kidnapped. Being a shifter. Why you didn't want to hug her. Have you even *considered* telling her?"

Now he was looking at her like she was a bug-eyed alien. "No, of course not."

"Well, why don't you take a moment and consider it?"

He didn't take a moment, but immediately replied, "She can't know any of that. For her own safety."

"Is it really keeping her safe, though? Remember her saying she was fleeing her home, and asking how knowing why would make her *less* safe? You didn't answer her. Do you have an answer?"

"She's too young, and it's too dangerous. And that's that." He sounded annoyed, which was fair; she was annoyed at him too. She thought for a living, and he was literally refusing to even *think* about a very important matter.

Tirzah opened her mouth to point out that being kept in ignorance might be more dangerous than knowing what was up, then closed it. That might well be true in the long run, but for now Caro was in a top security building, guarded by three ex-military bodyguard shapeshifters with magical powers. At this exact moment, it was literally impossible for her to get into any trouble.

Besides, she was skating perilously close to criticizing

someone else's parenting, which she knew was obnoxious. Especially since she wasn't a parent herself.

Instead, she said, "Is she going to sleep here? Where, on the sofa in the lobby?"

Pete looked relieved at the change of topic. "No, we have a place for clients who need protection and don't have anywhere else to go. It's a bedroom and bathroom. Roland fixed it up. He said anyone who used it would be scared and desperate and need a place that felt safe and cozy. So he put a deadbolt on the inside and a patchwork quilt on the bed and pajamas in all sizes in the closet."

"That sounds nice," Tirzah said, though she bet Caro wouldn't still enjoy it once she realized her father was leaving her there.

They reached the client room. The door was shut. Pete knocked. "Caro? It's me."

"Just a second!" Caro yelled through the door. She heard thumps and scuffles and a door slamming. Then the deadbolt slid back and she opened the door.

Tirzah spun her chair around on the hardwood floor, admiring the room. It really did feel cozy, with a big four-poster bed, blue walls, a big window (made of bulletproof glass, no doubt) with a great view of the city, and framed paintings of cozy scenes: a red barn in a snowy landscape, a white sailboat in a clear blue sea, a meadow of wildflowers with a brook running through it.

A tall bookcase held a very wide selection of books for every taste, from classics to fantasy to murder mysteries to popular nonfiction. The bottom two shelves held books for children, from picture books to young adult novels. There was a small table with a few chairs, a larger armchair, a TV, a closet, and a dresser. Caro had placed her jewelry box atop the dresser, and had Merlin's laptop on the bed.

"Hope you didn't break Merlin's bank," Tirzah said. "Get anything nice?"

Caro nodded, grinning, and turned the laptop to show Tirzah a billowing white nightgown trimmed with lace and tiny pink roses.

"Very pretty," Tirzah said.

Pete barely glanced at it. "Listen, Caro. Tirzah and I have to go away for a couple days. You need to stay here. It's completely—"

"You're DITCHING me?" Caro interrupted.

Tirzah winced. This conversation was obviously going to go exactly how she'd guessed.

Pete's voice also rose. "It's for your own safety! My team will be guarding you the entire—"

"You're ditching me AGAIN?!" Caro yelled.

"I'm not ditching you! I'm keeping you safe!"

"Why don't you keep me safe yourself?! Why are you foisting me off on your co-workers?!"

Pete lowered his voice. "I have a job to do, and so does Tirzah. You know you can't come along on my jobs."

Caro glared at him so hard Tirzah half-expected to see sparks fly out of her eyes. "Of course I know that! So tell me what the job is, if it's real and not just an excuse to DITCH me!"

Tirzah tried to catch Pete's eye. But he wasn't looking in her direction. Arms folded, he said, "I can't tell you that."

"You mean you *won't*! This isn't the military—it's not top secret! And it's not about Tirzah's privacy, because I know *she'd* tell me! You just don't want me around!"

With that, Caro jumped up from the bed. Snatching her jewelry case from the dresser, she ran with it into the bathroom, slammed the door, and locked it.

"Lina! Get back in here!" Pete yelled.

"My name's not Lina!" Caro shouted from behind the door.

After that, there was only silence. For the third time that day, Tirzah was in the uncomfortable position of being an onlooker to some intense emotional scene between other people. She was tempted to just leave, but if she moved, that would only make them remember she was there.

Finally, Pete said to the closed door, "I'll call you, all right? Okay, Caro? I love you, and I'm *not* doing this because I don't want you around. There's some serious stuff going on that has nothing to do with you."

There was no reply, but the silence had a distinctly sulky atmosphere.

"Good-bye, mija," Pete said.

"Bye, Caro," Tirzah said. "Um... If you like Harry Potter, you should try Percy Jackson. The second shelf has the complete series."

"I've already read it!" Caro snapped from within. "Twice!"

Pete silently beckoned to Tirzah, and they left the room. He closed the door a little louder than necessary—not slamming it, but making sure she heard they were gone.

Once outside, he sighed. "She's usually much better-behaved than this."

Tirzah nearly had to bite her tongue not to say "I told you so." Instead, she said peaceably, "I know, Pete. She's stressed and upset and she just had to flee her own house with nothing but that jewelry box. If it'd been me at that age, I'd have been curled up sobbing in a corner. All things considered, I think she's doing fine."

"I wish I could send her to Arizona to be with Mom," he said. "I could get one of the guys to escort her. But I can't risk someone trying something at an airport."

"Or on a plane," Tirzah agreed. "Come on, let's grab the kittens and get out of here."

Pete nodded. "You want some spare clothes or a tooth-brush or anything like that? We keep them here for clients."

"Nah, I have everything I need at the cabin."

Pete went to get a gun, a cell phone, and other equipment from the office supply room, and Merlin went with Tirzah to corral Spike and Batcat into the suitcase, which he'd already helpfully punched holes in with a screwdriver. Tirzah was just crossing her fingers they could both go in without a fight, because the backpack couldn't be comfortable for poor Spike.

They found the winged kittens snoozing on a desk, bellies rounded with all the ham they'd gobbled down. They were at opposite ends of the desk, but Tirzah decided to take it as a positive sign that at least they weren't at opposite ends of the *room*. She slid them into the suitcase with no trouble at all.

"Sure you don't want to leave them here?" Merlin asked hopefully. "They'd be safer."

"You mean, you want to kitten-sit," Tirzah said.

Merlin grinned, unabashed. "Of course I do."

"Pete's dead-set on making sure Caro never finds out about shifters or magic or any of this," Tirzah said. "These little guys are escape artists, and they meow. If they stay here, it'll all come out. Anyway, if I trust Pete to protect me, I trust him to protect them."

"Can't blame a guy from trying." Bending over the suit-case, Merlin called, "See you later, little guys. Maybe I'll have a little friend for you to play with by then!"

She and Pete met up in the lobby, where Roland was waiting for them.

"The cameras outside the building don't show anything suspicious," Roland said. "I think you'll at least be able to get out of the parking lot without any trouble. Hopefully out of the city. After that..." He spread his hands. "I know you can handle yourself and protect Tirzah. And there is a real danger of any of us getting within range of a mind-controller. But all the same, call us if you need us."

"I will," Pete said. But Tirzah had the distinct impression that he was just saying it to get his boss off his back. She'd yet to see him call for help under any circumstances.

But that didn't scare her any more than she was already scared. If Pete couldn't protect her himself, nobody could.

They got in his car and stashed the kitten case in the back seat, and Pete drove away. At first his attention was completely on the road, watching for ambushes or cars following them or gargoyles in the sky. But once they were on the freeway and heading out of the city, toward the forests and mountains and small towns that lay to its north, she saw him relax a little.

"Caro's a lot like you," Tirzah said.

"That girl is smarter than I'll ever be. Her mother's a high-powered lawyer now."

"Hey, don't put yourself down," Tirzah said. "You're plenty smart. But she's also got your stubbornness. And your temper."

"All my worst qualities," he muttered.

Tirzah gave an exasperated huff of breath. "Don't be like that. My point is that you're clashing now because you're so much alike, neither of you will give an inch. But you're so much alike, you're bound to come back together in the end."

Pete glanced at her with his big brown eyes, and she saw she'd given him some hope. "Yeah. I guess so. And you're right. If my dad had hustled me off and stuck me with his co-workers, I'd be plenty pissed. Then again, his co-workers were Marines, so I guess once I'd cooled down, I'd get them to teach me hand-to-hand combat or to disassemble a rifle blindfolded."

"Just wait till you see Caro's new skills when you get back," Tirzah teased. "She'll probably be a black belt."

"I don't think she's interested in that stuff. But Merlin might teach her some gymnastics. I could get her riding lessons or gymnastics lessons, but I couldn't afford both, and she picked riding. I don't know where Merlin learned—he claims he got taught by trapeze artists in that bullshit made up circus of his—but he's good."

"There you go." Tirzah patted his thigh. "You'll come back to a very happy girl who can fly through the air and has a complete set of the girliest clothes she's ever dreamed of. Possibly including a pink leotard."

Pete nodded, smiling at last. "I can't believe I'm saying this, but thank God for Merlin. And if she actually wants to hear his circus stories, and I think she will if he makes up some pretty pretty performing ponies, his life will be complete."

Tirzah smiled. Then she remembered what she'd been meaning to ask Pete, before Caro had distracted her. "Hey! What was going on when you shook Roland's hand? Does it still hurt?"

The hard planes of Pete's face were transformed by joy, like the sun rising over a mountain range. "No! Sorry, I didn't get a chance to tell you. Caro hugged me in the garage, and that didn't hurt either." He shook his head in wonder. "Didn't hurt. Man, that's an understatement. It was like when I first held her, when she was a baby."

"Oh, Pete." Tirzah couldn't give him a real hug, since he was driving, but she did her best. "I'm so glad."

"I wish I knew what changed. Just so I could stop worrying that it was a one-day fluke, and tomorrow it'll be back to the way it was before."

But the moment he said, "what changed," Tirzah's mind

was leaping ahead. "Pete, what changed was the Shoulder of Strength! You never did that before, right?"

"No, but I don't see what that has to do with..." His eyes took on a distant, inward-turning look. "When I did it to you, your emotions had a kind of... physical feeling. Like, your fear felt like it was cutting me. Your anger burned. I think maybe I always had the Shoulder of Strength, sort of, but it wasn't working right. I couldn't turn it off, and I couldn't do anything useful with it, and I couldn't feel anything positive or even know what I *was* feeling. Whenever I touched anyone, it turned on automatically, found whatever negative stuff was inside them, and threw it back at me as pain."

"So Jerry was telling the truth!" She grabbed his arm, excited by her favorite thing: all the pieces of a puzzle falling into place. "Remember, he said you had two powers, and one wasn't working right."

"Oh, yeah. I'd forgotten about that. I just figured he was making it up to mess with me."

"But why not me?" Tirzah asked, more thinking aloud than to Pete. "It's not like I don't have any negative feelings."

Pete started to smile, then got that distant look again. He suddenly blinked, then a look of understanding came across his face, as if he'd heard some inward voice. His cave bear talking to him?

"Earth to Pete," Tirzah said. "Someone talking to you?"

His face went deliberately blank. She gave an inward sigh. One more thing he wasn't going to tell her. Rather than argue about it, she changed the subject. "So what was it like being inside Ransom's head? You looked pretty shaken up after that."

"It was like walking into a giant store with thousands of TVs stacked up at every wall, turned up so loud they hurt your ears, with every single one playing something different.

I always figured when he used his power, it was like typing into Google and seeing what comes up. But I think it's more like having everything anyone's ever searched for on Google dumped into your head and trying to sift through it for the answer to your question."

"As someone who does a lot of weird searches on Google, that does not sound fun."

"It really, really wasn't."

They had now left the city limits, and the freeway was beginning to climb to a higher elevation. The skyscrapers were gone, replaced by small towns in between long stretches of fields or woods. The trees blazed with the reds and golds of late autumn. The frenetic energy of Refuge City had been replaced by something quieter and more restful.

"Look at those leaves," Tirzah said. "I'm glad I got a chance to get out of the city before they all fell."

"I never got a chance to ask," Pete said. "But... you own a cabin? What is it, family property?"

"No. I bought it. I used to work for a cryptocurrency startup. It turned into something like PayPal, and I made a mint. In fact..." Tirzah smiled, realizing that she'd completely forgotten to mention this little detail. "...I also own my apartment building."

"You do? I never realized. The other tenants don't act like you're their landlord."

"They don't know." Tirzah had to laugh at Pete's surprise. "I started off as a tenant. We had an absentee landlord who never repaired anything. He eventually put the building up for sale, and everyone was worried that we'd get someone who'd raise the rent and drive us all out. So I bought it under a company name I made up. I hired an apartment manager who's never met me in person. I pay for all the upkeep, and I've never raised the rent. When prospective renters come in to look at an apartment that's opened up, I drop on by and make sure they're nice people who'll fit in."

"And nobody knows who's cashing their checks?"

"Nope. I thought it might make things awkward. Change our relationships." She shrugged.

Pete was smiling. "I think you just like having secret identities."

"No—well—maybe," she admitted. "Okay, fine. When I was a kid I wanted to be a superhero. Wear a mask, bring villains to justice—stop laughing, smarty-pants, I know you did too."

"Of course I did. But you're the one who actually did it. I'm impressed, seriously. All you need is a Bat Cave."

"I have a Batcat. And I sort of do have a Bat Cave—that's my cabin." Looking at the road up ahead, she admitted, "I miss it. I'm glad you're driving me there. I'd thought I might never come back."

It was true. But she didn't tell him that she worried about how she might react when they hit the stretch of highway where her car had gone off the road. With any luck she'd be fine with someone else driving. And if not, there was always the Shoulder of Strength.

"How come you haven't fixed up your apartment to make it more accessible?" he asked. "There's no landlord telling you not to change things too much. And if you can afford the entire building, you can afford to renovate."

Tirzah had once dreaded him asking that question, as it could so easily lead to "So what happened to you, anyway?" But now that she'd already told him her story, she was able to answer easily. "I didn't want to move out of my apartment while the renovations were going on, so I kept putting it off and putting it off. And everyone in the building was happy to open doors and reach things down for me, so it didn't seem that pressing. A family's moving out of one of the three-bedroom apartments, though, so I might take that one over while mine's getting fixed up."

"You don't mind asking people for help." It was a statement, not a question, but Pete sounded like that was incomprehensible to him.

"No, not if they don't mind giving it. Why do you mind?"

"Because..." His voice trailed off, then he finally said, "I guess I want to know I'm self-sufficient. That I don't have to depend on anybody."

"I don't *have* to depend on anybody," Tirzah pointed out. "Well, other than to drive. But I don't *need* you to open the car door for me or stash my wheelchair in the trunk. It's just a nice thing you do, that saves me the effort."

Pete still seemed baffled by this, as if she'd told him that two plus two equaled orange. Finally, he said, "Yeah, I can see how that works for you."

But not for you, Tirzah thought. She could vividly remember Pete not only refusing to ask for help, but refusing to accept it when offered until he literally collapsed. That had to be such a hard way to live.

"Can you do me a favor?" she asked.

"Sure."

"When we get to the cabin, ask me to do something for you."

"Like what?" Pete asked.

"That, my friend, is up to you," Tirzah said, grinning. "And you already agreed to do it, so now you have to."

A sweet smile lit his face and warmed his eyes. "Okay. I'll see if I can think of a good one."

They drove for another hour, until Tirzah said, "This is the last town before we get to my place. We should stop and get milk and butter and anything else perishable we might want. There's coffee and canned stuff and so forth in the cabin, but my refrigerator was empty when I left that last time."

"Last *town?*" Pete looked around. "This is a town?"

Tirzah, looking at it through his eyes, noted the one small market next to a small gas station, with fields full of grazing cows bracketing the road, and the mountains rising above it all. "Yup. I told you this was remote. No one to go berserk but the cows."

Pete eyed them suspiciously. "I wouldn't want to get charged by one."

They checked the kitten suitcase (they both seemed to be napping), then cracked the window, fueled the car, and made their purchases. By the time they got back in the car, the afternoon light had turned the fields to gold.

Despite the danger they were still in—despite everything —Tirzah was inexplicably filled with a sense of happiness and peace. She and Pete were on this adventure together, on the way to her own special place that she'd never taken anyone to before. But rather than feel like her space was being invaded, she was glad to have the opportunity to share it with him.

As he drove, she kept sneaking glances at him. His dark hair, clipped so short that she could see the individual hairs standing up. His expressive brown eyes. The tiny cleft in his chin. The stubble just starting to come in that would make his cheeks feel rough if she touched them. His wrists so thick with muscle that she couldn't close her fingers around them.

He'd held her, once. He'd stepped inside her mind. But that hadn't felt invasive either. It had felt like she'd invited him in rather than that he'd barged in. More, he'd felt like he belonged.

Despite everything he'd told her, she sensed there was more than he wasn't saying. Did he still worry that she'd judge him? Was he still judging himself?

What did he *really* feel about her?

What did she *really* feel about him?

The one-lane highway narrowed as it began to climb the mountains. Cliffs rose up on one side of the road and dropped away on the other. There was no guardrail. If the car hit ice and slid, it would go right over, tumbling and tumbling to smash into the ground below...

Pete laid his hand on her shoulder. "Hey. You doing okay?"

Tirzah gulped for air. "N—not really."

"You want some help?"

"If you go inside my head while you're driving, you'll go off the cliff!" Her voice sounded shrill, and she winced at it.

"Wasn't what I meant." Pete squeezed her shoulder. "We'll do this old school. First, close your eyes so you're not looking at the drop."

She did. Immediately, she felt lost in darkness, which made her panic even worse.

Pete went on, "Focus on my voice and my hand on your shoulder. Take a deep breath. All the way in, until you can feel your stomach puff out. Then slooooowly let it go. Take another breath, from the stomach again. As deep as you can..."

Tirzah followed his instructions. His hand was warm and strong on her shoulder, and she could sense his presence beside her. His voice was a lifeline, easing her panic. As she breathed deeply, her pounding heartbeat slowed and her sense of suffocation went away.

Pete kept on talking, calm and kind. She could hear that he wasn't judging her for her fear, any more than he'd judged Ransom for whatever was going on with him. He'd seen that they were in pain and that he could help, and he'd stepped up to the plate. And that was what Pete was: compassionate, confident, and courageous.

Now that he'd gotten her past the worst of it, she knew she could open her eyes and manage her own fears without his help. But she liked hearing his voice, liked feeling his touch. Even though they were driving into danger, she was happy, because it meant they'd get to spend more time together.

I love him.

The realization came both as a shock and as an undeniable truth. Oh, she'd liked him before, she'd thought he was hot, she'd enjoyed his company, she'd had an enjoyable little crush on him. But this was more. This was the real thing.

I love him, she thought. *I want to spend my life with him.*

If he doesn't feel the same way about me, it's going to break my heart.

Tirzah swallowed. Pete was still talking, coaching her breathing. But she was now balanced on a precipice even more terrifying than the actual cliffs that had almost killed her. Now that she understood her own feelings, she also knew that she couldn't keep them hidden for long. Much as she liked having secret identities, she'd never kept her feelings and emotions a secret. People might not know that Tirzah was Override, but they sure knew that Tirzah believed in the same things that Override believed in. She had her secrets, but she didn't lie.

She'd have to tell Pete how she felt. And then she'd find out what *he* felt.

By the end of this day, she'd either be happier than she'd been in her entire life, or her heart would be smashed into a million little pieces.

If their mind-controlling enemy didn't kill them first.

CHAPTER 23

*P*ete could feel as well as hear and see when Tirzah's panic left her, but he kept on talking. He figured she'd tell him when she wanted him to stop. But she was so quiet and still, breathing deeply, that he was beginning to wonder if he'd actually lulled her to sleep when the steep road leveled off, and they left the cliffs behind.

She opened her eyes. "Thanks, Pete. I really appreciate it."

"Any time. And hey, you got through it without even needing the Shoulder of Strength."

"Sorry I snapped at you about that. I should've known that wasn't what you meant."

"Don't worry about it," he said. "I didn't take it personally."

"You know, I never asked. What was it like being inside my mind? Was it just a bunch of feelings that hurt? Or was it more than that?"

"More. Much more. It was like... the essence of you."

"Even more Google than Ransom?" she teased.

Caught between blurting out that he'd fallen in love with

her at that moment and saying literally anything else (which would be a lie), he only shook his head.

Of all things, the GPS she had programmed with the directions to her cabin came to his rescue. Its sing-song mechanical voice said, "In point three miles, take a right turn."

"Little dirt road," Tirzah added. "You'll want to slow down. It comes up fast."

He slowed, then took a sharp right on to a very rough dirt road. It wound through a forest of green fir and maples decked in red and gold. This late in autumn, the leaves were beginning to fall, carpeting the forest floor and blowing in drifts across the road.

"It's beautiful," he said. "You sure picked a nice spot."

Her house was at the end of the long driveway, an old-fashioned log cabin. It was, he noted approvingly, fairly defensible. The walls and roof were thick, and as it was atop a hill, anyone trying to sneak up on it would be easily spotted. If you had to hole up in a civilian building where an enemy might catch up with you, you could do a lot worse.

They got out, and Tirzah gave an irritated glance at the front door. "What is the point of thresholds, other than to make things difficult for people in wheelchairs? I'll have hire someone to get rid of that."

"To keep snow from blowing in, I think." Pete examined it. "I could take it off for you today. I've got some carpentry tools in the trunk."

"Thanks. I'd appreciate it."

Pete straightened up and looked around the front door, then gave a chuckle. "I should've asked you if you already had a security system and cameras. I brought them with me from the office."

"Oops," Tirzah said. "But yeah, no need. I've already got

them, state of the art. With no neighbors to keep a lookout and me not here most of the time, I figured I needed them."

She punched in a security code to turn off the alarm, then unlocked the door. He helped her wheel over the bump so she didn't get jarred too much, and then she closed the door and re-armed the alarm.

He'd expected the air inside to be musty, considering no one had been in it for a year, but it wasn't; Tirzah had left some windows open when she'd gone on that shopping trip so long ago. They were screened, so no leaves had blown in. The air inside was fresh and clean, if a bit chilly.

The cabin was small but cozy, with an open kitchen, a living room with a fireplace, and doors leading to a bathroom, a bedroom, and an office crammed with computers and other electronics. Dolls sat, legs dangling, on the mantelpiece, and several plastic ninjas were caught in the act of climbing the curtains. It was a distinctly Tirzah cabin.

Pete glanced up. "Where's the stairs?"

"Stairs?" Tirzah asked blankly.

"It looked like there was a second floor."

"Oh, that's the attic." She wheeled over and pointed upward, at a dangling rope with a handle. "Pull on that."

Pete gave it a tug. A panel slid to the side, and a rope ladder fell down.

"Even more useless now than when I bought the place," Tirzah remarked. She returned to the living room, where they'd left the kitten suitcase. Pete followed. "All the doors and windows closed?"

"Sure. Go ahead and release the kittens."

Tirzah giggled. "That sounded like 'Release the kraken!'"

"Not much difference, with these little hellraisers."

She flipped open the suitcase. Two pairs of enormous yellow eyes stared accusingly at him and Tirzah, and two rose-pink mouths opened to make sad little meows intended to strike guilt into the hearts of the monsters who had locked them in a suitcase. Then, moving in tandem, they launched out of the suitcase and flew straight up through the trapdoor and into the attic.

"Anything up there they can get into?" Pete asked.

"Nothing breakable, I think. I've only been up there once. The person I bought it from had furniture stashed up there that I guess he didn't want to deal with trying to get down the rope ladder, and I felt the same way."

Pete waited apprehensively for the sounds of mayhem, but there was only silence.

"They're probably plotting something," Tirzah said. "At least here we don't have to worry about anyone seeing them."

That was, in fact, a weight off Pete's mind. He'd spent so much time dreading Caro finding out about all the weird stuff he'd gotten tangled up in, and so getting pulled into danger. It was a huge relief to know that she was safe with his team, Mom was safe all the way across the country, and there were no neighbors or passersby to get caught up in anything that might happen.

Just to be sure, he took out his cell phone and messaged Caro, Mom, and Roland while Tirzah took off to check her computer room.

Mom wrote, *Everything's fine. I've arrived at Elena's place and am arranging for grocery delivery. Are you and Caro in the city?*

Pete knew Mom would tear him a new one when she found out what was really going on and that he hadn't told her, but he preferred that to her worrying. So he wrote back, *No, she's with friends.*

It wasn't *technically* a lie. She was with friends. His friends. If you stretched a point to call them that.

Roland wrote, *Caro's fine. She's all settled in and playing cards with Merlin.*

Caro wrote, *I'm fine dad. Merlin is teaching me to play poker. Better watch out!*

Tirzah came back in. "Computers are all good! No sign of the kittens. You see 'em anywhere?"

"No—" Pete began.

Just then, the kittens came zooming back in, green and black wings flapping madly. They chased each other around the cabin, meowing and occasionally bouncing off the walls. Finally, they tumbled together to the sofa, where they began grooming each other. Pete and Tirzah watched, fascinated, as Batcat pinned the larger Spike down with a dainty paw and licked him all over, while Spike craned his neck to groom her belly fur. That task done, the kittens wrapped their arms around each other and fell fast asleep.

"Isn't that sweet?" Tirzah said. "I'd started thinking they'd never get along."

"And all it took was getting locked in a suitcase together for hours."

"Don't knock it. We got locked in an apartment together for a week, and…" Her voice trailed off, and her cheeks flushed pink.

The air in the cabin no longer felt chilly, but hot. Or maybe it was just him. Tirzah was silent, looking up at him. Her beautiful brown eyes seemed to look straight into his soul.

Now, rumbled the cave bear. *No more secrets.*

"You asked me what I saw when I was inside your mind," Pete said. "I didn't see your thoughts, or your secrets. I saw *you*. I saw what makes you Tirzah. I saw courage and brilliance and kindness. I saw strength and humor and determination, and… you. You're more yourself than anyone I've ever met."

She was watching him, lips parted, intent on his words.

He felt so connected to her, he imagined that he could feel every breath she took.

"And I loved you," he said quietly. "I don't know if I fell in love with you then, or if I had some time before and that was when I realized it. I love you, Tirzah. That's my last secret. Now you know everything."

Tirzah opened her mouth, then shook her head, as if she felt too much for speech. But she didn't need to say a word. He could see her love shining like stars, so strong and passionate and true that he couldn't understand why he'd ever doubted it.

He leaned over to kiss her, but before he could, she caught his hands and pulled him down until he was kneeling before her chair. The imprint of her fingers was as intense a pleasure as touch had once been pain. It took his words away too, along with his breath.

He didn't know if he reached out to her, or if she pulled him in, only that her soft lips were molded to his, kissing him with a passion that undid him. Pete's head swam. If he hadn't already been on the floor, he would have dropped to his knees. He'd never felt anything like the soft wet heat of her mouth.

He didn't want to move—he didn't *ever* want to move—but he wanted to make sure she was comfortable.

"Should I carry you?" His voice was hoarse. "To—to the bed?"

She shook her head, sending the silken curls of her sweet-smelling hair brushing against his cheeks.

"Right here is fine." Her voice was husky too, velvety, almost a purr. "Here..."

She slid out of the chair and into his arms. His senses reeled at the weight of her, her sweet-spicy nutmeg scent, the softness of her skin, the heat of her body, her lush curves. Tirzah, his love, in his arms at last.

She hauled his shirt off, then traced her fingertips lightly over the bandages. "Do they hurt?"

He shook his head, though the truth was that he wouldn't have cared even if they had. "You can do anything."

"Anything…" There was that purr of hers again. It drove him wild. "You too. What do you want?"

"To touch," he whispered.

She was wearing a blouse that laced up the front, displaying her lush cleavage. "Here." She handed him the ties.

He gave them a tug, and they unraveled. Another tug at the blouse, and it fell away. Tirzah wriggled in his lap, making him gasp, as she reached behind her back to unsnap her bra. One more wriggle as she discarded both blouse and bra, and then he had the soft globes of her breasts in his hands. Her nipples were brown as maple wood, and when he touched them, they hardened and she gasped.

He could feel her heart speeding up, feel the pulse of her blood, feel her breath catch in her chest. Her eyes were wide, her hair curling tighter as she began to sweat. He watched a lovely pink flush wash over her face and then spread across her chest, like a tide. It was such an incredible turn-on to actually be able to see her arousal.

They lay down. The floor was hard and cool, but he barely noticed. All the while he never stopped kissing her, reveling in her passion, her desire, the startling strength of her hands.

He stroked every curve of her body, glorying in the feeling of her smooth skin, trying to convey the love he felt for her through the very pores of his skin. And as he explored her body, she explored his. Everywhere her fingers touched, he could feel their traces even after they were gone, like trails of light. After all that time of deprivation and lone-liness, at last he was getting everything he wanted—everything he *needed*. But the joy of giving Tirzah what *she* wanted, what *she* needed, was even greater than receiving it himself.

He caressed and kissed every bit of her, from the downy skin at the nape of her neck to the sleek column of her spine, from the tips of every one of her fingers to her deliciously plump belly. When he moved lower down, he felt her stiffen for the first time.

"Don't you like that?" he asked, glancing up.

She gave a nervous giggle. "Oh, *that* isn't what I was thinking. And yes, I like it a lot! It's just... I used to love my legs. Wore little '50s-style dresses to show them off."

Oh. In that case, he decided to put off where he'd been heading at first. Instead, he slid even lower. He'd seen her legs bare before, when she'd worn his WORLD'S BEST DAD shirt and nothing else; they were both badly scarred, and the right visibly thinner from lack of use. But at that time, he'd been distracted by other things.

"You should still love them. I do." Pete reached up and caught Tirzah's hand, bringing it to his barbed wire scar, then placed his other hand on the surgical scar running from her hip to her ankle. "These are all battle scars."

Her breath went out in a long sigh. "Guess we match."

"How's the sensation in your right leg?"

"I have some. Not as much as the left."

"Want to find out exactly how much?"

She smiled. "Go right ahead."

And he stroked and kissed her legs, the places that were scarred and the places that weren't. They were all beautiful, all part of his beloved Tirzah, who had saved herself and saved him.

CHAPTER 24

$\mathcal{T}$he last of Tirzah's self-consciousness vanished, washed away in a tide of love and pleasure and all things good. Pete loved all of her, body and soul. He knew her secrets—he'd literally been inside her mind—and it had only made him love her more. And the way he was kissing and caressing her dispelled any shred of doubt about how much he wanted her.

Just as intensely, just as passionately, she wanted him. She'd longed so desperately to touch and be touched, not just little pats on the shoulder but kisses and caresses over naked skin, and now she could. Her hands roamed over his hard muscles, skating around the edges of the bandages of the wounds he'd gotten protecting her. His dog tags, which were the only thing he was still wearing, were as cool as his skin was hot.

She hated to interrupt the moment, but she had to before it went so far that she forgot everything but the pleasure of the moment. "Hey. I'm not on the pill, so..."

"You don't have to be." Pete pulled his wallet from his back pocket and flipped it open, showing off a strip of condoms. At her raised eyebrow, he said, "Hey, a guy can dream."

"And sometimes dreams come true," she said with a snicker. "Seriously, I'm glad you have them."

"Don't need 'em yet, though."

As Pete had promised, he dipped his head down and tasted her. Tirzah gasped at the jolt of pleasure. She lost herself in the heat of his mouth, the caress of his tongue. He seemed to know exactly where to touch, when to be gentle and when to be rougher, when to go fast and when to go slow. She arched her back and moaned as he brought her to an explosive climax.

Her eyes had closed as her orgasm had shaken her body, but she opened them now. She wanted to see Pete, wanted to watch *him* come. His pupils were huge, his eyes like dark wells. His expression was like nothing she'd ever seen before, a passion so intense it might have been scary, if it hadn't been matched by her own.

"Tirzah," he said, and his voice sounded like a growl. "I want you."

"I want you." Her voice had dropped low too. "Now!"

He reared up above her. He'd already put on the condom, she noticed. Some other time, she'd have wanted to slow down and savor the sight of his naked body. His scars, so like her own. But now, she just couldn't wait. Desire crashed through her body like an avalanche, wiping out everything but pure need.

He filled her with one powerful thrust, and they both gasped, their heads rocking back with the fierce pleasure of it. She had never felt such intensity, such passion, such joy. Such love. And when she looked into Pete's eyes, she saw her own feelings reflected in their depths.

"Come on," she urged, or maybe it was Pete who spoke. She couldn't tell where her body ended and his began. They were melded together as one, two people with a single heart.

And then there was nothing but white-hot ecstasy, and an overwhelming love.

Much as Tirzah could have happily snuggled with Pete for the rest of the day, eventually her post-lovemaking haze faded enough for her to notice that the floor was hard and uncomfortable. She squirmed to get into a better position, and got yanked painfully back by the lock of her hair that was trapped under Pete's shoulder.

"Ow!"

"Sorry." He lifted his arm, releasing her. "Want to take a shower?"

"If you can do me a favor and help me keep my balance while I take it. I don't have a shower chair here."

He gave her that warm, sweet smile that she hoped she'd get to see for the rest of her life. "That's not a favor, that's a treat. Shall I carry you there?"

"Knock yourself out, big guy."

Tirzah knew Pete was strong, but she hadn't realized just how strong until he carried her to the bathroom, set her down on the granite counter by the sink, got the shower to just the right temperature, and then scooped her up and stepped into the shower with her.

Still reclining in his arms, tilted her head back and let the hot water pour over her hair. "Now that's what I call luxury. Who knew a little cabin in the woods would have five-star service?"

"I'll even shampoo your hair, how's that for service?"

"Definitely five-star."

He sat down on the shower floor to do it, with her in his lap. His fingers stroking through her hair was as sensual in its own way as his lovemaking. She could feel how much he loved to touch her.

When he was done, she wriggled around. "I'll do you now."

"Barely enough hair to do," he said, adding quickly, "But don't let that stop you."

"Oh, it won't." She rubbed shampoo into his short hair, massaging his scalp until he moaned with pleasure.

"We *are* a perfect match," she remarked. "You're touch-starved, and I'm handsy."

He chuckled. "I don't know whether you touching me all the time before now kept me sane or nearly drove me crazy. Maybe both."

"Well," she said. "We can touch all we like now."

She'd never tire of that particular look of his, as if he was astonished that the happiness he was feeling was really possible. Though she hoped one day he'd start realizing that it *was* possible, and no longer be surprised.

The hot water soaked his bandages loose. He peeled them off, and Tirzah was glad but startled to find that his wounds had healed to pink scars.

Pete did not seem surprised. "I told you I healed fast. Best thing about being a shifter, by far."

"Yeah, that's pretty great. But don't you like being able to turn into a bear at all? I always used to daydream about being an animal when I was a kid."

"No kidding? I did too. Thing is, I don't really remember being the bear. Maybe I like it while it's happening." A shadow darkened his face. "I hope not. I mean, considering what it does…"

"You ever try turning into the bear on purpose? I mean, when nothing violent or dangerous is going on?"

An involuntary shudder ran through him. "No."

The water had begun to run cool. Pete lifted her, sat her

down on the granite counter, snagged a towel from the rack, and gently dried her off. Then she grabbed her own towel, and did him. He knelt to give her access to his hair, which was short enough to dry instantly. She stroked it, reveling in its velvety texture and her newfound permission to touch him as much as she liked.

Pete handed her a bathrobe while he wrapped a towel around his waist. Then, taking her hands, he said, "I can tell you now why I could always touch you. My cave bear told me while we were driving up here. He says it's because we're mates."

"Mates?" Tirzah repeated blankly. "Oh—that was in the Apex file." She called it back to her memory, and quoted, "'Ability to recognize or bond with their mate has been severed.' But what *is* a mate?"

"It's what shifters call their true love. I already knew about the mate-severing thing. Lamorat told us that when we were squaring off with him at the Apex base. He said it like it was going to completely destroy our morale once we knew." Pete laughed. "We had no idea what it meant, so it fell completely flat. By 'we,' I mean my team. The west coast team all seemed to know. I asked them later, but I kind of blew off what they said. It seemed so..." He shrugged.

"So what?"

"Romantic," Pete said after a pause. "You know, I used to be a pretty romantic guy. I don't mean roses and candles and walks on the beach. I believed in love that lasts forever. I believed if you really love someone, you'd be willing to die for them. Well—I guess I still do believe in all that."

"Me too. At least, I do now."

Pete kissed her. "Anyway, the west coast team said everyone has a true mate, and when they get together, that's the kind of love they'll have. They said shifters recognize their mate the very first time they look in their eyes. They always fall in love at first sight, and they never fall out of love."

Fascinated, Tirzah said, "But you didn't fall in love at first sight with me."

"No," he admitted. "I guess that part really did get turned off." Then, like that made it better, he said, "I did think you were hot at first sight!"

She laughed. "Not the same thing. Though I did too. Hot stuff."

"Even with a faceful of flying kitten?"

"Oh, sure. I could still see the rest of you. Speaking of which, you should probably order some clothes. I've got stuff for me, but, well..."

"What?" Pete said in a mock-injured tone. "You don't think I'd look good in a '50s mini-dress?" Then he said, "No need. I have emergency supplies in my car. Clothes included. I'll get them now, actually. And your chair."

He returned as promised, with her wheelchair, their discarded clothes, and a duffel bag slung over his shoulder. He lifted her into the chair, then put his clothes back on. She watched him dress, unashamed of the enjoyment she took in it, like he was doing a reverse strip-tease.

In a sudden impulse, Tirzah said, "Were you serious when you said my legs were still beautiful?"

"Yeah, of course."

"Follow me." She led him to her bedroom, then said, "Turn your back."

When he turned, she opened the closet. There were all the clothes she hadn't worn in a year, but she knew exactly where a certain dress was. She balanced on her left leg to grab it, then shucked out of the bathrobe, put on fresh underthings, and then wriggled into the dress. She put on shoes, finger-combed her hair, then spun her chair around without looking in the mirror.

"Turn around."

Pete turned and saw her. If she'd ever had any real doubt that he'd meant when he'd said, it melted in the heat in his eyes as they traveled up her body, from her sparkly shoes to her legs to the cherry-red minidress to her cleavage to her face. And then to all of her, all at once.

"You look good enough to eat." He sounded distinctly hungry.

"You can have seconds later." She glanced at herself in the mirror. She *did* look good, if she did say so herself. Legs and all. "Too bad I didn't bring any jewelry. This dress really needs a necklace."

"Here you go." Pete lowered his head, took off his dog tags, and hung them around her neck. They fell right between her breasts, giving her a delicious little chill. The fire in his eyes burned even hotter. "They look good on you."

"Very punk. I like it." She sighed, glancing at the dimming light outside the window. "I should probably get to work now. I just thought you'd enjoy that."

"Oh, I did. Is the dress comfortable to work in, or do you need to change?"

"Eh, work is just moving my chair to the computer room. It's fine. Actually, it's nice to dress up again. I haven't in a while."

"Bring the dress back with you," he suggested. "I'll take you to a restaurant."

"Good idea." She beckoned him over, and they kissed.

Then she headed for the computer room. She'd already booted everything up, and made sure it was in working order. She settled down in front of a laptop and got to work. If Apex had left any online traces beyond that one file, she was going to find them.

Tirzah quickly became absorbed in her work, barely

noticing as the light outside the windows darkened, then turned to full night.

Her fingers flew across the keyboard. And then struck painfully against something hard as a rock. At the same moment, the screen went black. And not just the screen. The entire laptop had gone black, keyboard and all, with a distinctive glassy gleam.

Her laptop had turned to stone.

CHAPTER 25

"*P*ete!"

Tirzah's cry jolted adrenaline through his body, bringing him to instant combat-readiness. He bolted to her computer room, drawing his gun as he went.

Pete realized what had happened even before he saw the strange glassy shine of the computers; his gun was abruptly heavier in his hand, as was the cell phone in his back pocket.

Instinctively, his gaze flashed to the window. A hideous and all too familiar shape was silhouetted against the full moon: membranous wings spread wide, a whiplike tail ending in an arrowhead shape, clawed hands and feet, and distorted features. The gargoyle gave a mocking screech, and flew out of sight.

"Come on!" Pete said.

He grabbed the handles of her chair and pushed it into the living room, then the open kitchen. Batcat and Spike flew after them, meowing frantically. Batcat dove into Tirzah's lap and Spike landed on Pete's shoulder the instant Pete stopped moving. Pete put down the solid stone sculpture in the shape of a gun that he'd been holding and snatched up a chef's knife.

"Was that Jerry?" Tirzah gasped. "I thought he was dead!"

"I don't know. Either Jerry, or some other gargoyle and they can all do that."

Outside, the gargoyle screeched again.

Let me out, his bear growled. *I already killed one stone-wing. I can do it again!*

Pete couldn't tell if the surge of protective fury was his own or his bear's, or if there was any difference.

"I'll go out," he said. "Don't want to break the walls in here."

"Wait, wait!" Tirzah clutched at his arm. "Don't just rush out. We need a plan—"

It was hard for Pete to think over the bear roaring and snarling inside his head. "We *had* a plan. It didn't work. I'll just—"

"Valdez!" The voice came from right outside the front door.

Tirzah's fingers closed convulsively over his arm. Batcat let out a shrill squeak and dove into the front of her dress. Spike did the same with his shirt, becoming a warm spiky lump in the small of Pete's back.

Pete's blood instantly went from boiling with rage to icy cold. It wasn't that the enemy was close. It was that he knew who the enemy was.

"Gorlois," Pete said, as much to Tirzah as to their unseen foe.

"What?" Tirzah gasped. "From Apex?"

"Not Apex," came the voice of Gorlois.

There was a crash as something big slammed into the front door, knocking it off its hinges. Gorlois stepped inside the cabin. He was dressed as Pete remembered from when he'd been held captive, in a long white coat embroidered with strange symbols.

Tirzah gave a yelp and flung her arms protectively over her head, curling her body inward. The dog tags around her neck jingled. Pete stepped protectively in front of her. She must be so scared. It made his heart ache, as well as enraging him.

A contemptuous sneer spread over his enemy's face, and he sniffed, "Ah. The crippled hacker female. She's wise to fear me."

Hot anger rose up in Pete. "Don't you talk about her—"

"Pete, don't talk to him like that!" Tirzah interrupted.

"Heed her," said Gorlois. He spoke to Pete alone, as if Tirzah wasn't even worth looking at. Not that Gorlois could probably see much of her behind Pete's back. "As I was saying, we are not Apex. The council of wizard-scientists infiltrated Apex and took it over. Their experiments and military bases made useful tools for us, no more. We are far, far older than Apex, as well as far, far more powerful... and ambitious."

As Gorlois spoke, Tirzah's hand crept under his shirt, just to the side of where Spike nestled. She began to lightly scratch on his back with a fingernail. At first he didn't know what she was doing, then he recognized the shapes of letters. On his bare skin, she spelled out STALL HIM.

Pete had to swallow past a thickness in his throat before he could speak. Tirzah wasn't terrified after all—or if she was, she wasn't letting it control her. She was planning something, and he bet it was something good.

How had he been lucky enough to find such a brave and quick-witted woman? How had he been lucky enough that she loved him?

"Who *are* you people?" Pete asked, figuring everyone likes to talk about themselves.

"We are ancient," Gorlois said loftily. "More ancient than you can imagine. Or rather, from a time you probably believe was no more than imagination."

"When's that?"

The wizard-scientist's thin lips curled with hatred. "The time that you fools named for our greatest enemy. The time you believe belonged to King Arthur."

"What?" Pete exclaimed, genuinely startled. "You can't be serious. That was thousands of years ago. You're not *that* old."

"Fool!" snapped Gorlois. "Our *order* is that old, not us personally. Did you believe I am the Gorlois of that time?"

Pete, who had never heard of anyone else by that name, shook his head.

"Of course not," Gorlois said. "We took on the names of our predecessors from those times. We fought Arthur then, and we killed him. But it was a Pyrrhic victory. He and his knights had already killed many of us, and his pet magician—"

"*Merlin?*" Pete blurted out.

"Merlin!" Tirzah exclaimed. "You'd really *go to Merlin* to try to scare us? *Merlin, now?* Bullshit! There's no way *Merlin*—"

"Silence, female," said Gorlois. "Your betters are speaking."

Kill him now, snarled the cave bear.

Pete started to take a step forward, but Tirzah yanked him back by the belt. Realizing that she needed him to stay close so they could communicate, he restrained himself.

Kill him, his cave bear roared. *He insulted our mate!*

Not yet, Pete replied. *Our mate has a plan.*

Then, realizing a silence had fallen, Pete said, "Merlin? *The* Merlin?"

"Yes, *him.*" Gorlois looked like he was tempted to spit on the floor. "He cast a spell which unwove ours. We were forced to retreat, and it took us a thousand years and more to regroup. But we have, and we have learned new skills that weren't known then. Once we have our Dark Knights, as Arthur had his bright ones, we will bring about a new age—an age of magic—an age where we will rule!"

Pete was so boggled that he just stood there with his mouth open until Tirzah nudged him and again scratched out, STALL.

"Uh, the Dark Knights," Pete said hastily. "Who are they?"

Gorlois didn't answer immediately. Instead, he gave Pete a look that chilled him. His eyes held a cold, penetrating intelligence, as if he could look right inside Pete's mind and see things even Pete didn't know... and would be happier never knowing.

"The Dark Knights," Gorlois repeated. "Let me tell you about them. But first, let me tell you about *you*."

The wizard's eyes were deep, deep, deep. They were holes in the world. They went down forever. Looking into them made Pete feel like he was falling, but he couldn't seem to look away.

"You've never found your true place in this world, Valdez," Gorlois said. "Isn't that true?"

Looking into those eyes, Pete had to admit to himself that what the wizard was saying was true. Pete *hadn't* ever found his place in the world. He'd tried being a cop, and that hadn't worked out. He'd tried being a Marine, then a bodyguard. But some part of him had always been discontented.

"All that anger within you," Gorlois went on. "Doesn't it feel good when you let it out? Isn't it frustrating to always have to hold back? Think about it."

Pete thought about it. That, too, was true. It was the last thing he'd never admitted to Tirzah. It *did* feel good, on some level, to lose himself in rage. And it *was* frustrating to forever be holding himself back and trying to think before he rushed in.

"I recognize what you truly are," said Gorlois.

Pete no longer saw his face. His eyes seemed to have enlarged to fill his entire field of vision, until the blackness of their pupils swallowed up everything else. Pete stood in total darkness, listening to the wizard's voice.

"You're a weapon. Swear your allegiance to me, and I will wield you. I will let you unleash your true nature. You will be the first of the Dark Knights. You will be what you were always meant to be. You will be Rage."

Pete could feel his own anger, burning within him like a fire that sometimes was banked but never went out. It *would* feel good to let it go, to be nothing but a roaring, raging wildfire. To be the roaring, raging cave bear. There would be no more pain, no more fear or sorrow or worry or guilt or boredom. No more little daily annoyances and frustrations and responsibilities and chores. He'd be free of everything that hemmed him in and tied him down.

He heard a voice, so faint that it was almost inaudible, calling, "Pete! I love you! Come back to me!"

It was Tirzah's voice.

He realized with a shock of horror that he'd forgotten about Tirzah. He'd forgotten about Caro too, and his mother and teammates and friends and pets.

Whatever spell had been cast over him had led him down a path where all he could see was darkness. Sure, if he took the wizard's offer, he'd never again feel pain. But neither would he feel joy or love. He'd be alone forever. Even worse, he wouldn't care.

Some immense pressure was bearing down on him, pushing him to say, "Yes."

With a wrench that felt like it tore every muscle in his body, Pete forced himself to say, "No!"

245

He staggered, suddenly aware of his body and his surroundings. Spike was on his shoulder, alternately biting his ear and howling into it. Tirzah had her arms wrapped around his waist and her face pressed into his side, calling out, "Pete, Pete, come back! I love you! Come back to me!"

"I'm back," he gasped. "I'm back."

The wizard's face twisted in fury. "How dare you defy me! Well, even though you refused my offer, I still have my power. I can drive anyone into a mad rage. I'll make you kill the female you seek to protect!"

Pete, still dizzy, was unable to do anything to stop the wizard before he made a dramatic gesture with one hand.

Nothing happened.

Gorlois stared at him, looking baffled. Then, scowling, he made the same dramatic gesture at Tirzah.

Nothing happened.

"Impossible!" Gorlois exclaimed. "You should be trying to murder each other!"

We are mates, the cave bear rumbled.

"We're mates," Pete said. "Asshole."

The wizard's expression of baffled anger would have been funny under other circumstances. "But we severed that ability! Even at the cost of damaging your ability to use your powers, the mate bond was deemed too powerful to allow."

"Oh, so *that's* what was wrong with Pete's power?" Tirzah put in. Her voice had a familiar tone, the delighted triumph of figuring something out. He loved that she could still be thrilled at discovery, even now when their lives were on the line. "You tried to make it impossible for him to bond with his mate, and that screwed him up in general?"

The wizard started to nod, then scowled. "Why am I even talking to you two? You're useless to me now, and a danger to boot!"

Under Pete's shirt, Tirzah scratched, BEAR. NOW.

He heard wheels skidding over the floor as she threw her chair backwards. He trusted her to have a plan. And at last, he trusted himself and he trusted his bear.

As he shifted, Pete realized that it was the first time he'd ever done it deliberately. All the previous times, it had happened because he'd gotten so angry that it had just... happened. But this time, though anger burned hot within him, he became the bear because it was what he chose to do.

And this time, he didn't lose himself.

He roared, loud enough to shake the rafters, and lunged at the startled wizard. Pete raised a huge paw, intending to swat his enemy right out the door.

Before Pete's bear, which was big and strong but not fast, could react, Gorlois darted back. Standing framed in the doorway, the wizard reached beneath his cloak. He pulled out a gun.

In his cave bear form, Pete didn't feel pain. All he felt was a hard impact as the bullet struck him square in the chest.

CHAPTER 26

*T*irzah heard the gunshot, and saw that the wizard had fired at point-blank range. It seemed impossible for him to have missed. But for a wild moment of desperate hope, she was able to imagine that he had. Pete didn't fall, nor did she see any blood on his shaggy fur.

He roared, a terrifying sound, and his front feet came down so hard on the floor that the whole cabin shook. Gorlois turned and bolted outside, his coat streaming behind him.

Once he was outside the house, he turned into an immense dinosaur, like a pterodactyl but far bigger.

A pteranodon, Tirzah thought dazedly.

The dinosaur that had been Gorlois opened his great beak, let out a mocking screech, and took to the skies. There he was joined by the gargoyle. The two flying monsters wheeled and screamed in the air, seeming to mock Tirzah and Pete.

"Pete!" Tirzah called.

The cave bear turned, his heavy head swinging, and nudged her. Her gaze swept the floor beneath him. Blood

248

was dripping down from his chest and starting to pool on the floor.

"Pete... Oh, Pete..." She remembered him saying that he couldn't feel pain when he was a bear, and said, "You're hit."

The bear gave her chair a hard nudge, shoving it away from the door and farther into the cabin. She didn't want to make him work when he was wounded, so she moved in the direction he'd pushed her, until she heard him make a rumbling noise. She stopped. The rope ladder to the attic dangled in front of her.

"Do you want me to climb it?" she asked. "But I can't...*You* can't..."

Spike flew up into the attic. A moment later, his head appeared at the trap door, meowing urgently.

The cave bear gave her another nudge, not forceful enough to move her chair. His intent was clear: *go up.*

Tirzah twisted around and threw her arms around his shaggy neck. "Pete, there's no way I can get up that! And even if I could, I'm not leaving you!"

The cave bear vanished, and Pete stood in its place. He staggered, then clutched at her chair for support. His skin had paled to a frightening ashen color, and a blood stain was rapidly spreading across his shirt.

"Oh, Pete," Tirzah whispered.

He shook his head, wincing. "There's no time. We have to get up into the attic. It's the safest place."

Tirzah looked up at the flimsy ladder, the terrifying height. She had no use of one leg—she'd fall for sure! The thought of that fall made her almost as sick with terror as the sight of Pete's red-stained shirt. "I can't—"

He didn't raise his voice, but the intensity in it felt like a physical push. "You *can*. You're stronger than you think. You've been moving that chair around all year."

"But—"

"If you really can't, I'll carry you."

That got her going. There was no way she was going to burden him with her weight when he was wounded—he'd fall and break his neck! She grabbed on to the rungs, stood up on her left leg, and began to climb.

If it wasn't for the knowledge that every second she wasted was a second Pete remained in danger, she'd never have managed it. In order to move her legs up a rung, she was forced to support her entire weight with her arms and lift her left leg, with her right trailing as a dead weight that did nothing but threaten to tangle in the rungs. Her hands and arms burned with effort.

"You can do it," Pete said, his voice both confident and comforting. "I'm right behind you."

She looked down. He was standing and holding tight to the rung beneath her. He looked paler than ever, and she could hear his ragged breathing.

"Don't talk," she said. It was obviously costing him too much energy. "I can do this."

Looking down was making her dizzy, so she closed her eyes. It came as a shock when her blindly reaching hand touched the wooden floor. She braced her hands on the floor and dragged herself up, wriggling forward until she was out of Pete's way. Lying on her belly, she watched the trap door anxiously until he appeared in it. He stopped, gathering his energy, and hauled himself in. She grabbed his arm and helped pull him up. A moment later, they both lay on the floor, gasping for breath.

Tirzah moved first, yanking the rope ladder and the pull cord in and slamming the trap door shut. They were left in silence and near-darkness. There was a small window in the attic—thankfully small, Tirzah thought, no flying monsters would be able to get in that way—but the only light it provided was a square of moonlight on the floor. She could see nothing but the vague shapes of furniture.

She felt around until she found the light switch and flipped it. A single bulb illuminated Pete sprawled on the floor, eyes closed. Spike crouched beside him, nuzzling his cheek and meowing anxiously.

Tirzah longed to go to him immediately, but she had to ensure his safety first. She looked desperately around at the beat-up old furniture that cluttered the attic. It was all either too heavy for her to move, or too light to block the trap door. Then she spotted an old bookcase. She couldn't lift it, but she didn't need to. Tirzah gave it a hard shove, and it tipped over with a tremendous crash, falling directly on top of the trap door.

She crawled over to an old trunk and opened it. To her annoyance, it was the one with Christmas tree ornaments. But the second one was full of sheets and quilts. They were holey and smelled like mothballs, but she was immensely grateful for both the laziness of the first owner of the cabin and her own in never getting around to throwing them away.

She shoved the lot over to where Pete lay, then crouched beside him. He didn't stir, but turned into her hand when she stroked his soft hair and sweat-dampened cheeks. His skin was cool to the touch, drained of its usual warmth.

"Pete? You awake?"

Without opening his eyes, he mumbled, "Yeah. Jus' tired."

"Okay. I'm going to take off your shirt, all right?"

He made a sound that she took for assent. She tore off his shirt so she wouldn't hurt him taking it off, then coaxed him to roll on to his side. There was a bullet wound in his chest and another in his back, neither bleeding much. She tore up the sheet into strips and bandaged them.

"I put a quilt down for you to lie on. Just roll over, okay?"

He rolled over on to the quilt, and she covered him with another. He reached out for her, and she pulled him into her lap and put her arms around him. Pete lay still except for the steady rise and fall of his chest. Spike curled up at his side.

Now that she had time to sit still and think, the terror she had pushed aside crashed over her. Their enemies wouldn't be able to get into the attic easily—as humans, they wouldn't be able to reach the attic at all, and as flying creatures, they couldn't fit through either the window or the trap door. But neither barrier would hold them off forever. And once they got in, neither Tirzah nor Pete could fight them.

But even the knowledge that they had only bought themselves some time faded before her fear for Pete. Even with his shifter healing, he was badly wounded and had to be in need of actual medical attention. Tirzah was sure a clock was ticking on that, and not knowing how long he had only made it worse.

His hand closed around hers, startling her. She looked down, and saw that his eyes were open.

"Hey, Pete," she said softly. "How're you doing?"

"Been better."

The sound of heavy footsteps below sent a jolt of adrenaline through her body. Pete too started, his muscles tensing.

"Valdez!" It was Gorlois. "It's not too late. I'm giving you some time to consider my offer."

"Take your job and shove it," Pete muttered. But it was either too soft for Gorlois to hear, or he chose to ignore it.

"Lie there and slowly bleed to death if you like," the wizard went on. "Or surrender, and take my offer. I'll be generous, and throw in the life of that crippled female. If she surrenders the file and all its copies, she can live."

Neither Pete nor Tirzah replied.

"Think about it," Gorlois said. "I can remove you both

from your filthy little crawl space any time I like. But if you make me do it rather than coming out of your own accord, I will show no mercy."

There was a long silence, and then the footsteps retreated.

Wincing, Pete tried to pull himself up. She supported him until he'd managed to sit leaning back against her chest. Tirzah followed his gaze as he scanned the attic. "You made a barricade. Good work. That... that pterodactyl-thing..."

"Pteranodon," Tirzah said absent-mindedly. "They're like pterodactyls, but way bigger."

Pete managed a smile. "Trust you to know. Well, it'll have a hell of a time trying to get in, once he gets bored with waiting for us to surrender."

"Yeah, but it's just buying time."

"That's all we need. If I can just rest an hour or so, my shifter healing will kick in and I'll be able to fight again."

"Really?" Tirzah wasn't sure if he knew something she didn't or if that was just Pete being Pete.

"Well—hopefully."

So, just Pete being Pete. "Oh."

He squeezed her hand. "Don't give up now. We made it this far."

"Who said anything about giving up? If they break in and you can't fight, I'll throw old Christmas tree ornaments at them. If I time it just right, maybe I can toss one right down their gullet and choke them."

"You do that." He smiled, but she could hear the pain and exhaustion in his voice. Before she could say anything more, his eyes closed, and his body relaxed as he sank into sleep.

She eased him back down with his head in her lap, and pulled the quilt back over him. He didn't stir.

Tirzah too was exhausted, but she didn't dare sleep. It wasn't as if she could fight off their enemies, but she felt like she had to guard him. She forced her burning eyes to stay open and her aching body to stay upright as she sat stroking his hair and holding his hand, and listening to their enemies screeching outside.

CHAPTER 27

"*D*iscussion topic!" Caro announced as Merlin began setting takeout hamburgers around the table in the boardroom. She pointed to his *Harry Potter* shirt. "Do you all agree that the velociraptor patronus is blue?"

"Yes," said Roland, beginning to smile.

"Blue as a blueberry," said Merlin.

Ransom, who looked like he'd been forced to the table at gunpoint, gave a cautious nod.

"Are we all seeing the same color?" Caro asked. "Or are we all seeing different colors, but calling them all 'blue?' Support your reasoning."

"Yes, of course we're all seeing the same color," said Roland. "If we weren't, we wouldn't all call it by the same name."

For the first time, Ransom looked interested. "The ancient Greeks wrote about the 'wine-dark sea.' What did they see? No wine is the color of the ocean."

Merlin chimed in, "And in Japanese, 'ao' means 'blue or green.' So if someone says a coat is 'ao,' you don't know if they mean blue or green or blue-green."

"But they're still seeing the same color, regardless of what they call it," Roland said.

"Not necessarily," said Ransom. "They might be colorblind."

"Or they might see more colors than normal!" Merlin said. "Like when I—"

Ransom reached for the fries. His elbow hit Merlin's soda and overturned it into his lap. Merlin leaped up with a yelp.

"Oops," Ransom said, not sounding particularly sorry.

"Don't worry about it," Merlin said, mopping his chair and clothes with a wad of paper towels.

"Caro?" Roland asked. "Are we all seeing the same blue, or not?"

Since Merlin and Ransom had staked out the "no" position, Caro sided with Roland. "Yes, we are. How can we know that some people are colorblind? Because in fact, we *can* determine that they're not seeing the same colors as the rest of us! Therefore, unless we're colorblind, we're all seeing the same colors."

"You didn't specify that you're leaving colorblind people out," Merlin said.

"What if everyone else in the world is seeing the color you see as red, but they're calling it blue?" Ransom asked.

As Caro responded to those valid points, she heaved an inward sigh of relief. Finally, she'd managed to get Ransom and Roland to talk to her like she was a person, rather than a representative of that alien race of non-adults (Ransom) or someone who had to be protected like she was made of glass (Roland). That made the dinner about 1000% less awkward.

Though she did wish she knew what Merlin had been about to say before Ransom had interrupted him by deliberately knocking over his soda. However nice they were all being, they were obviously hiding something. Even Merlin, who *seemed* forthcoming, would distract her with stories about ponies or circuses or circus ponies whenever she asked about anything he didn't want to talk about it. He was as cagey as the rest of them, just better at hiding it.

As soon as dinner was finished, Caro stood up. "Thanks. I think I'll go read and then go to bed. Good night! Have sweet dreams of blue, which as we now know is definitely the same color for all of us. Unless you're colorblind."

They all wished her good night.

"Call if you need anything," Roland said. "Any time."

"I'll be fine," Caro said. "I'm thirteen, not seven."

"Even thirty-year-olds sometimes wake up in the middle of the night and want a drink of water or a snack or some company," Merlin pointed out. "Anyway, we'll be around."

Caro went to her rooms, bolted the door, and immediately headed for the bathroom, where she had left Moonbow after releasing him from the jewelry box she'd hurriedly repurposed as a tiny flying pony carrier. She'd felt bad about punching holes in it, but not *that* bad. What was an inanimate object, however much sentimental value it had, compared to her living winged stallion?

She opened the door and smiled to see him peacefully munching on the grass clippings she'd left in the bathtub. He looked up at her and nickered softly, and she scratched behind his ears until he returned to grazing.

Restless, she wandered back into the bedroom. Despite the assurances she'd given Dad's teammates, it *was* strange being in this room by herself (well, except for Moonbow). It felt kind of like being alone in a hotel, though of course she'd never done that either. Caro flopped down on the bed and gazed at the ceiling. She'd wanted so much to know more about Dad and his work, but now that she'd met his teammates and his client and was even staying at his office, she felt like she knew *less* than before, not more.

Secrets! She felt suffocated by secrets.

Moonbow flew out, his opalescent tail and mane streaming, and landed on her bed. Stroking him, she murmured, "Except for you. I *love* you."

Though she didn't love having to keep him secret. She'd almost had a heart attack when Dad had tried to hustle her out the door without Moonbow.

She wished she hadn't yelled at Dad when he'd left. He was going to do something dangerous, obviously, and she hadn't even said good-bye.

At least he'd hugged her that one time in the garage without stiffening up like he wanted to get away from her. That had been more like her old Dad...

...the Dad from when she'd been a little kid. From when she'd been Lina.

If she'd been younger, it would have made sense for Dad to treat her like a kid who needed to be protected from everything, even knowledge. If she'd been older, maybe he'd trust her judgment more.

"Thirteen is the worst age," she sighed to Moonbow.

Moonbow's ears pricked forward, and he trotted to the edge of the bed. His elegant neck stretched out as he looked up at the big window, then he glanced back at her. The moon had risen, and hung in the night sky like a pearl.

Caro smiled ruefully. "*You* can go flying if you like. But I can't come with you. If I get stuck outside when the moon sets, there's no way I'd ever be able to explain it."

She got up and went to the window. Turning back, she called to Moonbow, "Well? Want to go?"

Moonbow gave an eager whinny. Smiling, Caro turned to open the window.

Some flying *thing* smacked into the screen.

Caro leaped back with a strangled gasp, clapping her hand over her mouth to stifle a scream. Her heart was hammering so loudly that she could hear nothing else.

The thing clinging to her window flapped its wings and pressed its whiskered face into the screen. It wasn't a *thing*, it was a kitten. A tiny, adorable kitten with wings, clutching a silver necklace in its mouth.

Caro's adrenaline rush subsided so fast it left her dizzy. She felt her lips part in a half-disbelieving, half-delighted smile. A flying kitten! Was it a friend of Moonbow who had come to visit him? Or had she somehow become known as a rescuer of lost magical creatures?

Moonbow flew up and tapped on the glass with one hoof. It rang sharply, like a wind chime.

Caro opened the window, and the kitten flew inside. Once it was in the light, she could see that it was pure black and very fluffy, wings included. It landed on her shoulder. She reached up to pet it, and it released the necklace it held in its mouth. Cold metal fell into Caro's outstretched palm with an oddly familiar jingle. She lifted the chain, letting the pendants dangle before her eyes.

They were her father's dog tags.

CHAPTER 28

*P*ete slept without dreams, as deeply and heavily as if his own shifter healing was grabbing him by the scruff of the neck and yanking him in every time he closed his eyes. He woke several times, always when their enemies scraped or banged against the trap door or attic. But they always failed to get in, then retreated, presumably to figure out a new approach.

Every time he woke, Tirzah was holding him. It felt to him as if he was being healed less by rest and his own power than by the touch of her skin and the force of her love. She looked exhausted, with black smudges under her bloodshot eyes, but she always refused his suggestion that she get some sleep herself.

He'd stood guard over wounded Marines, and now she was standing guard over him, unarmed yet undaunted. His heart felt like it would burst with love for her.

Next time I wake up, he thought as he slid back into sleep. *Next time, I'll be able to protect her...*

He was shocked out of sleep by the sound of shattering glass. Pete sat bolt upright, instinctively reaching for a weapon he didn't have. The snapping beak of the flying dinosaur, sharp as a razor and long as a baseball bat, had stabbed through the window and into the attic itself.

Tirzah screamed. Pete grabbed her and they both scrambled backwards, though they were already out of reach of the beak. They fetched up against the opposite wall.

Spike, who had been curled up next to him, took to the air with a yowl and shot a fusillade of cactus spines at the beak. They all bounced off. The beak opened menacingly, displaying a gaping red maw, then clacked together with a sound like a gunshot.

Then it withdrew. Pete saw the pteranodon flying away, its immense wings beating heavily. Cold air blew in through the shattered window. The glass on the floor glinted in the moonlight. Outside the window, Pete could see the full moon, and the black silhouettes of the pteranodon and the gargoyle as they flew across it, screeching.

"I should block that." He stood up, ducking to not hit his head on the ceiling, and took a step toward an old dresser.

Dizziness swept over him. His knees hit the floor hard enough to make his teeth click together. He would have fallen over entirely if Tirzah hadn't grabbed him.

"Goddammit." He felt weak and cold, and involuntary shivers shook his body. His chest hurt so badly that it was hard to catch his breath. But the worst part was the frustration of being unable to protect Tirzah when she needed him.

"Take it easy," she said. "It can't get in."

The window was suddenly filled with a giant reptilian eye, yellow and cold. Both Pete and Tirzah jumped.

Pete nudged Spike. The cactus kitten puffed up, but the eye vanished just as he fired his spines. It was replaced by a set of huge claws gripping the windowsill. The spines also bounced off the thick scaly skin of the flying dinosaur's foot.

Tirzah's curly hair brushed Pete's face as she put her

mouth to his ear and whispered, "What do you think he's doing?"

Pete started to shrug when a tremendous bang and impact rocked the attic. Tirzah jumped, and Pete held her tight. Another bang and impact. And another.

The tip of the pteranodon's beak broke into the thick log walls of the attic. Like some monstrous woodpecker, it was using the window to perch and was pecking its way in.

Pete's nerves went ice-cold with fear and anger.

Kill it, his cave bear roared. *Protect our mate!*

Bang! An entire log fell away, pecked through at both ends and pried out of the wall by those huge claws.

Tirzah tugged at his arm, pointing to the trap door: *should we go down?*

Pete forced himself to stop and think before leaping into action. If they went back down, he could fend off the pteranodon as a cave bear, as it was too big to evade him within the house. But Gorlois could easily turn back into a man and shoot him—or worse, shoot Tirzah. But if they stayed in the attic...

Another log fell out of the wall. Five more minutes, and the entire attic would be open to the sky.

Pete turned to Tirzah and shook his head. Putting his mouth up against her ear, he whispered, "Wait. Once he breaks a big enough hole in the attic and sticks his head in, I'll become a bear and break his skinny neck."

It was a terrifying gamble to take. He'd have just one shot to evade the pteranodon's beak, and he already knew the creature was faster than he was—and that was before he'd been wounded.

Another log fell away.

Pete jerked his thumb at the corner of the attic, the farthest from where the pteranodon was steadily pecking through the wall. Tirzah pressed a kiss on his mouth, then scooted into the corner and huddled there, where she'd be out of the way of the bear.

The heat of her lips lingered on his, long after she was gone. She didn't know it, but it was almost certainly the last kiss they'd ever share.

The systematic way Gorlois was going about breaking through the wall made Pete certain that he wouldn't be stupid enough to just stick his head in. No, he'd wait till enough of the wall was gone that he could get his whole body in. Then he could use both beak and claws, or sweep them out with his great wings. And Pete wasn't strong enough yet for a real fight. He could make one move, and then he'd collapse. So he had to make that one move count.

His sole advantage was the cave bear's massive weight. If he leaped at the pteranodon, his momentum would knock them both right through the hole in the wall. If Pete grabbed the beast and hung on, they'd crash into the ground together. The fall would most likely kill them both. But at the very least, it would break the pteranodon's wings. And then Tirzah would have a chance to escape.

The hole in the wall was now big enough for him to see his monstrous enemy crouching in it, blocking almost all of the night sky. One more log, and Gorlois would make his move; one more log, and Pete would too.

The last log fell away. Pete readied himself to shift.

A voice he'd thought he'd never hear again broke the tense silence. "Get away from my dad, you *thing!*"

"Caro!?" Pete called incredulously.

He was answered with, of all unlikely sounds, a fierce neigh. And then the flapping of wings, and a sharp thud like a baseball bat whacking a slab of meat.

The pteranodon screeched and jerked like it had been goosed. Then, hissing, it launched itself backward out of the huge hole in the wall.

Through the hole, which was more like a missing wall, he saw the star-spangled night sky and a full moon. Between the moon and stars, he could see almost as easily as if it was day.

His daughter Caro was in the sky, riding a white horse with feathered wings. Batcat clung to her shoulder for dear life. Her long black hair streamed behind her as the flying horse swooped and dove, harrying the pteranodon with fierce kicks and bites. It was far smaller than the dinosaur, but also far, far faster, easily evading its beak and claws. Its hooves struck the beast again and again, making it screech in pain and rage.

The gargoyle circled around the fight, apparently too nervous of getting within range of the hooves to do anything.

Pete could do nothing but sit and stare, torn between astonishment, fear for his daughter, and pride in her. He had no idea how she'd found him or where the winged horse had come from, but she was clearly in her element, fearlessly riding her flying steed to his defense.

Tirzah came up beside him. "What the…?"

Pete shook his head. "Your guess is as good as mine."

He again looked around the attic for some weapon, and again found none. But there was no need. Urged on by Caro, the flying horse arrowed in and kicked the pteranodon right in the side of its hideous face. With an anguished shriek, the flying monster turned and fled, its leathery wings flapping with all its might. The gargoyle followed after. A moment later, both had vanished from view.

Batcat left Caro's shoulder and flew to Tirzah's. She pushed her face into Tirzah's neck and purred loudly. The horse flew up to the attic and hovered. Pete and Tirzah scrambled aside to give it room. It landed with a sharp click of its hooves against the floor.

Caro slid off its back and threw herself into Pete's arms. He held her as tight as he ever had in his life. She was the infant he'd held in his hands and couldn't give up, the toddler he'd swung over his head while she'd laughed with glee, the child he'd read to at bedtime, and the tempestuous, brave, stubborn, whip-smart teenager she was now. She was all of them at once in his eyes, the daughter he loved more than life itself.

Caro broke off the hug at last, then gave him a closer look. "Hey! Those aren't the same bandages you had at our house... are they?"

In the instant it took his mind to automatically weigh whether he should say they were or say he couldn't talk about it, he realized how ridiculous that was. Pete had meant well in trying to protect her with ignorance, but that was how you treated a child. His little girl had grown up. She wasn't an adult yet, but she wasn't a child either. She'd just protected *him!*

"No," Pete said. "I was shot."

Caro gasped, her hands tightening on his arm. "Oh, my God!"

"He'll be fine," Tirzah said. She shot Pete a *look.*

"I will." Pete gave Caro a pat on the shoulder. "Uh, I know because I can heal faster and better than I could before..."

"Before what?" Caro asked suspiciously.

"Before I got kidnapped on my last tour of duty by the thing you just fought, who experimented on me and gave me the ability to turn into a cave bear," Pete said, all in one breath.

Caro stared at him, incredulous and then indignant. "You can turn into a bear!? And you didn't tell me?!"

"For your own protection, yes."

Caro rolled her eyes dramatically. "How does not telling me anything protect me? You didn't tell me any of that, and I still just fought a pteranodon!"

"Well..."

Spike flew down from wherever he'd gone. He landed on Pete's shoulder, then stretched out his neck and gave Caro a cautious sniff.

"You have a flying kitten?!" Caro demanded. "You have a flying kitten and you didn't tell me?!"

"You had a flying horse, and you didn't tell me," Pete pointed out.

"Because you'd have made me give him to the government!"

"No, I wouldn't. Why would I do that?"

"Because you think authority figures always know best!" Caro proclaimed.

"No, I—"

Tirzah cleared her throat. "Guys, can we carry on this conversation later? We should get out of here. I don't know if the pteranodon and the gargoyle are gone for good."

Caro blinked at her, having clearly only just registered her presence. "Hey! Is that *your* flying kitten?"

"Yeah, I gave her Pete's dog tags and sent her to find Merlin," Tirzah said. "I did it behind Pete's back—literally."

"So that's why you needed me to stall," Pete said. He noticed for the first time that Caro was now wearing his dog tags.

"Wait, you didn't know?" Tirzah asked him. "Pete, I told you exactly what I'd done!"

"When?"

"In the attic, when… Oh. You were pretty out of it. I guess you don't remember. You said, 'Sounds good,' and went back to sleep."

That rang a faint bell. "Tirzah, I had no idea what you were saying. I meant the sound of your voice."

Tirzah smiled. "Honestly, I had no idea sending Batcat would work. I was just crossing my fingers she'd understand what I wanted. And remember the way back. And know

Merlin's name. I thought it was a great piece of luck when Gorlois actually mentioned Merlin himself, because that gave me an excuse to repeat his name. Only I guess Batcat went to Caro instead."

Caro nodded. "She appeared at my window with Dad's dog tags! Then she led us all the way back here."

"Smart kitty." Tirzah tickled Batcat, who arched her back and purred.

Caro took off the dog tags. Pete bent his head, and she put them back around his neck.

"So is Merlin a cave bear too?" Caro asked. "Are they all cave bears? No wonder they were acting so weird around me!"

"Er... Yeah, they're all shifters," Tirzah said. "I'll explain more later, but we really need to get out of here."

Caro glanced around. "How did you get up here in the first place? Oh, sorry, that was rude... right?"

"It's fine, Caro. I climbed a rope ladder. But..." Tirzah glanced at Pete. He wanted to say he could climb down just fine, but he wasn't altogether certain of that. Still, it wasn't as if there was another choice.

"Moonbow can take you both down," Caro said, quickly adding, "One at a time."

She chirruped to her flying horse and he obediently settled down to the floor. Tirzah and Pete looked at each other.

"I don't know about you, but I'm *dying* to ride the flying horsie," Tirzah said. She scooted over to him, clambered atop his back, and threw her arms around his neck. "Hi-yo Silver, away!"

The horse turned his head and stared at her. Pete didn't know if he was reading in expressions that weren't there, but the horse seemed to be thinking, *Really?*

Caro chirruped to him. "Take her down, Moonbow. Then come back up!"

The horse stood, spread its wings, and jumped out of the attic. Tirzah let out a strangled scream. Pete guessed that she'd been so excited by the thought of "flying horsie" that she'd forgotten that it would involve a height. But Moonbow landed lightly outside, then sat down. Tirzah slithered off, then looked up and gave a slightly shaky thumbs-up to Pete.

Caro whistled, and Moonbow flew back up, this time sitting down beside Pete. He still felt dizzy, and the surreal knowledge that he was about to ride on his daughter's flying horse didn't help. He got on and held tight. There was a sudden lurch, and then he was in the air. If he'd felt better physically, it would have been exhilarating. In a way, it still was.

And then Moonbow landed and sat down. Tirzah had to help Pete off. Even the small effort of holding on tight for thirty seconds had made black spots dance before his eyes. Spike jumped into his lap and nuzzled him.

"Caro!" Tirzah called. "I left my wheelchair in the kitchen. Can you get it for me, please?"

"Sure!" Caro shouted from the attic. Moonbow flew up and brought her down to the front of the house, and Caro ran inside.

"Thanks," Pete said quietly to Tirzah. "I'm not lying to her anymore. But I'd rather not scare her if I can help it."

"I figured," Tirzah said, also quietly. "Hey—that horse obviously can't carry three, so..."

Pete glanced at Moonbow, who stood looking up at the sky. He followed the horse's gaze, uneasily hoping it didn't know something he didn't. But there were no flying monsters in sight, only the bright stars and the last sliver of the setting moon.

Reluctantly, Pete said, "It could maybe take you and Caro."

Tirzah just rolled her eyes and didn't dignify that with a direct response. Instead, she said, "Do you think you can drive?"

Pete had been asking himself that exact question. "If you'd asked me before I rode that horse, I'd have said sure. But now that I have, I'm worried I might pass out over the wheel."

Tirzah shuddered, then swallowed. She took a deep breath, then lifted her head high. "I'll drive."

"But—"

"If you help me."

"Oh!" He nodded, relieved that she wouldn't have to try to force herself through terror and that he could help. "Yeah, of course. Caro can ride with us, and her flying horse can follow and guard the car." He chuckled. "There's a sentence I never imagined myself saying. I wonder how she found it. And how long she's had it."

"It can't have been long," Tirzah pointed out. "It's not like she could've hid him in her room, like a flying kitten."

Pete chuckled. "Yeah, no. Well, Caro won't have to bust out any of her conversation topics for the car ride back. We'll have plenty to talk—"

Moonbow stamped his hoof and whinnied. The sky darkened as the moon set. And, as Pete watched in astonishment, the winged horse shimmered, then shrank to the size of a kitten.

Caro came out, pushing Tirzah's wheelchair. "Sorry I took so long! The whole place was trashed. I had to get it out from under a sofa, can you believe—"

She came to a sudden halt, staring at Moonbow. Then she looked up at the moonless sky. In a small voice, she said, "Uh-oh. I was hoping we'd have more time."

Moonbow leaped into the air and landed on the hand rest of the wheelchair. Caro petted him with a finger.

"He's only big by moonlight?" Tirzah asked.

"Yeah."

"Don't worry about it," Pete said. "We have a—"

Some sixth sense honed by years of experience in combat made the back of his neck prickle. He looked around, then up. There was no sound, no shape, only a sense of movement: something black as the sky, black as obsidian, plummeting down like a hawk toward his Caro.

CHAPTER 29

irzah had never seen Pete move so fast. One second he was sitting beside her, the next he'd leaped to his feet and lunged forward. In the blink of an eye, he was the cave bear, rearing up and striking at the gargoyle plummeting toward his daughter.

There was a shattering crash. Fragments of something hard rained down all around Tirzah, making her duck and cover her face. It was only when she saw their familiar glassy sheen that she realized what had happened.

It had all happened so suddenly that neither Tirzah nor Caro had time to even scream. By the time the cave bear's front paws hit the earth again, it was all over.

Caro stared at the huge bear standing beside her. "Dad?"

There was no fear in her voice or expression, only amazement. She reached out a hand and buried it in the bear's shaggy fur.

And then Pete stood swaying with Caro's hand on his shoulder. But only for a moment. The next second, he dropped to his knees with a thud.

"Dad!" Caro exclaimed. "Are you all right?"

Tirzah scrambled toward them, half-crawling, half dragging herself by her arms. "Pete!"

He was pale and sweating, his eyes unfocused. Tirzah could barely catch his mutter of "Don't be scared."

Tirzah and Caro exchanged what Tirzah suspected were identical looks of worry and exasperation.

"Pete, lie down before you pass out," Tirzah said.

"But... I have to..." His voice trailed off into an inaudible mumble as his eyes closed. Tirzah caught him as he collapsed and laid him down on the ground.

Caro's eyes were wide and frightened. "Is he going to be all right?"

For the first time, Tirzah understood Pete's impulse to protect Caro by hiding things from her: she too had the impulse to make up something, anything to make the girl feel better.

Instead, she took Caro's hand and told her the truth. "Listen, Caro, I'm worried about him too. But I think he's going to be fine. See these?" Tirzah indicated the pink scars on Pete's chest. "They look like he got those a month ago, right? They're from the day before yesterday. He really does heal fast. He just wore himself out fighting when he was already hurt."

"Oh." Caro looked relieved. "But... What even happened?"

"The gargoyle went for you—"

"Yeah, I saw that. But... it turned into stone?"

Tirzah nodded.

Caro looked at the fragments of obsidian. "Is it dead?"

"I'm not sure. But even if it's not, I'm pretty sure it's down for the count." Tirzah levered herself into her wheelchair. "Can you stay with your dad? I'll go pull up the car."

"Sure."

Tirzah took the car keys from Pete's pocket and headed for the car. Her commitment to the truth had gone as far as she intended it to go: she'd answer any questions Caro asked, but she wasn't going to volunteer the information that she had a massive phobia about driving twisty mountain roads in general, and especially this specific one that had given her the phobia after she'd nearly been killed driving it, and she'd only agreed to drive it because Pete had said he'd use the Shoulder of Strength on her only that sure wasn't happening now, and oh by the way she'd had a panic attack just being a passenger on the way up.

She reached the car, opened it, stuck her chair in the trunk, and hopped to the driver's side. Trying very hard not to think about what she was doing, she adjusted the seat and mirrors, then crossed her ankles to touch her left foot to the gas pedal.

The instant her hands closed around the steering wheel, panic threatened to engulf her.

What if I have a panic attack and crash the car and get us all killed?

What if I hit black ice and the car goes off the road?

I can't do this.

Her hands felt icy. Her heart was pounding. She couldn't catch her breath.

Tirzah closed her eyes and recalled Pete's voice, deep and comforting and calm, talking her through the panic attack she'd had on the way up. She remembered the warmth of his hand in hers.

He needs me, she thought. *Caro needs me. And that's all there is to it.*

She opened her eyes, started the car, and carefully drove to where Caro sat with Pete. The car moved jerkily, hard to control with her legs crossed and her left foot on the pedal— and a weakened left foot, at that. She brought it to a some- what abrupt stop with the back seat door next to Pete.

Tirzah hopped out and helped Caro wrestle Pete into the

back seat. He woke up just enough to help them, though he seemed half-asleep and Tirzah doubted he'd remember it later, and closed his eyes again as soon as his head touched the seat. The best they could do was get him partially lying down with his legs on the floor and clip all three seatbelts around him. Spike curled up under his chin.

Tirzah touched Pete's cheek, but he was so deep in sleep that he didn't respond. His skin was cool and damp, his stubble just starting to come in and roughen his cheek. Reluctantly, she returned to the driver's seat. Batcat jumped into her lap.

Caro got in the passenger seat and whistled for Moonbow. The flying horse settled into her lap.

"Oh!" Tirzah's tension broke as she burst out laughing. "I knew he looked familiar! He was pretending to be a toy!"

As Tirzah started the car and began to drive, Caro laughed too. "Yeah, I had him hidden in my room. And then in my jewelry box."

"That was what the grass clippings were for!"

"Right!"

"Pete and I were hiding Spike and Batcat at the same time! Pete actually had them stuffed in his pillowcase when you came in and he said he was going to throw up!"

As they traded stories of what they'd been doing and how they'd acquired their magical pets, the car was filled with unexpected laughter. Tirzah didn't forget her fear, either for driving or for Pete, but it became more of a background anxiety than a presence so overwhelming that it threatened to swallow her whole.

The stars went out as the black sky brightened to the pale gray before dawn. Caro kept twisting around to check on Pete, since Tirzah didn't dare take her eyes off the road.

"How is he?" Tirzah asked.

"Still asleep." Caro rubbed her jaw in a gesture that Tirzah recognized: it was one she'd seen Pete do. "You know what's even weirder than finding out that Dad can turn into a cave bear? Being able to help out when something's going on, instead of Dad refusing to even tell me what's going on."

Tirzah shot a quick glance at Caro to see if she was being sarcastic, but she looked completely serious. "You really do like that better, huh?"

"Yeah, I do. I get that there's adult stuff I shouldn't be involved in, like... uh... rent and insurance and stuff." Caro's voice began to tremble, as if she was on the verge of tears. "But Dad was acting so weird when he came back this time, and he wouldn't tell me anything, and I thought he didn't like me anymore and he didn't want to say so!"

"Caro." The voice came from the back seat. Tirzah's gaze flicked to the rear view mirror, where she saw Pete pushing himself to a sitting position. "Mija. I love you. That stuff was all me. It was..." He stopped to catch his breath. "Cave bear stuff. I'll explain later. It had nothing to do with you."

"Yeah, but I didn't know that!"

"You're really okay with all... this?" He made a vague gesture, encompassing himself and the flying pets.

Caro beamed. There was no mistaking the sincerity in her voice as she said, "Kittens with wings? You being able to turn into a cave bear? Me getting to fly to the rescue on my *flying stallion?* This is the greatest year of my life!"

Tirzah suppressed a giggle at the sight of Pete's face in the mirror. He was clearly torn between relief that Caro wasn't traumatized, pride in her, and horror at the thought of her making a habit of flying to the rescue.

To save him from having to respond, Tirzah said, "Like father, like daughter. Pete, didn't you wish you had a flying pony when you were her age?"

"I wished I had a pet wolf. But close enough." He rubbed

his jaw, then caught her eyes in the mirror. "Nice driving, Tirzah."

She smiled. "Thanks."

They could have the real conversation about that later, in private. But she could see that he was proud of her. She'd never been afraid of driving before her accident, and a little of her old confidence had returned to her, though her body ached from the awkward position and her weak left leg ached more.

I'm going to go to a therapist and get some real therapy, she thought. *Maybe some anxiety meds, so I don't have to rely on Pete always being with me. And then I'll get the car with hand controls out of the garage. And then I'll make some major repairs to my cabin, and—*

In the rear view mirror, she saw a black shape appear in the sky over the hills. It was the pteranodon.

"Oh, shit!" Tirzah burst out. "Sorry, Caro."

"Drive faster!" Caro yelped.

"Keep calm," said Pete. He laid a comforting hand on Tirzah's shoulder, and on Caro's. "Once we're off the mountain, we can go off-road. It's too big to get through the trees."

But there was still a lot of mountain left to drive. And the pteranodon was coming in fast, its great leathery wings beating against the pale sky. It loomed larger in the mirror as it came closer. Tirzah realized that it was bigger than the car.

The animals in the car were either aware of the pursuit or else their owners' tension had transmitted itself to them. Moonbow snorted, his ears laid back against his head. Batcat meowed and flapped her wings. Spike bristled until Pete had to nudge him away.

"It's getting closer!" Caro called.

Gritting her teeth, Tirzah pushed even harder on the gas. Her foot ached fiercely but the car did speed up. But she couldn't go any faster along these hairpin curves without risking a crash.

The pteranodon put on a burst of speed, and its shadow passed over the car.

The pets went berserk. Tirzah had no idea if they were trying to escape because they were panicked, or trying to escape so they could fight the pteranodon. But either way, the result was the same. Two flying kittens and one kitten-sized flying horse began madly flapping around the car, meowing and neighing, smacking against the windows and windshield with hooves and paws and spines, banging into Tirzah's head and swooping in front of her face, and shedding choking clouds of fur and downy feathers.

"Grab them!" Tirzah yelled.

In the rear view mirror, she saw Pete trying to corner Spike against the rear window and only succeeding in getting cactus spines in his hands.

Caro grabbed Moonbow and clutched him tight. He struggled, kicking her in the stomach with an opalescent hoof. "Ow!"

Batcat leaped on to the dashboard, directly in front of the steering wheel, puffed herself up, spread her wings, and hissed.

"Caro!" Tirzah shouted. "Get Batcat!"

Caro clutched Moonbow to her chest with one arm and grabbed Batcat by the scruff of the neck with her other hand. Batcat yowled and scratched as Caro yanked her off the dashboard, fighting so furiously that Caro lost hold of Moonbow. The tiny stallion flew up and kicked the windshield, cracking it.

Caro let go of Batcat and grabbed Moonbow, clutching him in both hands.

"Caro, hold your horse!" Pete yelled. "I'll get Batcat!"

Tirzah heard a click as he released his seatbelt. "Pete, no—"

He made a grab for Batcat. The kitten evaded him, diving downward into the wheel well, where she crawled under the gas pedal. Tirzah was forced to let up on the pressure or squash her. The car slowed drastically.

"No!" Caro cried. "Speed up!"

"She's under the gas pedal!" Tirzah shouted.

Caro shoved Moonbow into her father's reaching hands, bent over, and plucked a thrashing, spitting, hissing Batcat out from under Tirzah's foot.

The pteranodon swooped lower, its talons spread wide as if it was going to try to snatch up the car. Tirzah stomped on the gas as hard as she could, whipping around a curve far faster than was safe.

And was faced by the same cliff she'd skidded over a year ago.

Her heart seemed to stop. Her hands went cold and numb. She couldn't tell if she was still holding the steering wheel until she looked down and saw her fingers clenched around it, knuckles bloodless and white.

I can't move my hands, she thought. *We're going to go over the cliff all over again.*

She could feel the stomach-dropping sensation of falling, the terror of the anticipated impact—

And then a pair of warm, strong hands were on her shoulders, and a deep voice murmured in her ear, "You can do this, Tirzah. Just breathe…"

…and then she was past the cliff, turning another corner, and heading into the long, straight downward slope toward the base of the mountain.

Her breath went out in the biggest sigh of relief in her life. But she couldn't relax just yet. They just had this last stretch to get through, and then they could go off-road, as Pete had suggested.

She was almost standing up in the car, pushing the gas pedal into the floor. Out of the corner of her eye, she saw that the pets were nowhere in sight, but Caro had her arms clutched around her own body, imprisoning a writhing, thrashing, yowling, squealing, whinnying mass underneath her shirt.

And that was when the pteranodon landed on the roof of the car.

CHAPTER 30

$\mathcal{T}$he pteranodon rode the car like a skateboard, shoving it off-road. It skidded toward a tree.

"Brake!" Pete yelled.

"Buckle your seatbelt!" Tirzah shouted as the car slowed, brakes screaming.

Pete fumbled for his seatbelt. The smell of burning rubber was strong and acrid. He clicked it into place a second before the car slammed into the tree.

There was a tremendous jolt, and everyone was jerked forward. But Tirzah had managed to slow the car drastically by the time they'd struck. The pets had gotten loose and were madly flapping around the interior, but no one seemed hurt.

"Are we safer staying in—" Tirzah began.

A gigantic claw punched through the roof of the car. Everyone ducked, and Caro screamed. With a nails-against-metal screech, the pteranodon began dragging his claw through the roof, slicing it like a can opener.

"Tirzah, I'll carry you," Pete said. "Caro, as soon as I say go, run for the woods. I'll be right behind you."

"It'll grab us as soon as we get out!" Caro said, her face pale.

Pete leaned forward, patting both her and Tirzah on the shoulder, and gave them the slightest smile. He unsnapped Tirzah's seatbelt with one hand, and with the other, using his body to block the pteranodon's view, he pulled something from the glove compartment.

It was a steel window-punch, which he kept so he could easily break the car windows in case his car crashed into water. His hand flashed up, past the pteranodon's claw, to stab the window-punch into its chicken-like foot.

The pteranodon let out an ear-splitting screech and sprang into the air.

"Go!" Pete shouted.

Caro leaped out of the car and bolted for the woods.

Tirzah opened her door and scrambled out just as Pete jumped out of the back seat. He swept her into his arms and tore after Caro. He took just one backward glance to see the pteranodon in mid-air, bending its beak to try to yank the window-punch out of its foot like someone trying to remove a splinter with tweezers.

And then oaks and cedars rose up above them, and moss was soft underfoot. They had made it to the relative safety of the woods.

Pete had meant to keep going, but the adrenaline rush that had enabled him to pick up Tirzah and run abruptly wore off. His head spun, his vision blurred, and his knees felt weak.

"Caro!" The name came out in a gasp.

Pete sat down hard on the mossy ground, about one second before he would have passed out. He felt Tirzah pull away from him, but he could see nothing. Dizzy and sick, he put his head between his knees.

"Caro, help Tirzah," he said. "She... she can hop if you support her. Go farther into the woods."

He didn't hear the sound of footsteps, but his pulse was pounding hard enough to cover them. Pete tried to make himself breathe deeply, gathering his strength for one last shift.

We can't, rumbled his cave bear. *Our strength is spent. If you try to force the shift, you'll only faint.*

Pete gritted his teeth. If his cave bear was advising against the shift, he had to be right. He fumbled around the forest floor, eyes still closed, searching for a rock, a branch, *anything...*

A soft hand touched his shoulder. He didn't have to look up to know whose it was. He'd recognize Tirzah's hand anywhere.

"Don't be an idiot," she said. "We're not leaving you."

Pete forced his eyes open. Tirzah sat beside him, the pets were circling protectively overhead, and Caro was running around, gathering rocks and branches and dumping them at their feet.

Like father, like daughter, he thought.

He supposed he could keep on insisting that they leave him and save themselves, but he gave up on the idea as soon as it occurred to him. They were his family. They loved him as much as he loved them, and they weren't going to abandon him any more than he'd abandon them.

"I love you," he said.

A tremendous noise of snapping branches drowned out their replies as the pteranodon forced its way through the woods. Pete snatched up a rock. Maybe he *could* throw it straight down the monster's beak and choke it.

Bang!

A hideous screech rose up, along with the distinctive sound of a ricochet.

The gunshot had come from behind them. Pete twisted around, and saw the very last person he would have expected: Carter Howe, in polished shoes and a three-piece suit, with some weird-looking modified rifle strapped to his back. He was holding a pistol.

The pteranodon stuck its hideous head out from between the trees. Carter calmly fired again, but the beast whipped its head around. The bullet again struck its beak and bounced off.

"Damn," Carter said. "Okay, fine. We do this the hard way."

He unsnapped his harness, and tossed it and the rifle down to the ground. For a moment Pete had no idea what he was doing. Then he remembered that not all shifters could take their clothes or weapons with them when they changed. Even in the midst of the battle, he couldn't help a spark of curiosity at the realization that he was *finally* going to find out what Carter's shift form was.

"Pick on someone your own size!" Carter shouted, then ran off into the woods just to the side of the pteranodon.

The dinosaur gave an uncertain hiss. Its head weaved, as if it wasn't sure whether to pursue Carter or go after the prey in front of it. Then its reptilian eyes narrowed, and it withdrew its snaky neck.

Bang!

Another ricochet as it blocked the bullet with its beak. And then it vanished into the woods.

There were more gunshots, more ricochets, Carter's shouted taunts, and the sound of breaking branches. Pete realized that Carter was leading the pteranodon away from them. He was grateful, though uncertain what good it would do if he still couldn't stand up.

Well. He'd just have to, wouldn't he?

Pete reached out and pulled the rifle to him. He gave it a

quick glance, saw that it was actually a harpoon gun with a silvery tip, and wondered why Carter hadn't tried it on the pteranodon. Maybe, since it only seemed to have one harpoon, he hadn't wanted to risk a miss.

Pete slung it over his back and braced his palms on the ground. "Caro, help Tirzah."

"*Caro?*" an incredulous voice said.

Pete's head jerked up. Merlin ran out of the woods, his soft-soled shoes almost soundless over the moss. He was carrying a pair of crutches. As Pete stared, Merlin gave Tirzah a hand up, then passed her the crutches. She held them a little awkwardly, obviously not really comfortable with them. But just as obviously, she did know how to use them.

"We all thought you were still at the office," Merlin said to Caro.

"Umm..." Caro squirmed. "Nope!"

He glanced at her little pony. "*That's* new."

"His name's Moonbow," Caro said proudly.

"Pleased to meet you." Merlin crouched beside Pete and helped him to his feet, then supported him. "Come on. Carter's distracting it. Let's get to our car before it remembers the rest of us."

"How—" Caro began.

"Later," Pete said.

But they hadn't taken more than a few steps when Carter's yells and gunshots abruptly ceased. They were followed by a spine-chilling sound, part howl, part scream. The pteranodon screeched in a note that sounded like shock. And then the sounds of a tremendous battle rose up: not just snapping branches, but falling trees and the heavy thud of flesh against flesh. And over it all, that terrifying wail that sounded less like any animal Pete had ever heard of and more like some beast out of nightmare.

Tirzah froze. "What *is* that?"

"No idea," Merlin said. "I mean, I don't know specifically. But it's Carter's shift form, so... it's friendly!"

Pete knew what Merlin meant, but that nerve-shattering howl sure didn't sound friendly.

"Is the rest of the team here?" Pete asked.

Merlin shot an exasperated glance at Caro. "No, Ransom and Roland stayed at the office to guard Caro's empty bedroom. Roland somehow managed to find Carter, and sent him because he's shown resistance to mind-control before. He sent me because if I got mind-controlled, at least I wouldn't set anything on fire."

"What's your—" Caro began.

Merlin turned to her. Smoothly, he said, "So I guess Batcat went to you after me, huh? What's your shift form, Caro? Some kind of bird?"

"I don't have a shift form." Indicating her tiny pony, Caro said, "I rode him. Moonbow can change his size under the moonlight."

It was the first time Pete had ever seen Merlin look genuinely surprised. "I'll be darned."

Merlin was leading them on a wide curve, presumably to a vehicle parked by the road. Though Caro and the pets followed easily, Tirzah was panting and sweating, struggling to keep up. He could see why she didn't normally use crutches: they required her to lift her entire body weight, as if she was doing a push-up with every step, then put it down on her weak left foot.

"Hang in there," Pete said to her, or tried to: his words died away as he too gasped for breath. Despite his support from Merlin, he too was winded. Every breath felt like it was stabbing a red-hot dagger through his chest.

"You too," Tirzah said.

By the time they broke out of the woods and back on to

the road, it was all Pete could do just to stay conscious. The company van, a big SUV, was parked by the side of the road. Pete knew it had extra weapons and emergency supplies, including a military-grade first aid kit. Much as he disliked being a patient, the thought of lying down on the seat under a blanket was sounding awfully good right now.

"Uh-oh," Merlin said in his ear.

That was not a word that Pete wanted to hear. "What?"

Merlin abruptly set him down on the ground, none too gently, and started backing away from them. His normally pleasant expression was twisted, angry. "Get—get—"

His words became a hiss. The next instant, he was a velociraptor the size of a man, black hide gleaming, needle-fanged mouth gaping. He hissed again, his taloned hands flexing.

"He's mind-controlled!" Pete gasped.

The velociraptor sprang.

Pete scrambled as much as lunged into its path, grabbing it around its legs in a clumsy tackle. He expected to get his head bitten off at any second, but the velociraptor thrashed around awkwardly, its jaws snapping shut on air. Pete realized that Caro and Tirzah had also grabbed it, Tirzah lying on the ground and clutching each of its taloned hands in her strong grip, and Caro on its back with both her forearms across its neck. The velociraptor struggled and hissed, writhing and snapping, but was unable to get to any of them.

"Pete!" Tirzah called. "Get in his head!"

He had no idea if that would actually work, but it was a good idea and worth a try. Pete slipped into Merlin's mind.

He found a very familiar white-hot rage, blazing until everything else vanished within its brightness and roar. Pete had to look hard to find a bewildered Merlin stumbling around in the middle of it, vainly searching for a way out. Merlin was like a river, all quick currents and sparkling surface and unseen depths. Pete loaned Merlin his strength, allowing him to douse the fire within himself.

And then Pete was sprawled on the ground, gasping, his hand cupping a velociraptor the size of a hamster. Its little claws pricked his hand like Spike's fur.

The next moment, the velociraptor was gone and Pete had his hand curled around Merlin's ankle. All of them were lying on the ground in a heap, with two kittens and a pony circling and squealing overhead. Carter, bruised and bloody and wearing nothing but a pair of tattered dress pants, stood over them, unarmed, fists clenched.

And facing all of them was Gorlois, back in human form, complete with embroidered coat. He too was battered and bleeding, but his familiar contemptuous expression was unchanged.

"Pathetic. Writhing on the ground like a bunch of worms." Gorlois pointed a disdainful finger at each of them in turn, first to Tirzah, Caro, and Pete. "A cripple, a child, a beast." Then to Carter, Merlin, and the pets. "A monster, a liar, and three escaped experimental subjects. I shall retrieve the magical animals—we can still make use of them—and dispatch the rest."

And then Gorlois vanished, and the pteranodon once again loomed over them.

"HEY!" Caro yelled unexpectedly. "Don't you call my dad a beast! Or Tirzah a cripple! And I'm not a child, I'm THIRTEEN!"

While Caro was shouting, Carter's bare foot slid backward and nudged his weird harpoon rifle against Pete's hand.

Here goes nothing, Pete thought.

He whipped up the harpoon gun and fired. The silver tip of the harpoon struck the pteranodon in its soft belly. The dinosaur let out a screech. Silver light flared around the harpoon, growing brighter and brighter until Pete was forced to close his eyes.

There was a soft *whump*, like a pool of gasoline igniting. When Pete opened his eyes, there was nothing left of the wizard but black dust gently drifting down.

CHAPTER 31

irzah was so exhausted that she couldn't even climb into the SUV by herself. Merlin had to lift her. Then Carter went off to fetch her wheelchair from Pete's wrecked car while Merlin gave Pete first aid in the back seat.

"Caro…?" Pete mumbled, fighting to keep his eyes open.

"I'm here, Dad," Caro said. "I'm fine."

"Tirzah…?"

Tirzah squeezed his hand. "I'm fine too. Go to sleep, Pete. You saved us all. You can rest now."

Pete gave a sigh, and his eyes closed. He didn't stir while Merlin applied new bandages to his wounds, but Tirzah could see his steady breathing.

"Can you take him to a hospital?" she asked.

Merlin shook his head. "It wouldn't be safe. But Roland's already called in for medical help, just in case. They should be arriving at the office right about the time we do. Just keep an eye on him. I'll call Roland now and give him an update. And tell him he can stop guarding Caro's room."

Tirzah and Caro sat by Pete, Tirzah stroking his hair and Caro directing the pets to cuddle with him.

"It would make *you* feel better if had two flying kittens and a magic flying mini-stallion curled up next to you, right?" Caro inquired.

"Absolutely," Tirzah replied.

Caro rubbed her jaw. "Um... So, you and my dad... PLEASE NO DETAILS but you *are* dating, right?"

"Yes, we are," Tirzah admitted, inwardly crossing her fingers that Caro wouldn't have a problem with it. "It's pretty serious—"

"NO DETAILS," Caro reminded her, then cast a speculative glance over the flying pets. "But, without details, is there any chance he might move to Refuge City? Like, to be with you? And I could move too?"

Tirzah repressed a gulp. It was one thing to daydream about adopting, and another to have her possible new stepdaughter quizzing her about their living arrangements. Cautiously, she said, "Pete and I haven't discussed it yet. Would you like to?"

"YES." Caro beamed. "Could I have my own bedroom?"

"You'll have to discuss that with your father," Tirzah said firmly.

To her relief, Caro seemed content with that. Maybe parenting wasn't that scary after all. Especially when you were a step-parent and could offload the major decisions onto their dad.

Carter returned with Tirzah's chair, which he loaded into the SUV. As Merlin took the driver's seat and pulled out, Carter began rummaging through the duffel bags and boxes of equipment in the back. A grin began to spread across Tirzah's face at his expressions of disgust and annoyance as he pulled out desert camouflage, jungle camouflage, bulletproof vests, and rainproof ponchos.

"I thought we—you—did a lot of undercover," Carter

called. "Where do you keep clothes for going undercover at a decent restaurant?"

"What, like a chef's hat?" Merlin inquired innocently.

"No!" Carter finally uncovered some plain black clothes, which he pulled on. They gave him the appearance of an irritated ninja.

"What was that harpoon thing?" Tirzah asked.

"It was tipped with shiftsilver." Carter shrugged, spreading his hands. "I have no idea what happened. Shiftsilver stops mythic beasts from shifting, so I thought even if it just got off a glancing blow, it might make an animal turn back into a human. I had no idea it could make you spontaneously combust!"

"Shiftsilver interferes with magic," Merlin corrected him. "Mythic shifters use magic to shift, so it stops them from shifting. Gorlois was a wizard, so shooting him with a shiftsilver harpoon must have interfered with a whole bunch of his spells."

"The way a bucket of water interferes with a grease fire," Carter said.

Tirzah realized that both Carter and Merlin seemed to know a lot more about shifters, not to mention magic, than Pete did. She recounted what Gorlois had told them about the ancient order of wizards who had fought King Arthur, and what he'd tried to do with Pete.

"Just great," said Carter. "Now we've got a thousand-year-old wizards' order after us."

"Coooool," Caro murmured, then looked abashed. "I mean, not cool that they're trying to kill you!"

"So have either of you ever heard of it before?" Tirzah asked.

Carter shook his head.

Merlin said, "I haven't heard of it *exactly,* but my name

isn't a complete coincidence either. There are legends that say that Merlin—I mean Arthur's Merlin, not me-Merlin—was the first shifter."

"Really?" Tirzah asked.

"Absolutely. You see, when I was with the circus—"

"Oh, God, spare me," Carter groaned.

Caro piped up, "I want to hear!"

Merlin went on over them both, "—there was a trapeze artist whose ambition was to train a troupe of flying squirrels..."

Tirzah's attention drifted from the conversation. She hadn't wanted to let on, so as not to upset Caro, but she *was* worried about Pete. He looked pale, and she couldn't tell if he was unconscious or just very deeply asleep.

When Caro got a conversation going on the subject of "Would you rather be attacked by twenty pteranodons the size of hamsters or one hamster the size of a pteranodon?" Tirzah made sure to participate enough that her distraction wasn't noticeable. But inside her mind, she was leaping up and down in frustration, waiting for the car to get a move on already.

Pete still hadn't awakened when they finally, *finally* pulled into the underground parking lot at Defenders, Inc. But it felt like a huge weight was lifted off Tirzah's back when she saw Ransom and Roland waiting for them, along with one male and two female strangers.

"Those are the paramedics from Protection, Inc.," Merlin explained. "And their ride."

While Carter unloaded Tirzah's wheelchair and helped her into it, the tall white man and short Latina woman rapidly examined Pete, started an IV, and loaded him on to a stretcher. From the ease of the way they worked with each other, with barely a word needing to be exchanged, Tirzah guessed that they were either close friends who'd been working together forever, or else romantic partners.

Mates, she corrected herself as the man tenderly brushed away a lock of the woman's hair that kept falling into her eyes. *They must be mates.*

Tirzah went with the two of them in the elevator, while everyone else took the stairs. She had been too nervous to ask before, but once she was alone in an elevator, the question burst out of her. "Is he going to be all right?"

"Oh, sorry!" the woman said. "We should've said right away. Yeah, he'll be fine. We'll stick around for a couple days to make sure there's no complications, but his shifter healing should take care of everything. Just make sure he rests, even if you have to tie him down." She laughed.

Tirzah felt her entire body relax. She was so overcome with relief that she couldn't even speak, but just reached out and brushed her fingers over Pete's cheek. He didn't open his eyes, but this time he must have sensed her, for he turned his face into her hand.

"I'm Tirzah Lowenstein," she said belatedly. "His mate."

The word came naturally to her lips, and the two paramedics simply nodded as if it was natural to them as well.

"We're mates too," said the man. His face looked forbidding, and his ice-blue eyes only added to that impression. But she'd seen him caring for Pete, and his touch had been gentle. "I'm Shane Garrity, and this is Catalina Mendez. We're from Protection, Inc."

They were met by the others at the lobby. They moved Pete into one of the client rooms, where the paramedics put him in the bed.

"His color looks better," Roland said, peering down at him.

"He'll be fine," Catalina said, her voice pitched loud enough to carry to everyone. As if that was an invitation, a flying kitten swooped down and landed on her shoulder. It was as small and furry and black as Batcat, but it had butterfly wings, swirled orange and black like a Monarch's. It stretched and meowed.

"Oooh," Caro began. Her delighted exclamation rose to a higher pitch when a gray tabby kitten with moth-like wings drifted down and landed on Shane's shoulder, silent as falling snow.

"That's Shadow," said Shane, indicating his own kitten. Pointing out the butterfly kitten, he said, "And that's Carol Danvers."

A musical note pierced the air. A lovely blue miniature dragon flew in and perched on the outstretched forearm of the third stranger, a woman with long silver hair and glittering silver tattoos that swirled up her neck and shoulder. It stretched out its elegant neck and trilled again.

"This is Doina, my dragonette," said the silver-haired woman in a slight accent which made Tirzah think of the musical sound of her dragon's voice. "And I am Raluca."

Caro stared at her. Even apart from Raluca's unusual hair and tattoos and voice, she was dressed to the nines, complete with expensive-looking high heels. It was quite a contrast to the paramedics, who were both in jeans and T-shirts.

"Are you a bodyguard?" Caro asked.

"No, I'm a fashion designer," Raluca said. "I brought Shane and Catalina here. My mate Nick is a bodyguard at Protection, Inc., but he's a wolf. The only dragon on the team is currently on an assignment abroad."

There was a brief silence while both Tirzah and Caro processed this, and then Caro said, "You're a *dragon?*"

Raluca inclined her head in a nod.

"*I'm* a bodyguard," Catalina put in over her shoulder. Or rather, behind her shoulder, as Raluca was nearly a foot taller.

Raluca smiled at Caro and added, "But I used to be a princess."

"A *dragon princess!*" Caro stared up at Raluca with visible awe, then extended some of it to cover Catalina.

Ransom cast a glance at Merlin. "You have officially been upstaged."

"Yeah," Merlin admitted. "It's kind of an unusual feeling for me."

"Oh, hi, Merlin," Catalina piped up. "Did a magical pet ever find you?"

"No," Merlin said glumly.

Shane started to nudge his mate, but Catalina went tactlessly on, "Oh, what a shame! But don't give up hope. You were at the lab when we set them free—maybe one imprinted on you. I mean even Pete's mate got one, when she wasn't there when they all got loose and her only connection with them was that she was *going* to be Pete's mate in the future—"

"Catalina," Shane said, as Merlin heaved a gloomy sigh.

Hurriedly, Catalina said, "Well, I'm sure it's not too late. I bet you'll all get one eventually! And I bet your mates will too!"

"I don't want any furry pests flittering around and shedding on my suits and messing with my stuff," Carter said.

"I don't believe in mates," Ransom said flatly.

Roland said, "If I ever had a mate, she's dead."

That brought the conversation to a sudden halt. Then, as if that was a signal, everyone drifted out, striking up conversations or asking about acquaintances on Protection, Inc. Tirzah only half-heard the snippets of conversation as they left:

"...Rafa's family is absolutely crazy over their little Gabriel..."

"...Haley can sit up all by herself, and Elliot says 'Ma...'"

"...Destiny has some contacts in India. I'm sure she could put you in touch..."

And then the door closed softly behind them, leaving Tirzah and Pete alone together. Batcat had flown out with Carol Danvers, but Spike stayed at Pete's side.

Tirzah wasn't sure if she heard a change in his breathing or some more subtle shift in the atmosphere, but something made her ask, "Are you awake?"

Pete's eyes opened. He looked very tired, but better than he had in the car. "Yeah. Couldn't cope with that crowd fussing over me."

"You'll have to tomorrow, you know. Faking unconsciousness only lasts so long."

He was quiet for long enough that she thought he was falling asleep again, but then he said, "I was awake a bit in the car. Enough to hear some stuff, anyway. I wanted to say something, but I couldn't manage to get my eyes open."

"Oh?"

He nodded, and even managed a faint smile. "Got any three-person apartments open in your building? I know a certain thirteen-year-old girl who really, really wants a Refuge City apartment with her own bedroom."

Tirzah's face nearly cracked with her grin. "I do! You'd move into the city for me?"

"The cactuses are getting a bit old." Spike let out an indignant meow. Pete lifted one hand to pat him. "Not you."

"How will your mom feel about it?"

"I think she's ready to have a life of her own." Pete smiled again, this time more widely. "I can't imagine what she'll think when I tell her... everything."

"I can't either," Tirzah admitted. "But I bet she'll *love* Spike."

Spike gave a wide yawn. So did Pete.

"Lie down?" he asked.

Tirzah climbed into bed and put her arms around him. She nestled her head into his shoulder, in that hollow that seemed made for it, and let out a sigh. "So glad I hijacked your laptop."

Pete's amused exhale was warm on her throat. "Me too."

EPILOGUE

$\mathcal{P}$ete shook a frying pan over the blue flame of a gas burner. The hash browns were nice and crispy, just the way Caro and Tirzah liked them.

Right on cue, Tirzah and Caro came wandering into the kitchen, yawning and rubbing their eyes. Tirzah was in a nightie, but Caro was already dressed for school. Moonbow looked up from his planter box of grass, snorted, and trotted up to Caro, who bent to stroke his wings. Batcat launched off Tirzah's shoulder and joined Spike in weaving in and out of Pete's ankles.

"Morning, Caro. Morning, Tirzah." Pete held the frying pan out of the way as he gave Tirzah a kiss and Caro a one-armed hug.

"Can't believe you've got me getting up this early," Tirzah muttered. "This can't be good for you."

"Discussion topic," Caro said, her jaw audibly cracking with a huge yawn. "Forcing teenagers to go to school in the morning when their circadian rhythms are optimized for late night: a bad idea, a really bad idea, or the absolute worst idea?"

"I don't think the 'threat or menace' formula is really meant to provoke a discussion," Tirzah said.

Pete handed a toasted bagel with lox and cream cheese to Tirzah, who didn't like eggs. She took it to the kitchen table, where her steaming mug of coffee was already waiting. Pete flipped Caro's cheese omelette, then slid it on to her plate.

"Ready for the computer science test?" Tirzah asked Caro.

"*Now* I am," Caro said. Tirzah had been tutoring her, with much better results than Pete had gotten. He had steadfastly not inquired whether Tirzah was teaching her any hacking tricks on the side.

Pete was the last to join the table, with two fried eggs. He sat between Tirzah and Caro, pushing aside Mom's house-warming gift of an inconveniently sized cactus. The kittens lurked, vulture-like, their yellow eyes fixed on Tirzah's lox.

"Discussion topic," Tirzah said. "What food is to humans as lox is to flying kittens?"

That occupied the rest of breakfast. Just as Caro finished her orange juice, there was a knock at the door.

"Caro?" a girl's voice called.

"Just a second!" Caro shouted.

Pete snapped his fingers twice. The air around Batcat, Spike, and Moonbow shimmered briefly. When the shimmer faded, Pete could still see them, but Caro's friends wouldn't be able to. Apart from getting him back on his feet, one of the most useful things the visitors from the west coast office of Protection, Inc. had provided was to let them know that the magical pets could be trained to become invisible at will to people who didn't already know about them.

Caro petted Moonbow and cast a pleading look at Pete. Softly, she said, "No one will see him, so can I take him to—"

"Absolutely not," Pete said firmly.

"You never let me do anything fun," Caro said, but she

was grinning. She picked up her backpack and went to the door, where she was greeted by Jamal, Hannah, and Sofia.

"Finally!" Jamal said. "I thought you'd never talk your dad around."

"I'm right here," Pete said. He was roundly ignored.

"Check it out," Hannah said, holding up her hand with Sofia's, displaying their matching nail polish. "We'll do yours on the subway."

"Awesome," Caro said.

Bang!

The door slammed behind them. A second later, it opened again and Caro popped her head back in. "Don't forget the cook-off this weekend with Abuelita!"

"Don't worry, I—" Pete began.

Bang!

She was gone.

Pete stared at the closed door. "I still can't believe she talked me into letting her ride the subway alone."

"She didn't," Tirzah reminded him. "Jamal and Hannah and Sofia's parents did. And she's not alone, she's with three friends."

"I still can't believe it," Pete said. "I want to get up and haul her back right now."

Tirzah cleared her throat. "Who came to your rescue on a magical flying horsie? Who shoved you into the back seat of a car when you couldn't even stand—"

"Low blow."

"And her cell phone is loaded up with every possible in-case-of-emergency hack, and she has a one-of-a-kind personal alarm system disguised as a pen and designed by Carter Howe himself," Tirzah pointed out. "And she's getting self-defense lessons from Marines. Should I go on?"

"No, no. It's fine. I know the other kids' parents wouldn't let them do it if it wasn't safe."

And if anyone even thinks of harming her, I will tear them limb from limb, rumbled his cave bear.

That too, replied Pete.

Aloud, he said, "She's not going to keep three magical pets secret from her new best friends forever, you know."

"Yeah, I know. But I think it'll be all right. Hannah and Sofia and Jamal are smart, responsible kids. And if we ever fly anywhere—I mean on an airplane—we'll need a pet-sitter. And Lola's allergic."

"Not to Spike," Pete said.

"Spike wouldn't want to be parted from Batcat and you know it."

When Mom had come back from visiting her sister, whose foot was healing nicely, she'd taken the flood of revelations surprisingly well. Like Caro, she'd been relieved to learn what his problems really were and that they weren't as bad as she'd been imagining. And she'd been delighted with Spike, though she instituted a rule that no flying animals were allowed in rooms with delicate glass cacti.

Tirzah scooted her chair closer, nestling into him as she sipped her coffee and surveyed the apartment. "I love what you did with the place."

Pete too looked around, satisfied with his work. With the help of a crew of workmen, he'd made their new three-bedroom apartment completely accessible. The shelves and cupboards were all within Tirzah's reach now, and had kitten-proof latches. He'd built her a new cupboard himself, shaped more-or-less like R2D2, as well as a wooden cabinet to hide the litterbox.

"By which I mean your dollhouse," Tirzah said, nudging him.

Pete glanced at his military base for action figures, currently half-done on one of his work tables. "Please. It's a war game miniature."

"If it has little beds with teeny people in them, it's a dollhouse."

Since the part of the base that was completed was the barracks, and Drill Sergeant Nick Fury was about to surprise a number of sleeping superheroes, Pete found this difficult to argue with. Instead of trying, he resorted to changing the subject. "Quickie before we go? It'll be good luck for your first official day on the job."

Tirzah wound her arm around his neck and purred, "Thought you'd never ask."

Pete picked her up, bending to breathe in the scent of her hair.

Knock-knock!

With a sigh, he put her back down, then snapped his fingers to command the kittens and Moonbow to become invisible. Tirzah opened the door and found Esther, Tupperware in hand.

"Could you spare half a stick of butter?" Esther asked. "I'm making latkes, and I'm just a bit short."

"No problem." Pete headed for the kitchen. As he collected the butter, his sharp shifter hearing caught Esther's whisper of, "My my, your young man is certainly very nicely built! And good with his hands. Look at that beautiful cupboard!"

Tirzah whispered back, "Confess. You came to check out Pete, not for butter."

"I *am* making latkes. If I happen to notice that my neighbor has found herself a true mensch who's handsome as well, what's the harm in that?"

Pete returned with the butter, suppressing a grin as he handed it to Esther. "Good luck with the... what were they?"

"Latkes," said Esther. "Potato pancakes. I'll bring you one!"

"Not today," Tirzah said firmly. "We're about to go to work."

She shut the door behind Esther, then held up her arms to Pete. "Where were we...?"

"On our way for a quickie." Pete picked her up. "What's a mensch?"

"A good guy. A person with honor and integrity. Esther is very observant."

Pete took a step toward the bathroom.

Knock-knock!

"Let's see who it is," Tirzah whispered.

Pete tiptoed to the door and held Tirzah so she could peek through the peephole. She shook her head and pointed to the bathroom. He carried her to it and closed the door firmly behind them.

"That was Khaliya with a package," Tirzah said. "I'm sure it's something delicious, but she can wait till I come home. They all want to check you out, you know. Make sure they approve."

"I know. You need a 'do not disturb' sign."

She smiled. "Make me one. But first, the quickie!"

Once they got in the shower, their quickie turned out not to be so quick after all. As Pete combed his fingers through Tirzah's drying hair, feeling the curls spring into life, he could hardly believe how lucky he was.

"When my cabin gets repaired, want to leave Caro with Lola and let your bear come out to play in the woods?" Tirzah asked.

Yes, rumbled the bear. *I would like to play and catch fish and run and sleep in the sun.*

"Yeah. I would." He repeated what his bear had said, marveling at how far they'd come. Like Pete himself, his bear was meant for more than just fighting.

They took Tirzah's car to the office. She drove with caution but confidence with the hand controls, navigating the madhouse that was Refuge City traffic like a pro.

At the office, a hand-lettered banner was hung in the lobby. It started out with neatly written letters in black Sharpie, but the black started to fade out on the second word, and switched to red partway through the third.

Welcome To Defenders, Tirzah
Hope You Survive The Experience

Tirzah laughed. "A+ X-Men reference. That was you, Merlin, right?"

Merlin gave a modest nod, adding, "Ransom did the lettering. And Roland made the cake."

Pete eyed the rather lopsided cake with the icing sliding off, and hoped Roland had remembered to put in the sugar.

Roland snapped his fingers, and everyone yelled, "Welcome, Tirzah!" in a somewhat ragged chorus.

The front door banged open in the middle of this, and Carter stared from the cake to the banner to Tirzah. "What's going on?"

"Tirzah's our newest Defender," Roland explained. "She'll do research, hacking, and cyber security from the office."

Carter's jaw dropped. "What? But I do that!"

"Only when you're here," Ransom pointed out. "Nobody's seen you in two months."

"But—" Carter protested.

"I didn't mean to take—" Tirzah began.

Roland held up a hand, cutting them both off. "Want to join the team, Carter? Tirzah keeps her job, but we'd be happy to have you *too*."

"No," Carter said. "It's fine. Congratulations, Tirzah. I'm sorry I was ungracious. You're a better hacker than me anyway."

Tirzah glowed at the praise. "Aww, thanks."

"Have you found anything on the wizard-scientists yet?" Roland asked her.

"Not yet," she said. "I've resorted to combing conspiracy websites for any mention of them, but no luck so far."

"Which ones?" Carter asked her. "Because I have a database…"

Pete sat back in his chair, put his arm around her, and glanced around the office, from the haphazard sign to the melting cake to the live trap someone (presumably Merlin) had jammed into a half-open window and baited with a chunk of lox, a hunk of cheese, half a Hershey bar, and a small carrot. Pete had been to the west coast office of Protection, Inc., and had been impressed with its professionalism. Anyone walking into this lobby right now would probably run screaming.

Pete wasn't sure what it said about him that he felt as much like he belonged there as he did in his own apartment. But this gang of weirdos and misfits had welcomed his mate, protected his daughter, and saved his life. They might not exactly be a well-oiled team, but Gorlois had been wrong about Pete never finding his place in the world. It was right here.

Roland strolled to the window, removed the past-their-prime and odoriferous lox and cheese from the live trap, sealed them in a Ziploc bag like they were toxic waste, tossed the bag in the trash, then put a companionable hand on Carter's shoulder.

Carter jerked away. "Roland! You just touched—what the hell is that, anyway? Other than a stink bomb and a hazard to pedestrians?"

"A magical pet trap, of course," said Merlin.

"It should be bigger," Ransom said unexpectedly.

"What?" Merlin said, turning eagerly to him. "How much bigger? Full-size cat? Raccoon? Dog? Horse? *Elephant?*"

Ransom shrugged.

"Seriously, Carter," Roland said. "You might as well be on the team already. Why not make it official?"

"I'm *not* on the team," Carter said. "I don't *want* to be on the team! I only came in today because your systems... Well, never mind. Tirzah will take care of it."

"When I was in the circus," Merlin chimed in. "There was this one guy who kept hanging around the elephant tent, but whenever anyone offered him a job, he'd say—"

"Give it up!" Carter burst out, whirling on him. "I've had it with your bullshit stories about your non-existent circus! Anyway, I'm sick of circuses. Did you know some tacky circus *just now* put up its tacky billboard right next to our— your—office? They were finishing it right when I pulled up. Now we—YOU—look tacky by association!"

"Awesome!" Merlin exclaimed. "We all need to go. Maybe we can get a team discount."

He was heading for the window as he spoke. The rest of the team joined him. Sure enough, a brand new circus billboard was up in the space that had formerly been occupied by an ad for the Humane Society's new (Tirzah-funded) cat shelter, which was currently occupying Sucks To Be You Square.

Pete had figured that Carter's idea of tacky probably wasn't Pete's idea, but the billboard was, in fact, amazingly tacky. Enormous swooping letters in red highlighted with gold proclaimed:

THE FABULOUS FLYING CHAMELEONS!
World-famous circus on a special US tour!

The rest of the billboard was crammed with colorful

illustrations of clowns piling out of a clown car, a ringmaster cracking a whip at a tiger that looked like it was about to bite his head off, trapeze artists in spangled leotards, a seal balancing a ball on its nose, and more. Much, much more. So much more that it reminded Pete of a *Where's Waldo* illustration.

"Aren't you going to say that's your circus, Merlin?" Pete teased.

He'd expected Merlin to reply immediately with something like "No, that was the rival circus that we had a feud with which culminated in the riot police getting called out when the seals rampaged through the seafood section of the city's biggest grocery store. Let me tell you how it all began..."

Instead, there was a long silence. Then, in the smallest voice Pete had ever heard out of him, Merlin said, "Actually... it is."

It was his tone more than his words that made everyone turn to stare at him.

"What?" Merlin asked. "Did you guys think I was making it all up?"

A NOTE FROM ZOE CHANT

Thank you for reading *Defender Cave Bear!* I hope you enjoyed it. If you'd like to read about the west coast heroes—and catch the introduction of Defenders—the prequel series, Protection, Inc., starts with *Bodyguard Bear*.

I also write the *Werewolf Marines* series under the pen name of Lia Silver. All my series have hot romances, exciting action, emotional healing, brave heroines who stand up for their men, and strong heroes who protect their mates with their lives.

Please consider reviewing *Defender Cave Bear*, even if you only write a line or two. Reviews are what help me keep writing.

The cover of *Defender Cave Bear* was designed by Augusta Scarlett.

MORE PARANORMAL ROMANCE BY ZOE CHANT

Protection, Inc. (prequel to Defenders)

Bodyguard Bear
Defender Dragon
Protector Panther
Warrior Wolf
Leader Lion
Soldier Snow Leopard
Top Gun Tiger